THE SIGHT

The Sight

V. H. Mizzell

CONTENTS

To Robert Heinlein for
giving away the racket.

ONE

SNAKE

Snake came to me in a dream, as she had many times before.

Always a premonition; this time a warning! She appeared as an anaconda but bigger, impossibly large, large enough to swallow me in one strike.

She gazed at me, watching every move, waiting for me to flinch. I knew that if I turned one way or the other to run, or so much as looked away, she would strike. I knew with the certain knowledge of a dream that she planned to do just that.

I had no choice but to return her gaze. Her eyes smiled at me, penetrating the deepest parts of my soul. I felt as if she could see into my heart, my mind, and my past, that I could hide nothing from her.

Fight, flight, or freeze, I froze. If it was an ordinary nightmare, I would have woken up at that point. Awake, but unable to move at first, stuck in dream paralysis.

Presently she said, "You must go into the Forbidden Land Rion. You must cross the Forbidden Mountains and enter the Kingdom of the Morifati."

"How am I supposed to do that?" I asked.

The Forbidden Land was forbidden because of radioactivity left over from the Great Third War. Nothing lived there except rapidly mutating plants and animals, there was nothing anyone could eat and no water that was safe to drink. The ground itself was not safe to lie on, so I could not camp there. Grandfather said that no citizen of the Free State had ever come back home after going into the Forbidden Land. My own Father went in and never returned.

"I will die in there." I added.

"You will surely not die!" she said.

"If you do not go, if you hesitate, the Morifati will come here to you. They take everything they want everywhere they go. They will kill, steal, and burn. All will die, everyone you love will die, the Free State destroyed, everyone lost!"

"How can I go in there?"

"You must, you must stop them before they find the way through!"

"There is no way through! Everyone who tries to go through sickens and dies!"

"Yes, there is a path. Take that path and stop them on the other side before they find the way through to the Free State."

"How am I supposed to do that?"

"I will show you. I will reveal all."

Then an image appeared before me. I no longer saw her, I saw a landscape. She no longer spoke, but she showed me where to enter. And then I could see myself flying over the mountains, I could see a path along a ridgeline.

The path traced the contours of the ridgeline for many miles until it ended where a great river cut through the mountains and divided them by a great canyon. I followed along the ridgeline path in the dream, then down another path to the river until presently, I came to the village of the Morifati.

"This path leads directly to their village and the path through the mountains directly to us. How have they not found it?" I said.

"They do not know the path along the ridge, but they know it exists. They are looking for it now, they cannot see its entrance."

"If they cannot see its entrance, how will I find it?"

"I will send you a guide. He will lead you to the path and be your companion along the way."

"Who will you send?"

"Wolf."

Then an enormous wolf appeared to me. It turned and walked away toward the Forbidden Land; it stopped and turned to look at me. I knew it wanted me to follow. I followed it into the forest that leads into the Forbidden Land and up the hill to the path along the mountain ridge, with the scene changing and unfolding as only it can during a dream. The Wolf and I walked along the ridgeline with the village spread out beneath us. Then I woke up.

I lay there stunned, then sat up slowly. The dream had felt real. I knew I would have to tell Grandfather about it. He knew how to interpret dreams.

TWO

GRANDFATHER

It was dawn outside the cabin. I lay on the bed for a while to give reality a chance to return. The dream had taken me somewhere else, I couldn't get up until I recovered from the shock of returning.

As I lay there, I thought about the dream. It was a dream, or so I supposed, and yet I felt I ought to treat it as real, as if I should go outside and start walking toward the Forbidden Land. I felt like I should pack up and go look for the entrance to the mountain trail.

I laughed it off, though. Some nightmares are so real that it seems like they really happened. This was one of those. Snake was just some dream symbol in my unconscious mind that kept recurring now and then. It was just a coincidence if anything she said came true.

Presently I got up and walked to the front door and out onto the porch. Grandfather was sitting out there, he was already up. He was smiling, but he looked a little concerned.

"You had a dream there, didn't you, Rion?"

"Yeah, yes I did. How did you know?"

"I could hear you trying to talk, moving around."

I walked over to him and sat next to him on a couch we put out there for that purpose.

"It was so real. Like it really happened. Like I was there in it. You want to hear it?"

"Sure. Go ahead. Tell it."

"This being came to me in my dream as a snake, an enormous snake, an anaconda I guess, but impossibly large, big enough to swallow me in one gulp. I knew somehow that her name was Snake, and that she is a Psychic. I've had some dreams about her before, but not like this. This dream felt real, like I was really standing in front of her, talking to her. I've heard people talk about the Psychics, but I've never seen one or dreamed about one this way. Are they real? Do the Psychics still live somewhere outside the Free State? Do they still practice their powers? Do we need to be afraid of them or is that just superstition?"

"There were no Psychics until about three hundred years ago. The world was a very different place then, and the only thing people believed in was Science. People used to think there was no psychic power, and no Psychics, they were wrong. But no one knows why there were a bunch of Psychics suddenly, even the Psychics themselves. It's thought now that people are born psychic. That it is genetic mutation. They gained their powers quickly, some say in a day, some say longer. But they didn't know each other, not at first. So they all went around trying to profit from their powers, each on his own, out for himself. That's what caused the panic. People didn't know, couldn't know what was going on, and the explanation was something that the scientists didn't believe in, a thing they said was impossible. But everything that the people had in their world that depended on knowledge of the future failed. They had a thing called the economy, and a thing called the stock market, and they had big lotteries and whole cities

5

where people would get together and gamble and all those things and places lost money, because the Psychics could see the future and knew how to win. They knew what all the numbers would be ahead of time. People knew everything was collapsing and failing, but they didn't know why. They didn't believe in psychic power, Scientists said that psychic power was impossible. The government said it was a computer virus, an attack on our computers by the Russians or the Chinese."

"What's a computer?"

"It's a machine that they had that could do all kinds of mathematics, and do it faster than any human could."

"So that's what started the Great Third War?"

"Yes. The USA accused Russia and China of launching an attack on the computers to shut down the economy, so the USA launched an attack on Russia's and China's computers. The Russians and the Chinese knew they hadn't launched an attack on USA's computers so they said that American's made it up to have an excuse for war, so all the countries that had nukes launched their nukes, and the death and sickness was great, so very great, greater than anybody had ever seen in the wars before that."

Grandfather paused then. I could see tears forming in his eyes. I had never seen him cry before for any reason. He was solid as an oak tree spiritually and the Chief of our village and served on the Council of the Free State. He was a powerful warrior in the past and had fought bravely against the Morifati. If he was this upset about the Great Third War, I knew it had been a terrible thing.

"It was a horrible time then, wasn't it Grandfather?"

"It was an atrocity! The greatest atrocity that the Human Beings have ever seen in all history!"

"How many died?"

"No one knows. Hundreds of millions, maybe a billion. There is no way to count the dead now because we cannot find their bodies. Records lost, people went missing. It wasn't just the nukes. After the nukes stopped, people started going crazy. Some formed into gangs, they went around looting, stealing, murdering, raping. They went from house to house taking everything they could, not caring whether they lived or died but trying desperately to survive like wild animals, not like men. They said, 'It does not matter if we die because death is our fate', and so they became known as the Morifati: those whose fate is to die. Their hearts became evil and corrupt, they worshipped death, they call death Than, and say Than is the only god. They say there is no heaven or hell, only this life and an eternity of death. They believe they can do anything they want in this life because there is no punishment or reward, only an eternity of nothingness."

"What did the people of the Free State do then?"

"Good people who were not Morifati fought back. The Morifati killed many people, but those who had weapons and fought back, those who believed that people should live together in peace with each other, protected by laws, they formed into tribes and nations and states. The Free State is one of these states. Men and women who wanted to protect their families and their children, their homes and their farms founded the Free State. Many knew how to use weapons and make weapons and how to fight, and they taught the others who did not know. They had to form new governments and militias. The Free State believes in freedom. We are against killing except in self defense, and we do not steal, even to survive. If we need something from another nation, we trade for it or work for it. We do not take it by force. We give freely to those who need our help. Our God is compassion."

"Grandfather, she said that the Morifati are planning to attack us!"

"So there is more in your dream? Tell me everything!"

"She said that there is a line of mountains from one end of the Forbidden Land to the other, and on this side is the Free State, and on the other side is the Kingdom of the Morifati. She said there is a trail along the ridgeline high up, high enough that there is no radioactivity. The Morifati do not know where it is, but they have heard that it exists. They are looking for it now. When they find it, they will use it to attack the Free State."

"How could anyone know this thing? How could you dream this?"

"I don't understand, Grandfather."

"There is a trail along the mountain ridge, but its location and its existence is a secret known only to me and some elders of the Council of the Free State. It has been our warpath to the Morifati for hundreds of years. We have kept it secret from the Morifati and the people all this time. We did not want anyone to know the way through the Forbidden Land. The Forbidden Land is a barrier to the Morifati that has kept us safe from their attacks. They have to travel far to the north and through other allied nations' territories to get to us. We also do not want anyone from the Free State to think they can hunt in the Forbidden Land, or to attack the Morifati without a decision of the Council."

"I see. I had never heard of this mountain trail before. I thought to enter the Forbidden Land meant death from radiation sickness. But Snake said that the Morifati are looking for the entrance to this trail and will find it soon and that I have to stop them, kill them before they find a way through. I don't know why I have to go and not someone else, but she said that I have to do this thing or the Morifati will find us and attack and she showed me where the trail is, we flew over it in the dream."

"Did she say how you should defeat them?"

"No, all she did, the only thing she showed me about the future was this being she called Wolf."

"She showed you the wolves?"

"She showed me an enormous wolf, a big male called simply 'Wolf', she said he would guide me through the Forbidden Land."

"I see. That is a great curiosity. There indeed are wolves in the Forbidden Land. They are not ordinary wolves, they are Psychics who have assumed the form of wolves. They can live there without radiation sickness. They usually stay far to the south, but they range over the whole territory. We agreed long ago that the Forbidden Land and the mountains would be their domain. They have sometimes been our allies but prefer to remain apart from us, they wish no contact with us, but they don't want war either. They hate the Morifati. The Wolf Pack and the Morifati are mortal enemies."

"So there are Psychics who can assume the form of wolves?"

"Psychics can assume many animal forms, but ordinarily one Psychic can only assume one form, the one that corresponds to their spirit animal. There are many advantages that they can gain by doing this. The primary advantage is concealment from ordinary people and from the Morifati. Many Psychics cannot bear the Morifati. They are too empathic to be near them. They must hide from them rather than fight them directly. The wolves live this way in the Forbidden Land. What concerns me, though, is this Snake. She may not be a dream. She could be a Psychic who is contacting you through your dreams."

"You think Snake is really a Psychic? I think she is only a dream. I have dreamed about her before."

"How could you dream all these things that are real, things that you did not know existed? And this Snake told you these things, you did not just see them in a vision of your own."

"Do you think I am I a Psychic?" I asked Grandfather. "Will I become a Psychic? The way people did in the before time?"

"You must find out for yourself, Rion, Grandfather said. You must complete this journey that Snake wants you to go on, not just to save us, but to find out who you really are!"

"I don't believe this dream is true. I don't see how it could be true. And why me? Why is it up to me to defeat the Morifati by myself?"

"Rion, if a Wolf appears to you and speaks to you with the voice of a man, you will know what to do."

While I thought his words over, Grandfather got up and went back inside the house.

THREE

WOLF

It was still early when Grandfather left me on the porch. I took a walk as I normally did first thing in the morning. I would walk along the treeline of the forest around the village, just to inspect things and get my blood flowing. When I got close to the woods on the eastern side of the village, a slow movement caught my eye. There next to the trees stood an enormous wolf. It was Wolf, from my dream.

"Don't be afraid, Rion," Wolf said.

He didn't open his mouth when he spoke, nor did he speak inside my head, instead he looked at me and I heard him.

"I come to lead you to the Morifati, as promised by Snake."

I stood dumbfounded. Snake was real. Wolf was real. I had been communicating with real beings in my sleep. Am I asleep now I wondered? I looked around to see what I could do to prove to myself that I was awake. Before I could act, Wolf spoke.

"You are not still asleep! Get ready for the journey ahead. We must leave soon."

"I cannot leave now, I am not ready."

"Gather your weapons and tools, prepare as if for a hunt. Tell no one you are leaving. We must go now!"

"Can I not leave a message behind? May I tell no one I am leaving? They will worry when they find I am gone."

"No! They will follow if they know where you are going and all will lose their lives. If instead, they find that you and your weapons are missing, they will think you went on a hunt by yourself."

I had to admit that made sense. It was not unusual for me to hunt alone. Still, I hesitated because it was all too sudden.

Could I trust these creatures? What were they, Snake and Wolf? They had to be two of the Psychics Grandfather explained to me about. I thought they were dream symbols, products of the unconscious, but here was Wolf in front of me, in the flesh, or so I supposed.

It occurred to me I should test my senses.

"I want to see if you are real," I said.

I walked over toward Wolf. He did not tense or growl or threaten me, but said.

"I am quite real, see for yourself."

When I got close enough, I held out my hand for him to sniff it, the way you would when you greet a dog for the first time. I could smell him, a smell not unlike the smell of a hunting hound. I felt his nose and his tongue warm and wet against my hand.

"It is our custom among the wolves to greet a stranger or a returning pack member by touching our tongues together."

I reflexively made a face.

"It is just a custom. To show that you do not mean to fight. Make no sudden moves toward a wolf's throat when you great them."

So I took one knee, and I let him touch his muzzle to my mouth. I stuck my tongue out, and he briefly licked it. He was definitely real.

"You may rise, Rion. Stroke my fur if you like. We are friends now, brothers."

His fur was thick and soft to the touch. I could feel taut muscles underneath. I did not want him as an enemy.

"Now that you know I am as real as you are, we must start our journey. Go prepare for the trip."

"How do I know I can trust you?"

"You don't Rion, not now, I will only be able to prove myself to you later."

"How will you prove you are trustworthy?"

"My words and my deeds will manifest themselves to you."

I stood and waited before turning to gather my hunting gear and leave with Wolf. I did not sense danger, but I was a little afraid of Wolf, he was a large and powerful wolf. He could over-power me or any other man in a fight if that man was unarmed.

"If you do not come with me, all who live in this village will die! Snake has foreseen it! She has that gift, the gift of Fore-sight. When she foretells a thing it comes to pass, but only if you take no action. The past is dead, but the future is still un-formed. Only the now is alive. Act now! You must trust us even at the risk of your life. You will lose everything if you do not. Go! Prepare for the hunt! We leave now!"

"Do we go to hunt? I thought Snake said to make war!"

"We go to hunt men! We go to hunt the Morifati!"

FOUR

DIANA

So I went back inside the house as quietly and as quickly as I could, so as not to wake anyone. You might say I stalked through the house, hunting what I needed for the trip. I grabbed my bow, my pack, tent, Grandfather's hunting knife, the one he gave me for my Order of Manhood, and my canteen, which I realized was empty. I would have to fill it at the well before I left. I took no food with me on a hunt, that was what a hunt was for, finding food. I always fasted on a hunt, it sharpened my senses. But no one could survive for long without water, and the water in the Forbidden Land was "hot" so I could not drink it. You could not trust any random source in there, maybe Wolf could sense the difference or knew a fresh stream. I had to fill the canteen, and without being seen, or I would have to tell a whopper of a lie about what I was doing and shake off whoever saw me so they wouldn't start following me. Also, from my memory of the ridgeline in the dream, there would be no streams along the trail, just rainwater if we were lucky. This time of the morning I would probably be okay unless someone was down there fetching water to cook with.

When I came back outside, Wolf had left, but no one else was out. It felt as though he was watching me, but I could not see him, even over near where he came out of the woods. While I stood there looking around for Wolf, I saw a beautiful raven fly past. It was very large and of a type I had never seen before. It flew quickly out of sight toward the woods. I had no time for curiosity though, had to get to the well and find Wolf.

The well had been dug near the edge of the camp, between the camp and the garden. I could enter through the garden, fill my canteen, and then leave through the garden without being seen. Then I could double back around to the spot where Wolf came out of the woods.

I wove my way through the garden. Luckily, the plants had grown tall. I got to the edge and paused, so I could look through the leaves and see whether anyone was there or whether anyone was coming.

No one was there, so I rushed out and began working the pump. It squeaked, of course, but that couldn't be helped. That noise by itself wasn't suspicious, it just made me nervous as I was trying my best to be stealthy and to stalk my way through and out of the village. I was already on the hunt.

I filled my canteen, slung it over my shoulder, turned to go, and when I turned, there was Diana.

"Rion!"

"I don't have time to talk!"

"Are you going hunting?"

"Yes."

She had lied for me. She would want to go with me, so I had to think of something to say to put her off the trail. It was normal for her to want to go along. She followed me around a lot. It was annoying. People assumed we were lovers, not hunting partners.

She wore her hunting gear. Odd that she should prepare to go on a hunt. She had long black hair, dark and shiny like a crow's feathers. She kept it in a warriors' braid but let the braid fall down her back. Her sky-blue eyes were as piercing as a cat's. She was carrying a bucket, so I knew she had come to fetch water for her Mother.

Maybe that's how I can get away from her, I thought? When she goes back with the water, I can escape quickly and cover my trail. But what if she tries to track me?

"Can I go too? Can I go with you, Rion?"

"No. Look, I've got to hunt by myself today."

She screamed, dropped her bucket, drew her machete and went into a stance. She stared behind me, horrified at something in the garden.

I whirled around to attack, and there was Wolf coming out of the garden.

"Do not be afraid, your Majesty," he said.

"What? He is talking!"

"He is a friend."

She looked unconvinced and continued to stand with her machete drawn. She glanced at me as if to say 'what should I do?'

"See." I said.

I walked over toward Wolf and he approached me and rubbed against me while I stroked his fur.

"You can pet him."

He walked over to her and sat in front of her, then lowered his head and lay down.

"I am at your service Highness. I have come to help your people and lead Rion through the Forbidden Land."

She lowered her machete and stepped forward. Wolf rose up on his haunches. She reached out and stroked his head and neck.

"I can't believe it," she said.

She put her arms around his shoulders and kissed his muzzle. The spontaneity of it surprised everyone, including her.

But even though he was large and fearsome, almost evil looking, he had a nobility to his bearing and when he spoke his face bore an expression of kindness. He leaned up and licked her mouth as he had done mine in the customary wolf greeting.

"Oh! I'm sorry! I just suddenly felt as though we knew each other somehow.", she said.

"You have a magnificent gift for feeling what others feel Highness."

"Why have you come here? You cannot enter the Forbidden Land, no one can, it is radioactive. What do you want with us? And why Rion?"

"All answers will be given to you in time. I do not have the authority to provide you with all the answers. You and Rion will have to discover some things for yourselves. Snake will teach you many things. I will take you to her when it is time. For now, I must take Rion to defeat the Morifati. He is the only one who can defeat them for us. I cannot attack them alone, and I will not lead my pack into a battle they cannot win. The other Psychics are too empathic to bear the presence of the Morifati and must retreat from them. Only Rion can enter their midst. You must remain here for your safety. Do not follow us and tell no one."

"Who is Snake?"

"Rion knows the one of whom I speak. She is a powerful Psychic with many powers. She has the Sight. She has seen your fate, and Rion's fate, and the fate of the Free State, and of the Realm of the Psychics."

"I want to go with you!"

"You cannot Highness.", said Wolf.

"Why do you call me Highness? If Rion is killed by the Morifati, it will ruin all our futures. They are so evil, I can't bear the thought of them. I have nightmares about them. Sometimes it's as if I can sense their thoughts. I feel like I can sense their presence on the other side of the Forbidden Land.", she said.

She straightened up, recovered herself, and held Wolf's head up so she could look into his eyes.

"You must protect him with your life."

"I will Highness, that is my purpose here. I will be his guide, bodyguard, and constant companion until we reach the Kingdom of the Morifati. When we find them, he must enter there alone. He will in time possess powers much greater than mine, and his fate is not to die at the hands of the Morifati. His fate is to lead us all, but he must face a great trial before he is ready to lead."

I stood and watched this exchange anxiously. I knew we must slip away now before anyone discovered us. I said, "Diana, I have been in contact with a Psychic for months now. A Psychic named Snake appeared to me in my dreams. I didn't believe she was real until now. I thought I was having nightmares. She would make predictions. Nothing proved she was anything more than a dream until this morning. Last night she said that I must stop the Morifati before they crossed the Forbidden Land to attack us. She said that Wolf would lead me through a mountain trail past the radioactive zones to the Morifati village. Then he appeared in my dream and showed me the path I must travel. As you can see, he is here with us now and he is quite real. I don't understand everything that is happening now. I mean, why me? But I know in my heart that we should trust Wolf. I must go with him now."

With that, I stepped forward and held her in my arms. She cried. I kissed her forehead. She looked up with eyes closed and offered her mouth. We kissed.

"Tell no one where I have gone. Do not follow me there!"

Then I turned to Wolf.

"We go, take the lead."

And with that, we crossed through the garden and entered the forest. Diana stood silent by the well and watched us disappear while tears ran down her cheeks. She had to take water back to her mother, but she had not promised me she would not track us.

FIVE

FIRST NIGHT

We traveled many miles through the woods, moving quickly. I could tell I was slowing Wolf down. I wanted to double back to make sure that Diana had not followed us, but Wolf said,

"Keep going."

"When will we camp?"

"There is a hill up ahead. The entrance to the path into the Forbidden Land is on the top of it on its eastern side. We will follow a trail up that hill until we reach a plateau. There is a cliff overlooking your land where we can camp for the night. We can watch this side of the trail so we will see anyone who follows."

"How much longer?"

"We should make it just before sundown. We must make camp quickly then, and no fire. We must make no sign at all."

#

That first night when Wolf and I camped on the cliff top, Snake came to me in a dream.

"You have chosen well, Rion."

"Did you doubt I would go?"

"You thought I was only a dream, or a nightmare, or a symbol in your mind until now."

"That's true."

"And even though you could see that Wolf was real, how did you know you could trust him? He could have killed you. He could kill you now."

"If you wanted him to kill me, he would have killed me already."

"So why did you trust him? Why did you agree to go?"

"I have faith in the Great Spirit. I know he will guide me. I know he will protect me from evil."

"I see. You believe in the Great Spirit."

"But why did you choose me?"

"Did I choose you?"

"Didn't you?"

"No. You are the one who I saw."

"I don't understand."

"Everything comes to pass in accordance with the decisions of the Great Spirit. But the entire future is too complex to be seen perfectly. There is always uncertainty about what path a being might choose to take or whether the outcome will fulfill our desires."

Then Snake showed me Diana walking alone along the way we had come, looking for signs that we had left, tracking us.

"Diana is coming."

"She didn't listen to me."

"She loves you. You must not hurt her, but you must not allow her to follow. You must face a trial alone, greater than your Order of Manhood."

"What trial is that?"

"You must allow the Morifati to capture you. They seek captives for their sacrifices to Than. They will not kill you until that time. They will keep you a prisoner and prepare you for sacrifice. You will escape from them. You will walk right out of their camp unharmed. You have a power within you, a special type of foresight, but you do not know how to use it now."

"What power? How will learn to use this power?"

"I will not tell you, I cannot help you. It is a riddle you must solve for yourself. A secret that is only revealed by a trial of mind and flesh and spirit"

Then I woke, and it was first light.

SIX

FIRST LIGHT

As I lay there, I thought, these dreams with Snake are not any normal dreams. She is speaking to me with her mind. This dream left me with my hands and feet tingling.

I had not bothered to set up the tent that I brought with me when I hunted. Instead, I lay down a ground cloth and covered myself with a blanket. Wolf lay down near me. He was used to living in the open, being a wolf, and I could hack it. A light dew had settled on us.

I had been on many long hunting trips since my Order of Manhood; which by itself was two weeks on my own.

I got up, stretched, and drank a little from my canteen. My stomach hurt a little from hunger since I did not eat at all the day before. We left in a hurry and I intentionally brought no food.

The night before Wolf said, "We should fast until we reach the Morifati's land. It is good to fast on a hunt, and we must travel fast and light. You do not need to be burdened with a heavy pack."

"I always fast on a hunt." I said, "Until I make a kill."

I walked over to the cliff. There below lay a wide valley. There was a meadow between the forest that surrounded my village and this cliff, which I was standing on. The cliff which begins the range of hills that run through the Forbidden Land. We had crossed that meadow at dusk the night before. Wolf knew a trail that brought us up the hill to this spot where you could look out over the way we had come. I felt Wolf walk up behind me.

"She is coming," he said.

I could see nothing beneath us.

"I don't see her."

"There, look back along our trail, watch for movement."

I scanned back along the way we had come. I saw nothing, then a glimpse of motion.

"She has a powerful spirit, but she cannot come with us, the danger is too great."

"She is such a pest, she follows me around all the time in the village," I said. "Everyone makes fun of me because of it."

Wolf snorted. I think he was laughing at me.

"I told her to stay behind, I will have to make her go back, or take her back myself."

"Let me handle it, Rion. We can't let her go any further than this. On the other side of the plateau is the Forbidden Land. I foresaw that this would come to pass. We will wait here and when she arrives I have made preparations for her. We cannot let her go with us, let her follow us, or let her go back and cause suspicion in your village. They would question her until she tells what she knows. I have a place prepared where she will be safe until she can rejoin us."

We watched her as she made it to the trail that lead up the side of the hill. I don't think she saw us, but I found out later she knew we were there.

"What should we do?"

"Just wait, take a seat."

Wolf went over and lay on his stomach where we had slept, facing the path where she would enter the clearing where we camped. I sat with my back against a tree like I was expecting a turkey or a deer to arrive. She reminded me of a doe; slender, with tapered legs and feet. She knew how to hunt, though. She always moved quietly went she tagged along with me. Wolf and I relaxed and remained quiet, saying nothing to each other, nor moving.

Presently, after an hour had passed, Wolf said, "You can come out now Highness, we were waiting for you to arrive."

She had been watching us from behind some brush. I could not see her, but I knew she was out there somehow. Wolf, with his keen senses and because he was a Psychic, knew exactly where she was and when she was coming.

"How did you see me?" she said.

I said, "Why did you follow? I told you to stay behind!"

"I cannot allow you to come with us, Highness," Wolf said.

"I am going to take her back!" I said.

"It's too late for that. The village has found that the two of you are gone. Some expect the two of you to marry now."

I had forgotten about that detail. After the two of us spent three days alone, that was the same thing as a marriage ceremony. Sometimes a man would intentionally kidnap his fiance because of this law.

"I am not going!" Diana said, "I won't. If Rion goes to that awful place, he will die! I have seen it!"

"You've seen that I will die? How are we supposed to believe that, are you a Psychic?"

"No, I am not a Psychic, you know I was born in the Free State. You remember when I was born, you remember when I was a baby. Rion, I see things somehow, I see things before they happen."

"What do you see now?" Wolf said.

"Nothing, I can't control it. I just have these visions, and they come true. I can feel things too, like when I felt you were good and I could trust you back at the village and I hugged you. I knew you wouldn't hurt me."

I said, "How am I supposed to believe that I will die at the Morifati village?" I turned to Wolf.

"Are you leading me to my death?"

"No, you will not die, Rion, I am taking you there to defeat the Morifati."

I turned back to Diana and asked, "So Wolf is leading me to my death at the Morifati village, and yet you say that you can 'feel' that he is good. So how do I die?"

"I don't know."

"Have you seen the manner of my death?"

She looked thoughtful for a moment while she remembered what she had seen.

"Try and remember, it could be helpful."

"The future you see with the Sight is a potential future Highness, minor changes can lead to big changes later on," Wolf said.

"I saw them capture Rion. I saw them take him to their king, an awful evil man, I can't bear to remember him, and their God, their God is Death."

"Were you asleep when you saw these things?"

"No, I was awake. I have visions. I go alone into the meadow or sometimes the woods. I rest beside a tree. I daydream, then the visions they come to me as real as you are now, as if I was there. It is horrifying! I feel as if I am there and the Morifati can see me. I am afraid of them, Rion. They are so evil. They have filled their hearts with murder, envy, and greed. They sacrifice their captives! They plan to sacrifice you!"

"She has the Sight Rion," Wolf said.

"What?" I said.

"She has the power of Foresight. Just like Snake does, and I do too. You may in time develop powers yourself if you choose wisely."

"Diana, tell me exactly what you saw," I said.

"I saw you a prisoner inside a dark room in an old hut that is guarded day and night. There is only one high window with bars. An old hag comes to feed you every day. They give you lots of food, but they never let you out."

"What happens after that?"

"I don't know, I can't see that far."

"How am I supposed to believe this?"

"I see them capture you, and take you to that prison! I see them bring you to their king! I see their awful ceremonies, their horrible faces! They will kill you if you go there! They kill and torture everyone they capture just as they have always done!"

While this was going on, I slowly became aware of the presence of others. I looked around and a pack of wolves stood behind me, waiting for Diana to finish. They had joined us silently as she spoke. Wolf was clearly expecting them, and Diana was not afraid this time. They all stood behind him in order to show respect. I could see right away that they were his pack.

"Highness, these are the wolves of the Forbidden Land, I am their leader. They belong to me and me to them. You must go with them. They will take you to our most sacred place and keep you safe from harm by the Morifati."

"I will not! I must go with Rion!"

"You cannot, I will not allow you to do anything that would lead to your death. You are precious to us. Our future, the future of all the Psychics, and the Free State depends on you and on Rion. Our journey over the mountain trail will take three days and will be very hard. At the end of this journey, Rion must go to the Morifati and surrender to them. You have seen it yourself. They capture him and hold him prisoner."

"Surrender? I thought I should defeat them!" I said. I had not taken the time to tell him about the previous night's dream and what Snake said in it.

"Do not contend against your fate, Rion. In order to defeat them, you must first allow them to capture you."

"But that is too dangerous! They will kill him! They plan to sacrifice him! Why cannot I go too? I may see more of his fate in time to save him!"

"You will not survive the journey. Not this time. And besides, the two of you alone for three days? You would be obligated to marry."

"But we are going to marry, anyway. I have seen it."

"Then you have nothing to worry about, he will survive."

Diana looked stunned at that remark. She was trying to understand all the things she had seen, or maybe dreamed in her future and mine. These visions didn't all fit together, didn't have resolutions yet, just as Wolf said.

I wasn't sure I understood myself. Until now Wolf had said nothing about allowing the Morifati to capture me, but then neither had Snake before last night. I started to press him on this, but before I could, he called to a large white she-wolf.

"Lara!"

She stepped forward and approached Diana.

"Greetings Highness. Come with me, please. Climb upon my back and hold on!"

Diana looked uncertain and went quiet. I could tell she didn't want to go but didn't know how to refuse all of us.

"Lara is my mate, Highness. You will be safe with her. She will take good care of you." Wolf said.

"Please go with them, Diana." I said, "I will return to you unharmed, and when this is over, we will marry."

28

I surprised myself when I said this. I had not until then considered any such thing, but it was the only way out of the deadlock we were in. She brightened up when I said it.

She said, "You will marry me when you return? You must swear it in front of all present!"

She had me. I had stepped in it.

"In the space of time, yes, I will. Now I must accomplish this thing. I must travel across the hills along the mountain trail through the Forbidden Land. I must go to the Morifati and let them capture me. I must escape from them somehow and prevent them from finding the way through the mountains at all costs, for if they find the way through they will attack the Free State. Then I promise I will return to you and we will marry."

"It is so, you understand your tasks, Rion," Wolf said.

Lara said, "It is so. All has been foreseen. Come with me, Highness. Delay no longer. Your love will return to you in the fullness of time. We must go now so that he may proceed."

Diana ran to me and embraced me. She was weeping. The force of her embrace knocked me a little off balance. Then just as quickly she turned and mounted on Lara's back.

"I love you, Rion! You will return to me!"

The wolf pack turned and leaped into the forest in an instant, making no sound. They suddenly left Wolf and I alone, looking at each other as his mate and my future wife rushed off into the wilderness.

SEVEN

THE TRAIL BEGINS

"You didn't tell me before that I would have to surrender to them."

"There is much that you will have to learn about them, that you can only learn first hand, by living among them."

"But how can I defeat them, how can I prevent them from finding the mountain trail if I surrender to them first thing?"

"They are about to depart. Their leader wants to go look for Snake so he can kill her. They also have some idea about the mountain trail, some legends, but they have never found it. They believe as you do that the Forbidden Land is radioactive."

"Isn't it?"

"Your arrival there will create a distraction for them. They will not want to leave to make war before they know exactly who and what you are and how you found them. They will suspect rightly that you know the mountain trail and used it to find them. They will not kill you as long as you can lead them to your people."

"But how can I ever escape from them?"

"I cannot tell you. Snake has warned me not to tell you or help you. It is something you must learn for yourself. No one can understand the truth of a thing unless they find that truth on their own. You have the power within you. You will defeat them, but you must face a trial as their captive first. You will be their captive for a month, from new moon to new moon. They will try everything they know to make you talk, but if you tell them nothing and if you endure until the end you will defeat them. Snake will tell you more about what she expects of you later. My task is to guide you through the Forbidden Land to them and wait for your escape."

"Snake came to me in a dream last night. I didn't have time to tell you about it with Diana tracking us. She told me I would have to let them capture me, that they will prepare to sacrifice me, but little else. She claims she foresaw me and these events. That I will have a type of foresight in time, but I can see nothing now. All of you seem to know what is going to happen, but I know nothing and you will not tell me how to learn. The only reason I am here is because I feel that the Great Spirit has led me this far."

"Do you believe the Great Spirit dwells within your heart?"

"Yes. Are we going to leave now?"

"Yes, you will lead the way."

"How can I lead the way?"

"You must learn to find your way through the wilderness by sensing what is ahead of you."

I shrugged my shoulders.

"You know we are going to the top of a mountain ridge. Look around, how would you find such a thing?"

So I looked around us. Although we were in a heavily wooded area, there was still a gradual slope through the woods to our northeast.

"That way. Where it slopes."

"Lead on."

We made our way along a faint trail that I found through the forest and the slope grew steeper. Presently, I heard a sound that I recognized as rushing water.

"There is a stream ahead." I said.

"Yes. Keep going."

After some more effort, we found the stream rushing down the slope, which by then was moderately steep.

"So what do we do now?"

"Look there."

He gestured with his head uphill. A tree had fallen across, making a natural bridge.

"We will cross to the other side."

"And follow the stream as far as we can up the mountain?"

"It will lead us to a point where we can see the way to the top more easily."

So we went up to the tree and crossed easily enough. On the other side was a worn trail leading up the mountain.

"There is a trail there, faint but still visible, is this it?"

"No, but it will lead us to the mountain trail. We wolves use this trail to follow the stream down to a place that is holy to us. Lara is taking Diana there."

"But we should continue uphill."

"It is so."

We followed the stream uphill and though the slope got steeper; it was never so steep that Wolf could not climb it. I could climb a cliff face if necessary, but wolves do not climb cliffs or trees as humans do.

The trees thinned out until there were none. The stream was just a trickle by then. It started as a spring from within the mountain higher up. There the stream was really just a small waterfall that fell down a cliff face. You could not follow it anymore unless you wanted to climb a sheer cliff. There was no point in that since the way the trail led was more gradual and got to the top of the ridgeline.

I could see the top of the ridge still higher up. I remembered in the dream how we walked along that ridge which widened into a plateau, narrowed into a ridge in other places, but was still passable along its length.

"That's where we are going, up there," I said, more a statement than a question.

"Yes, but we can camp just a little further along. We have a hard couple of days ahead of us."

We came to a place where the trail left the stream and went along the side of the mountain to a plateau. The top of the ridge was still hundreds of feet higher up, but within sight now.

"We will camp here," said Wolf. "This cliff will shelter us from the wind tonight."

An icy breeze blew as we neared the top of the mountain. I had not dressed for winter. I regretted I had not brought a coat. I wore a hunter's cloak for rain and snowstorms and I brought my tent to sleep in. I would have to use the breathing techniques that Grandfather taught me for the cold.

"It is going to get cold tonight, isn't it?"

"It will snow."

"Snow!"

"We are at the top of a mountain."

"I didn't expect Winter conditions. It is Spring in the Free State."

"It is still winter up here, but it will not last long, it will melt and we will get through."

"So we will camp here until it passes."

"The storm will have gone in the morning, only the snow will remain."

"Great."

A chilly breeze gusted around and the skies darkened overhead, but it came from the North, from the other side of the mountain. I thought I better prepare as best I could for a snowy night.

EIGHT

THE TWO MORIFATI

That night I dreamed again, only this time I dreamed of Diana. She was in an outdoor place that looked like a chapel, surrounded by walls of rock. She wore a long white dress with a white lace veil over her head, the kind women wear in a wedding ceremony. The wolf pack stood on both sides of her and everyone stood turned toward me. The Shewolves were on her left. Everyone looked as if they were waiting for me to walk toward them, but no one spoke.

Then the dream changed scenes as dreams will do. I was in an enormous courtroom with a throne on the end. On the throne lay Snake, coiled up with her head raised up regarding me. She was not enormous this time, not large enough to swallow me, but still big. She was the biggest timber rattler I had ever seen.

She regarded me as if waiting for me to speak.

"Why are you on a throne?" I asked Snake.

"I am waiting for you, righteous king."

I woke up then. To my surprise, Wolf had snuck into the tent during the night and lay curled up next to me. On the other side of me, away from Wolf, I felt cold air. I got up and wrapped my cloak around myself. I stepped outside. Snow lay everywhere around, about a half a foot deep. There was snow on top of the tent and all around the mountain, except for the stream. I could see the waterfall the stream made a little way off, putting off mist in the cold.

There was no breeze, so it was not too cold yet, although I was not sure how long I could last in conditions like this, with just my cloak and the hiking boots I was wearing. I had dressed for moderate cold, but not deep cold.

I began the breathing exercises Grandfather taught me. You can withstand long periods of deep cold if you breathe correctly and keep moving. It really wasn't deep cold up there but at that altitude, conditions can change fast.

I took a drink from my canteen. I tried to, forgetting that it was nearly empty. But the little water left in it had frozen.

I walked over to the spring. It flowed too fast to freeze. It lay a few hundred feet away. We had camped in the shelter of the cliff, well away from the water's flow, but not so far we could not find it.

As I got closer to the spring, I saw something that made me freeze in my tracks. Something that I should not have seen up there in the Forbidden Land. Two sets of human footprints. Along the side of the spring heading down the trail were two sets of human footprints, large enough to belong to two adult men.

I went back and woke up Wolf.

"I found something you need to see," I said.

When we got back to the prints, he began sniffing around them, following them up and down the trail.

"They are Morifati," he said.

"Are you sure? They should not be here." I said.

"There is no mistaking their scent. It is the smell of death."

"How could they be here?"

"These two have found the mountain trail somehow. There should be no others yet."

"What if there are?"

"I have seen no more, but the longer we delay, the greater the danger grows. This is why I wanted you to hurry. These two will find a way to the Free State, then go back to their village. They are scouts. They may even find the Forest Temple. We must find them. We must hunt them down and you must kill them both."

"I have never killed a man."

"You must kill them, or they will return and then all the Morifati will come back and attack the Free State."

"Wolf," I said, "I have never killed a man. I have killed many bucks and boars, once I killed a bear, but I have never killed a man."

"You will kill these two Morifati. It is a test for you. A trial you must pass. Everything depends on it. Not merely your life, but Diana's life and the lives of all your people. You will do this thing. I will not do it for you. I will go with you but you will do it alone."

"But how?"

"With your bow, then you will finish the job with your hunting machete. They cannot live or they tell the rest of the Morifati. Kill them now, and we will fulfill our mission. Let them live and they will know we are coming and know how to find their way back here."

#

So we set out to track them down. They had not gone far. The snow had fallen heaviest in the early evening and by early morning had stopped. They passed close by us in the night without seeing my tent, which was covered in snow. If they saw anything in the early morning darkness, they must have thought it was a snowdrift. When I found their tracks, they were still fresh.

When I found them, they were at the tree that made a bridge across the stream. I guess they were debating whether to cross there.

"You must advance on your own here, Rion, and make the kill," Wolf said.

I said nothing. I knew I had to do it, but the question was how? I wanted to do it, but I was afraid. The first time you kill anything is scary. Killing a man for the first time is the worst, even a Morifati. You know they have no mercy and are inhuman, but they still look human and on some level still are human even though they have degenerated into savagery.

I crept closer to them. They had stopped to make a fire to warm themselves next to the bridge. As I got closer, I could see that they had blood red paint on their faces. I had heard that they did this.

When I was as close as I dared to get, I was still a little too far to be certain of my bow. Did I need to charge into their camp? Should I try to catch them by surprise?

Suddenly, one of them got up and walked into the woods. He almost walked toward me. I crouched down low and when he passed and had his back to me; I got up and followed, checking first to see that the other was not watching.

I stalked him for some way until he paused at the edge of a clearing. He just stood there as if he were waiting for a deer or turkey to enter the clearing. I got my bow ready and crept closer.

Just as I got ready to take a shot at him, an arrow thudded into the tree I was hiding behind, just above my head. I wheeled around. The other Morifati who I thought had stayed by the fire was behind me. He had already prepared another arrow.

"Halt!" he said.

I froze. They had ambushed me. They had sensed me somehow and set this trap for me.

"Lower your weapon!" he said.

He called to the other Morifati, who rushed up to cover me from the side.

"Lower your bow. I will not ask again!"

I could kill one of them, but not both of them. I had lost the element of surprise. I never had it, really. I lowered my bow and took the tension off my string.

"We would speak with you, but if you make a false move or try to escape, we will kill you!"

"Who and what are you?" said the Morifati in front of me. He appeared to be the leader of the two.

"I am Rion, of the Free State."

"The Free State! What are you doing here in the Forbidden Land?"

"Hunting. But I should ask you the same thing. How did you get here?"

"We will ask the questions Rion of the Free State. You will answer, or die."

"But I don't know any answers, and you have asked no questions that are any of your business."

"You will answer my questions young hunter, or I will pin you to that tree with my arrows."

He paused then to let me think it over. His companion stood to the left of me and said nothing. He moved up, and they both stood, one on my left and one on my right where I could see them, but out of reach. They were close enough that if I shot one, the other one could rush me and I would quickly have to draw my machete out and kill him, before he could take a shot himself with his own bow. While I was thinking this over, the leader said.

"Drop your bow! Do it now!"

I had no choice but to drop it and wait for a chance to out-maneuver them.

"How close are we to your village?"

"Very far, I have been out for a week."

"You lie!" the other Morifati said.

"We have seen that this mountain ridge ends close by and there is a valley below. We know that you Freemen do not live here because of the radioactivity from the Great Third War. So your village and the Free State have to be down there. You will lead us there. You know a safe way through the fallout zones or you would not be here."

"I know nothing. I will tell you nothing. Kill me if you must."

"We will kill you, but not all at once. We will make you wish you were dead. You will beg us to kill you by the time we finish with you. Then we will roast your remains."

So there I was, in a standoff with them. I would not tell them anything. They would torture me since that was their custom. Grandfather had told me stories about the Morifati and their customs. They preferred to capture enemies rather than kill them. They enjoyed torture as part of their religion. They sacrificed to their god Than by roasting their captives alive.

"Walk back to our fire."

I turned.

"Slowly!"

It was not far. They followed close behind, but out of reach.

When I left Wolf, he had been watching their campsite from a distance up the trail. Was he watching us now, I wondered? I could not sense his presence. He would not allow himself to be seen. He said I had to do this by myself. So far, I had screwed up.

When we got back to their camp, we stopped.

"Slowly draw out your machete and drop it, then back away." the leader said.

I did as I was told. I had no choice at this point. Wolf meant what he said about me handling this alone, I guess. He was nowhere to be seen.

"Are you alone?"

"There is one other with me."

"Where is he now?"

"He has gone to warn the Free State that you are here."

That was a lie, of course. I had no idea where he was, but then neither did they. I didn't want them to get too comfortable. Maybe keep me here for a while, torturing me. Plus, I wanted to see how they might react to the news that help was on the way.

"Another lie." said the second Morifati.

"Yes." said the leader.

"How are you able to travel here, in the Forbidden Land?"

"I have a map."

"Show it to me!"

"I can't. It is back at our camp on the mountain top. You passed by us in the night. I saw your tracks in the snow and we tracked you here."

That would at least take them back in the wrong direction, but I didn't know what I would do when I got there, since there was no map. I could pretend I lost the map, I guess.

"We could make him lead the way without a map.", said the second Morifati.

"I don't trust him, not at all. He tells both the truth and lies. If he leads, he could lead us to a trap.", said the Leader.

"That's right I guess. And with a map, we might not need him anymore."

"Except to keep us fed on the trail."

They chuckled over that.

"We need to find the other one, and make certain that there are no others. Walk back the way you came then.", said the Leader.

I turned and started back up the mountain with the Leader behind me, keeping me covered. The second one gathered up what little belongings they had, my weapons, and quickly doused the fire. Then he caught up to us. I learned later that I was alone with them. Wolf had left me with them so I could prove myself. I would have felt less confident had I known that.

NINE

THE KING OF THE MORIFATI

By the time we got back to my tent, the snow had melted. The tent sat a little disheveled but still upright on the rocky plateau where we had camped. There was a small amount of earth up there and a little grass. Enough earth to stake a tent down, but not much else.

Farther up the mountain there was nothing but rock with only occasional flowers or grass persistently forcing their way through the cracks. The top of the mountain varied between rocky plateaus and jumbled boulders, which still formed a natural trail along the ridgeline.

We walked up to the tent and when we got close; I started to enter.

"Halt!" the Leader said.

I froze just a few feet in front of the tent. I turned around to face them.

"We can't see you if you go in there alone, and something doesn't feel right."

"I don't trust him at all, no further than I can throw him. He is a liar, this one, always scheming. I can see it. He plans to get away if he can. He would like to kill us. You can see it in his eyes. We won't get much information out of him, even through torture." said the Follower.

"What then?" said the Leader. "What do you propose we do?"

"I'll tear the tent down. Then I'll dig through his gear until I find that map. If he has really got one."

So the second Morifati went over and grabbed the front tent pole. I had jammed it in pretty solid so it wouldn't come out. He opened up the tent flap and tugged on it.

Meanwhile, I tried to stand where I could watch them both. I knew I was going to have to make a run for it soon. More likely, I was going to have to grab one of them and take his machete, or better yet his bow, and if possible, kill them both with it.

The Morifati stuck his head in under the tent flap to see what was holding it. He screamed and then gurgled out a terrified moan. He fell over on his back with Wolf on top of him. Wolf had his throat gripped in his jaws. While the Leader and I watched in horror, Wolf ripped the Morifati's larynx out in front of us, then looked up and snarled at the Leader.

I turned and lunged at the Leader then. That move would have worked on any ordinary man. He didn't have time to raise his bow. Instead, he did something to me with his mind. He knocked me backward without even touching me. He had teleported to the top of the mountain above us. When he teleported, there was a sound like a thunderclap as the air rushed together where he had been. There was another pop on top of the mountain where he landed. I lay stunned for a moment, my ears ringing.

Wolf came over and looked down at me.

"Get up!" he said, "We must follow."

Then he sat up and howled. His pack answered his howls from down the mountain. I got up and pulled myself to my feet. I turned to look up at the mountain. The Leader of the Morifati stood up there watching us and laughed at us.

The wolf pack had been waiting, just out of sight. They ran past us toward the Leader, intent on catching up to him. He laughed again and disappeared with another clap of thunder. I guess he went further down the ridgeline out of sight. I learned later he could not teleport over great distances, only from one place he could see to the next. The pack continued up. They wanted to make certain he had gone.

"I failed my test, Wolf."

"Yes. I hoped you would kill them, but I failed too. I did not realize their King was with them."

"That was their King?"

"A Psychic who uses his powers for evil leads them. His name is Blackheart John. He can teleport short distances, he has some limited powers of foresight, and he can look into your mind."

"What will we do now?"

"We have no choice but to follow. He hurries back to gather his people."

I doubted myself profoundly. I had not killed either of them and I could not kill their King unless I caught him by surprise. I was not entirely sure what Wolf and Snake expected from me. Were they sending me to the Morifati as a distraction?

"I don't know if I am the man you want to defeat them," I said.

"You are," said Wolf.

"You're certain."

"Snake is certain. I believe what she tells me. I have no other way to know except for glimpses of you in the future and what little I can see."

"So your pack will follow him and we will join them?"

"They will return here when they are certain he has retreated. They will come back here and guard this area since it is the entrance to our lands and yours. That spring is sacred to us, we think the Morifati may have defiled it"

"Is the stream hot?"

"No. That is an illusion that was created in their minds and yours to keep you out of our hunting grounds. The only radioactive zones are where the great cities used to be. You may drink from that spring in time, but not until your sanctification."

"We must kill Blackheart John before he gets back to his people," I said.

"We cannot. He is too fast. We will stick to our original plan."

"But the Morifati will return here at once!"

"They never undertake a war without sacrificing to their God first."

"But that shouldn't take long. What kind of sacrifice would keep them waiting?"

"Human. They will sacrifice you!"

"That makes no sense. How can I defeat them if I am sacrificed? If I die?"

"You have to solve that problem yourself. No one else can solve the riddle for you, or you will not understand it. You must gain understanding, Rion."

The wolf pack returned from over the mountain then.

"What news?" said Wolf.

"He hastens back to his people." said a large black wolf.

"You will all stay in this area, guarding against their return. If you see them and they are not too many, you will attack. If their numbers are large, watch them and wait for the opportunity to attack individuals and small groups."

"We will!" they all answered in unison, and then they all howled and scampered around.

TEN

ON THE MOUNTAIN TRAIL

So we gained the summit of the mountain. It was a narrow plateau there, which extended for a mile, then narrowed to a jagged peak. It was not straight, but meandered a bit. It got pretty narrow in spots, but was still passable. The elevation varied. It was higher up ahead. For that reason, I could not see to its end.

I scanned ahead, trying to spot the King of the Morifati, but he was nowhere to be seen.

A beautiful raven flew past. I wondered how it could survive in this cold so high up. It looked very much like the same raven I had seen on the morning of the day Wolf appeared to me.

It took no notice of me, but flew toward our destination. I looked around us. To the north and south were the mountains and hills of the Forbidden Land. To the east, a peak blocked our view. To the west lay the valley where my village and the Free State lay. Too far away to see the village now hidden in the wood already a great distance behind us.

"We have a long way to go before night."

"Keep going," Wolf said.

The way was much harder than I expected it to be. My canteen was empty, and we still fasted. The snow had melted, and it was completely dry up there.

"How much farther is it?"

"A day, a night, and a day at least," said Wolf.

We pressed on the rest of the day over rocky plateaus and narrow trails between the boulders which made up the jagged ridge until at last we arrived at a steeper trail which ascended the side of the peak that blocked my view earlier.

"We will camp here. The way is too hard now to try in the dark. We will start in the morning first thing." Wolf said.

I said nothing. I had doubted their motives, Wolf and Snake. What could I possibly do to defeat the Morifati? What is this test I have to pass? This riddle I must solve? I was neither the smartest nor the bravest among the soldiers of the Free State. Their mysterious answers had annoyed me.

Without setting up the tent, I threw down a ground cloth and lay myself down on it. There was no way to stake down the tent anyway, nothing but rock. I wrapped myself up in my cloak and fell into a deep sleep.

Presently I dreamed again.

Diana came to me in a dream. She appeared to be kneeling next to me while I lay asleep. She brushed my shoulder to wake me. I looked at her.

She said, "I love you, Rion."

"What are you doing here? You should be with the Wolves."

"I am with the Wolves."

"You are kneeling next to me."

"I wanted to tell you it is okay to trust the Wolves. Wolf will not ask you to do something unless he believes you can do it."

"What is this trial they want me to pass?"

"I can't explain. You must discover the answer for yourself. I have a way to watch over you."

"Diana, I lied when I said I would marry you."

"I know. You will have a change of heart."

I sat up at that point to look her in the eye. I wanted to explain myself to her. I looked at her, then I put my arms around her. I could feel her slender body, even though I dreamed. Then she faded away. I was awake and the scene on the mountaintop was otherwise just as I had pictured it in my dream.

The first light of dawn glowed in the sky to the east, but the sun had not risen yet. A thin, waning crescent moon hung in the sky; there would be a new moon soon. Wolf lay close by but was not awake yet. It was cold, so I wrapped my cloak around myself and practiced my breathing exercises. I had to condition myself for this cold and for what lay ahead.

After what happened the last time I met the Morifati King, I knew I must act differently the next time we met. I could not say what Wolf wanted me to do, but I knew he believed I could do it.

Diana said I could trust the Wolves, and I believed her. Was she trying to say that I could not trust Snake?

It was a curious way to say it. If that's what she meant. I had much to ask everyone involved. Wolf when he woke, Snake, and of course Diana. The only one I could speak to at present was Wolf. Diana was too far away now. Snake had only ever come to me in my dreams. Wolf and I were going to have a long talk when he woke.

I knew I shouldn't worry about how things would turn out. Grandfather always taught me to stay in the present. To plan, but not to obsess over my plan. To wait and see what needed to be done in the present.

"When the time comes, you will know what to do. Learn first, act later."

It was then I saw something peculiar. A raven, the same raven I saw before, flew past me and then flew on ahead.

Wolf still lay sleeping near me. Should I wake him now I wondered?

I knew that somehow I had to stop the Morifati from reaching my village. I did not understand why I needed to face them alone. Or why I should let them capture me.

All I knew was that Snake believed I could do this thing and so did Wolf, and now Diana told me I must go to meet them alone.

I did not know how I was going to do it.

When Wolf woke up, I let him stretch and go through his morning routine.

Then I said, "Why do I have to let myself get captured?"

"You have to learn how to defeat them," Wolf said.

"How can I defeat them by going to them alone, allowing them to take me back to the middle of their camp and imprison me?"

"You have the power within you to defeat them, you have the Sight."

"The Sight! I have no such power!"

"There are many who can see the future, but most can only glimpse the future of days or years ahead. Snake is one of these. Diana can and I can, to a limited extent, but you can see what happens next. You can see 'around the corner.'"

"I can't see anything. They will kill me and sacrifice me to their god."

"You will develop this ability. I and others have foreseen it."

"How!"

"I don't know. If I knew I could do it myself. All I know is that you can and you will."

"But first I must go to them alone and let them capture me? Why can't I defeat them now?"

"This power only comes to those who need it. Through the concentration of your mind, you will gain it. Then you can appeal to it when lost or trapped or cornered. You have it within you, you will find it when the time comes. Do not be afraid. You are enough to defeat them single-handed. Do it! Solve the Riddle!"

"I didn't do so well before."

"You will prepare."

"If you can't train me or prepare me, that's going to make it a lot harder to do."

"Rion, there is another reason you must not know too much. Their King, Blackheart John, he can look into your mind. If you know all now, he will see all when he captures you. He will search your mind, your thoughts, and memories. You can hide much perhaps, but this you must never show to him for then he will know it and become unstoppable."

"So you will not tell me how to do it? How to escape?"

"Rion, you will have a month. From new moon to new moon. They will not sacrifice you until the next new moon. And know this, if I knew this secret then I could do it myself. I would then become as great a warrior as you."

"Wolf, when I learn this secret technique, whatever it is, I will teach it to you."

"As you wish my Lord."

ELEVEN

WHITEOUT

The time to move on had come, so we broke camp. We set out toward the steep slope ahead of us.

"That peak is the last one on the trail." Wolf said. "After that it is a long climb downhill to the Great River, and on the other side of the river is a broad valley, which is the Kingdom of the Morifati. If you travel south along the river it will lead you to Snake's domain."

We found a path that meandered up the side, steep, but not so steep as to make me climb by hand or to make Wolf turn back. I looked around when I got high enough to get a view from behind to the west and north beyond the range of mountains. Dark clouds approached from the north and west.

"A storm is coming." I said to Wolf.

"Then we had better climb quickly." he said. "We can camp on the summit but we cannot climb if the snow is too thick, nor can we descend the other side."

This weather was worse than I had counted on. It was Spring in the Free State. We could not have made it through this mountain trail if it was Winter. The snow had melted up here, now it returned.

"Did you not foresee this, Wolf?"

"Yes, but only in part. It does not matter. We will face worse than this soon. You will face greater danger than the weather."

We made excellent progress up the slope. We moved steadily, as fast as we could walk uphill without winding ourselves. It was necessary to climb as quickly as possible as the storm would clearly overtake us soon, but we dared not exhaust ourselves either.

We continued and as we climbed; I took the opportunity, when the trail wound back to the north, to watch the storm approach. The cloud did not so much seem to rush toward us than it seemed to grow ever larger until it filled the sky. It appeared to be a deep winter storm. Not rain followed by sleet, followed by snow, but starting with snow. Gradually at first, just a few flakes, then falling thicker and thicker. No wet snow, no big flakes, just dry deep snow. This type of snow storm appeared to be a dust storm when it was far off, but as often as not, turned into a full-blown blizzard.

Soon this dusty looking cloud completely covered the sky overhead, and the first sparse flakes fell. We had a long way to go to the summit, too long to make it in time. I said nothing, but quickened my pace. The wind gusted and picked up. That was not a good omen.

There was nothing to do but to keep going. The snow fell thicker; the wind grew stronger and colder. I wrapped my cloak around me and tied it. Wolf seemed undisturbed, but his fur was standing up. Then the storm set in and the wind blew a steady gale.

With a gust of wind, the snow became so thick I could no longer see the trail ahead. I could not even see the trail beneath my feet. I stopped. I held my hand up in front of my face. When it was a foot away, it disappeared in the snow.

"Wolf!"

"I am behind you!"

"Can you come forward?"

"I will. I cannot see, but I still feel and smell."

He was not far behind, but I could not see him or the trail, and I didn't want to crawl back to him. Presently, he came up behind me, sniffing my legs. He brushed up beside me. I steadied myself on his back.

"That's it," he said. "Take hold of my fur. I will lead us forward."

"We should wait for it to clear."

"We can't. It will get worse before it gets better. We must make the summit or we will not make it at all. We must keep going. Until we reach the top."

"Can we climb fast enough? I can't see even a foot ahead of me. I dare not pick my foot up or set it down."

"Take a rope and tie a harness around me. Walk directly behind me. Take slow steps. Move your feet along the trail."

I did as he said. I had to dig one of the tent ropes out of my pack by hand. I tied it loosely around his neck with a knot that would not choke him.

"I'm ready. Let's go."

I felt him brush past, and the rope tugged. I rested a hand on his haunches to make sure I was behind him and was stepping in his footsteps. We plodded. The thought flashed into my mind that we would not make it.

I felt cold, especially on my feet and hands. I say cold, but what I mean is that they hurt. I had not prepared for deep cold like this, why had no one foreseen it? Could they be wrong? I knew the Sight wasn't perfect, that it was only a potential future, and a glimpse in part more often than not.

The idea entered my mind that they were wrong. Suddenly I knew it. We would not make it. I felt sick to my stomach, the pain in my hands and feet got worse.

"Wolf, we will not make it."

"Be silent. I must concentrate. We cannot stop. You must keep going. Even if I die here."

I had not thought of that. The thought of leaving him behind to freeze on the side of this peak gave me a pang of remorse.

"I won't leave you. You may have to leave me. I can feel myself freezing. My hands and feet are on fire. My cloak is not enough for this wind, this blizzard."

"I am not leaving you, and you are not quitting. Think of your people. Think of the Free State, think of Diana your mate."

That struck me. Suddenly I wanted to see her again more than I ever had before. How could I do it? I had to make it through this somehow. What if I collapsed?

"What if I fall? I know I must go on, but what if I pass out?"

"If you stumble, we can wrap the tent around you and let the snow pile on top of us the way the wolves do. I will keep you warm with my body. It is not too cold for me yet, but it is hard to sense the way so I must go slowly. Keep moving, don't stop. Keep thinking about Diana."

#

We were making slow progress when Wolf stopped. Minutes passed. I asked him, "What's wrong?"

"I can no longer sense the trail."

"Not at all? What's wrong?"

"I can't feel or smell anything but snow. I can't sense the way forward."

"What will we do now? I can't see in this blizzard, and now you can't!"

"We will wait. See if I can recover, maybe the storm will clear. If not, we will have to camp here like I said before."

"But that won't work Wolf, we will surely freeze to death here!"

He said nothing. I felt desperate. I hoped for a way out of this. My heart ached. I had visions. I saw the Free State; I pictured it in my mind's eye. I saw Grandfather and then Diana. Memories at first, then visions of them as they might be right now.

A vision of Diana appeared to me. I concentrated on it. It became more distinct. I longed to see her again. I had to get out of this somehow, some way.

The vision became more real, then suddenly dissolved. I looked around and I could see Wolf and the surrounding area in a golden glow. The snow still fell heavily, and the wind blew furiously, but I could see through it. The glow came from an object ahead of us. Floating ahead of us and above our heads was some being in the shape of a dove. It glowed brightly enough to illuminate the surrounding area.

I heard Diana's voice come from the Dove.

"Don't be afraid, Rion, and don't despair. You and Wolf will make it through this storm all the way to the summit, I will see to that."

"Diana? How can that be you?"

"I don't have time to explain now. You and Wolf must continue to the summit at once and make camp when you reach it. If you stop here, you will die."

"How are you able to do this thing?"

"I can't explain. I will illuminate your path. You and Wolf can see now. You will climb this mountain. You must climb this mountain and enter the lands of the Morifati."

"We will follow you, Highness.", said Wolf.

There was nothing to do now but continue up the mountain. She moved ahead of us along the way up the mountain. We kept to the portion of the trail that she illuminated for us. I forgot about the pain in my hands and feet, and the cold. I no longer felt any pain or cold. The golden light that emanated from the image of the dove did not just illuminate our path, it warmed us and gave us strength.

But how had she found us? How did she know we were in trouble? What powers were these she possessed? She claimed she wasn't a Psychic and here she was performing miracles. She was still a child in my mind. Now I knew she had hidden her true nature from me.

There were many questions I needed to ask her. There was a lot more going on than I was aware of, or that anyone had explained to me. I knew she wasn't just a pesky kid now.

#

At last, after a climb which could have taken an hour or some unknown time longer, we reached the summit. By some lucky twist of fate the storm subsided and we waded through waist deep snow until Wolf said, "Let us camp here, Rion."

I unpacked the tent and unfolded it on top of the snowbank. I could jam the tent poles down into the snow, so we had something to crawl into. Diana still kept the form of a radiant dove, illuminating the area while I set the tent up. When I had finished, she said, "I will go now, but I will keep watch over you, I will never be far from you."

Then suddenly she went.

"Wait!" I said.

It was too late. She vanished as incomprehensibly as she had appeared. The moonlight shone through the clouds so I could see just well enough.

"What can all this mean, Wolf? How can she do these things?"

"I don't know.", he said. "She must still be with Lara, but I know Diana has great powers."

"So much has been hidden from me. It's too much to take in."

"You must rest now, Rion."

"If these clouds have gone in the morning, the sun will melt the snow, we can make it down the mountain.'

"Yes. Let's sleep now. Tomorrow we may find new dangers."

So we packed it in. I fell exhausted into my bedroll and went into a deep sleep. This time with no dreams.

TWELVE

THE GREAT RIVER

We slept until after the sun came up. The sun had risen high enough for the snow to melt. It was still cold, but I could tell that it would warm up beyond the freezing point. The sky had cleared, so there was a view in all directions. We had camped a short distance from the eastern cliff.

"It is still too early to climb down.", Wolf said.

"I'd like to go over and see if I can find the way.", I said.

So I walked over to the edge as close as I dared go. The valley lay spread out before us. Down below, almost at the base of the mountain, was a big river which stretched from the north to the south.

"That is the Great River. It is the boundary of the Kingdom of the Morifati and the Forbidden Land. I will go with you as far as its west bank, but I must leave you there and you must go on by yourself. The rest of this journey you must complete alone."

"Thanks, I could not have made it this far without you."

I have to admit I dreaded going any farther. No one had explained to me why I had to let the Morifati capture me or how I was ever going to escape from them or defeat them, except to tell me that somehow I would learn or attain the power to defeat the Morifati by enduring some kind of ordeal.

I went over to the edge of the cliff as far as I dared. I looked around to see if I could see the way down. Over to the left were stone steps someone had carved into the mountainside long ago. They led off parallel to the cliff face.

In front of me, as far as the eye could see, was the Kingdom of the Morifati. It was dense woodlands, followed by large expanses of open grassland. And of course the Great River lay beneath us at the base of the mountain. I could not see any signs of their village or see any of them moving through the open country, or see any smoke from a fire. We were still too far away from their village at that point.

The river, the wood, and the plain were all beautiful at that height, as were the sun and sky that day. There was nothing threatening in that scene. No hint of evil men living there.

"It doesn't look so bad from here, Wolf."

"No, but the Morifati could lie in wait for you in that wood. That is their way. And after our encounter with their King you know they will soon return here in force. To make their way back along the mountain trail and find the way down to your village and the Free State."

"I wonder how long it will take them to return. Blackheart John moves fast since he can teleport. He has surely made it back to his village by now."

"They are on their way back here now. You can count on it."

We made good time going down the mountain. The shadow of the mountain from the setting sun grew in the afternoon, but before that the morning sun warmed the cliff face. It was still mid-afternoon when we got to the bottom.

The last few hundred feet of the trail hid behind a gigantic stone monolith that had sheared off from the cliff face in some past event, but remained standing upright. It was dark and cool in there. There were signs we had worked the stone in times past. The warriors of the Free State, or maybe someone before them, had used this trail often.

At the base of the mountain, the trail ended where a rocky shore had formed by sand deposited at a bend in the river. There were more rocks than sand there, so much so that we made no footprints. When I turned around, I could not see the trail up the side of the mountain, hidden behind boulders, and the little shore we stood on did not extend any further than the length of the bend, There was no shore on the other side of the river. The only way to get to where we were, someone would have to cross the river and land at exactly this little rocky beach. I realized then why the Morifati had not found it for such a long time.

"This is as far as I go, Rion."

I was at a loss to say anything in return. Looking out across the river, I could see that I could wade out a very long way, but before I could get to the eastern bank, there was a channel about sixty feet wide with a swift current. I would have to swim across that and would wind up somewhere downstream. The eastern bank was a dirt cliff with woods beyond. Dark looking woods that might contain swamps. In some places, trees had fallen into the river.

When I get to the other side, I had better backtrack upstream to a spot where I can swim back across; I thought. I would have to find some landmarks to get back here if I ever made it back from wherever the Morifati would take me. I dreaded what I must do now.

I turned around to look at Wolf.

"It looks like I can wade out a long way, then I will have to swim for it the rest of the way."

"You should leave your pack and your bow and your cloak behind. Stash them here where you can find them later."

"Maybe I can float them across. I could make a float out of my cloak."

"You will not need them on the other side and the Morifati will take them from you and you will lose them forever."

"I don't understand why I have to allow myself to be captured. How can I do this? Just walk up to them with my hands up?"

Wolf said nothing.

"Just go to them, surrender, and while I am their captive I will develop the Sight, and somehow I will defeat them?"

"No one can tell you how to do what you have to do, Rion. Figure out how to do it yourself."

"It would be helpful if someone would tell me something more than 'defeat the Morifati'."

"You have the power within you. I know you have it within you. Don't be afraid. None of us want you to fail. Do you think that Snake or Grandfather or Diana or I would send you to your death at the hands of the Morifati? You are the only one who can do this thing. You are unique."

"So I have to go to the Morifati and let them capture me. What happens after that?"

"They will capture you. They will whip you and throw you into a cell. The King of the Morifati will try to read your mind. He will try to control your mind. He has psychic powers that he uses for evil. The Morifati seek only to satisfy their own lusts in the here and now. They do not believe there is anything else."

"What if I fail?"

"Then they will roast you alive. They will cross the Forbidden Land and attack the Free State. They will invade Snake's domain so they can kill her."

"And the Wolves? What do they have planned for the Wolves?"

"They seek to hunt us. They want to find and destroy our holiest places and hunt us to extinction."

"Why me? How was I chosen for this?"

"It is your fate! You cannot fail! You will not fail! You must not fail!"

"You really believe that? You believe I can defeat them?"

"Yes. I know it. I know you have the power within you."

"You are a faithful friend, Wolf."

So I gathered my things together and wrapped them in a bundle with my cloak. I found a little cave to stash them in that the Morifati would not see and which probably would not flood.

"Goodbye Wolf."

"It grieves me to leave you here. It is not our way. It is not the way of the Wolves to let a brother hunt alone, to let a brother face enemies alone. We are a pack. You are a member of our pack now."

I felt pride mingle with my fear when he said that. We had bonded on the trail.

"And you and your pack will always be welcome in the Free State. The Wolves and the Free State are allies now. For as long as I am alive. I will tell Grandfather and the rest of them of your deeds. I will testify about you before the Council."

"Sometimes, one of us walks alone, hunts alone, lives apart from the pack. The ones who return become the ones who lead us later on. It is now your time to hunt alone. Remember, there are those who love you and watch over you. Like your mate, she guided us through the storm. You can call upon them, but they cannot help you directly now. You will not fail. I have seen it."

"I won't let you down. I will go now."

Without anymore goodbyes, I turned from Wolf and walked toward the river.

As soon as I stepped into the river, I realized it was freezing cold. I started breathing deeply in through my nose and out through my mouth, using the ancient breathing techniques that Grandfather taught me to adjust to the cold.

So I waded out into the river. When it got to be waist deep, I turned around to see if Wolf was still there. He sat on the bank, watching me cross. I guess he wanted to stay and see if I would make it.

When it got shoulder high, I pushed off and started swimming. The current was not too bad at first, but when it picked up, I turned and swam at an angle to the shore. It was faster than it looked, but the channel was deep, so there were no rapids. I swam faster with the current pushing me along.

It started carrying me downriver fast. I worried I had made a mistake crossing at this point. I could get carried a thousand feet downriver if the current was too fast, or get pulled under if there was an undertow. I knew the worst thing to do was panic or let myself become tired, so I swam steadily at an angle. The shape of the river helped me. It turned as I described before, and then it turned back. It got shallow again right in front of me, this time with a sandy bank. I walked out onto the sand, feeling the cold but fighting it by breathing deep till I felt warm. I had only traveled about three hundred feet downriver.

I don't think I could have made it through a current like that with a steeper river channel. So while it wasn't a perfect place to ford, it proved to be possible.

I couldn't see Wolf, so I howled to see if he could hear me.

"Rion! Did you make it across?"

I forgot he spoke with his mind, not his lungs. I pictured him in my mind, and in my mind and out loud I said, "Yes, I am okay. It was a little rough, but I'm okay. Will we still be able to speak this way?"

"It is possible, but it is better not to. You must learn many things now, and you must concentrate your mind on the dangers you face. I go now."

And that was it. If he heard me any more he didn't answer me. I turned my attention to the wood behind me. Was there a trail where I could enter?

I needed to double back upstream to see if I could find the way back across, too. I put my shoes and clothes back on. I had bundled them up and tied them to my back so I could swim easily. I could not see any entrance but the wood was open enough that I could enter it.

I thought I might have to wander blindly through the wood to the north, through an untouched forest, then I stumbled upon something which was both welcome and a bad sign. There was a well-worn trail that ran parallel to the river, but just out of sight of it. Hidden from above as well by the forest canopy a line of men could walk along it in broad daylight and walk unseen from the river or from above. It had to be a Morifati path that their hunting parties and war parties had made over the years.

It would lead me to where I wanted to go, so I followed it. I walked steadily and quietly, careful not to leave tracks or make noise. I lost sight of the river but I could hear it. I counted my paces so I would know when to turn back toward the river to see how far along the bank I had gone.

When I had gone about four hundred paces, I stopped cold. The smell of campfires drifted down through the wood.

THIRTEEN

I AM CAPTURED

I crept up the trail then and the smell of their fires got stronger and I heard them talking. I wasn't ready to reveal myself to them yet, so I stalked toward them to get a better look.

The trail ended at a clearing where they had camped, just at the edge of the wood. I could see the river through the trees just a little beyond. This must be the place where you have to cross to get to the mountain trail. If they camped here, they were getting ready to do just that. I had arrived just in time; I realized. Just before the entire war party crossed the Great River and make their attack.

This was the moment of truth. The timing of my arrival was perfect to accomplish my mission, to prevent them from crossing by giving them a distraction. They would not cross if they had me as their captive to take back to their village and present to their King.

But how to surrender to them and when? There were a lot of bad ways to do it and many things that could go wrong. How could I be sure they would capture me and not just kill me on sight?

The sun had almost set when I reached their camp. At least it had gone down behind the mountain far enough to cast its shadow over us. I could no longer see them except by the light of their campfires and the shadows they cast.

Their customs were strange and morbid. They all wore black clothes, and they painted their faces black with a red stripe across their eyes and a red stripe across their mouths. They painted their throats and hands and anything else they had exposed white, like a ghost.

At the center of the camp they placed a tall wooden totem pole that was painted black except for the features of a carved head which had red eyes, red nose, red mouth, and red ears. I knew it must be an image of their god Than.

They had built an enormous bonfire in front of it, which illuminated the center of the camp. This was not a permanent village, so I guess they planned to perform a ceremony before they launched their attack on the Free State. Did they perform a war dance before leaving? Will they make some kind of sacrifice?

I thought I better wait to see what they would do before I walked up to them. Was their King with them? I scanned the camp, but I did not see him. Maybe they still waited for him to arrive. I was pretty sure he was their chief priest and their King, but that was more often than not two separate jobs in most tribes.

They all gathered in a circle around the totem pole. There was quite a crowd of them. The gathering was twenty to thirty men deep. They stood silently. They were waiting for something to happen.

The crowd chanted. Quietly at first, so quiet I couldn't understand what they said. They chanted louder.

"Than! Than! Than!"

This went on for some minutes, getting louder and louder. They became more and more energetic. They were cheering as much as chanting. Finally, they stopped and cried out in unison,

"GRANT US VICTORY!"

They screamed out war cries, then they fell silent.

A path opened up between them as the ones in front of the wooden image of Than stood aside to let someone through. They all turned and held up their right hands as he passed through them. He walked between them and approached Than, bowed, and knelt on one knee.

A man painted all over in ghostly white paint except for red eyes and a red mouth. He wore a white robe that looked like a funeral shroud. He wore a headdress of black feathers.

It was not their King, Blackheart John. I knew what he looked like. This was another man. I guessed he must be their high priest. I was wrong about them. They separated the two jobs, like everyone else did.

He stood up and turned around to face them.

"You are all fated to die!" he said.

A great cheer and war cries rose from the crowd. They didn't stop until he raised his hands.

"That is why we are strong! We the Morifati do not fear death! Death is our god! We know that Than rules over all men and decides the fate of all men! He owns your soul, you cannot escape from him! He made the strong to rule over the weak. We, the Morifati! We are the strong!"

Another great cheer rose from the crowd.

"Than is your lord because death is your fate!"

"Than! Than! Than! Than! Than! Than!"

The High Priest of the Morifati held up his hands for silence.

"We are here to prepare to attack the Free State. They think they are free. They are not free! No one is free from Than!

Death is the fate of all men. Death is stronger than life! The fate of all men is to serve Than! No one can escape from Than!"

He paused to let that sink in.

"But Than will not punish them. Than does not punish. Than does not reward either. It does not matter what men do, neither the Free State nor the Morifati, nor even the Psychics. They will all live out their brief lives, then live for all eternity in the realm of Death, the realm of Than."

He gestured for the crowd to respond.

"Than! Than! Than! Than! Than! Than! Than! Than! Than!"

Their chant ended in a war cry.

"It pleases Than when men do their own will. It is the will of Than that we live as we please, that we do what we please, that we take what we please. It is his will that the strong survive! It is his will that the weak perish! We, the Morifati, may do whatever is necessary to survive! No one will stand in our way and live!"

The Morifati jumped up and down and made their war cry, just as if they had won a glorious victory. The High Priest let them go on. They all danced around the totem in a circle. Drums and horns played from somewhere out of sight.

The dancing went on for some minutes before he spoke again.

"There is an unbeliever in our midst! He watches us now. He waits because he is afraid. He hides because he is afraid. He is hiding in the wood there! Go! Find him and bring him before me!"

They all turned at once and ran toward me. I looked around for a place to hide. I knew running down the trail would not work. Could I escape through the wood by running deeper into it?

Before I could move, they entered the woods and the trail all around me. There was no way to run without running into them. I crouched low behind the brush I had watched them from. They crashed past me without seeing me. Would they all run past without seeing me and give me a chance to escape?

"Halt!" the High Priest called out. "Turn and search the area. Every tree, every bush."

They obeyed his orders and searched for me. I had no time. If they found me now, I would have to fight my way through them. But how could I do that? I had come there to be captured. If I escaped, I would have to return and still have to give myself up. I stood up.

"I am here!", I said.

They rushed me then, crying out their war cries. They grabbed me and bound me hand and foot. A crowd of them carried me over to the High Priest. They yipped and cheered the entire way like they had scored a glorious victory.

They threw me down at the feet of the High Priest. I had solved the problem of how to get captured without being killed on sight. Or had I? I still couldn't be sure whether they would kill me now or sacrifice me, or how I would ever escape.

"What should we do with this boy?"

"Sacrifice him! Make an offering to Than!"

"But we already have a captive to sacrifice."

"Sacrifice them both. Than will be pleased. He will grant us victory against the Free State."

"I am from the Free State! Take me to your King!"

"Silence! Do not speak unless spoken to! Who are you to demand to see our King?"

"My name is Rion. I am the grandson of the Chief of the village on the other side of the mountains. You must take me to your King. He has seen me before, in the Forbidden Land. He will want to speak to me again."

"What do you have to say to our King?"

"That is for the King's ears only. Send word to him. He will want to hear me."

"You will indeed be brought to him. Do not attempt to lie to him. He will know if you lie. His powers of insight are great. Greater than any power in the Free State. Greater even than the powers of the Psychics."

"The truth I have to tell he will not want to hear."

"Silence dog! You will see our power here tonight and you will learn to fear the Morifati, but nothing can help you now. We will bring you before King John and you will feel his wrath. Now, you will get to see what we do with captives! Bring forward the sacrifice!"

They brought a man forward bound to a long pole carried by two Morifati. Two more of their warriors walked behind them, carrying wooden posts that they had lashed together to support the pole at each end. Other warriors stirred the bonfire, which by that time had burned down considerably. They lifted me up and placed me on my knees, facing the fire.

As I watched, they stirred out a bed of coals, set the poles on either side and hammered them into the ground. They lay the man still bound to a pole on the ground at the feet of the High Priest. The man lay silent, but his eyes were wild. He was not from the Free State, at least not from our village. He must have been from the tribe to the north.

"Now, everything is ready."

The High Priest turned to the captive and said, "Do you accept your fate? Will you accept the will of Than?"

"Let me go! I have done nothing to your people! I have a wife and children. I was only hunting to feed them. I did not know I was on your land!"

"All land is our land! We do whatever we want, go wherever we want, all that we do is the will of Than. If you accept that this is our right, your death will be quick, but if you do not accept that we do Than's will and that this death is your fate, then you will die slowly over the coals."

The man was speechless. I did not know what to do for him.

The Morifati took the pole with the captive still tied to it and set him upright in front of the totem pole with Than's image on it. The High Priest took a long knife and a cup and stood in front of the victim.

"Will you accept your fate? Will you accept that Than rules all men's lives?"

"No! We men of the north do not fear your god or fear torture! My people will one day revenge themselves on the Morifati!"

My heart swelled with hope to see this man die this way. They wanted him to cower in fear and beg for mercy. He chose a hero's death.

"So be it. You will regret your decision soon."

The High Priest took the knife and made a cut across the man's chest. He put the cup underneath the cut and collected his blood. When the cup was full, he held it up over his head. The Northman did not cry out or speak during any of this.

Two Morifati moved in and took the pole with the Northman tied to it and placed it over the coals, face down. The coals were so hot I could feel the heat from where I sat on my knees, watching.

The High Priest muttered some kind of incantation, turned and sprinkled some of the man's blood on the image of Than as an offering. He went over to the fire and sprinkled the rest on the fire after taking a drink from the cup.

The smell was awful, the smell of human flesh cooking. I closed my eyes. I tried to imagine a way out of this. Was this to be my fate, too? I cried out to Wolf and Diana and Snake in my mind, but I heard nothing in response. I tried to see what would happen next. I was supposed to have the gift of "seeing around the corner", but nothing came to me.

"Open your eyes! Are you a coward? Accept your fate."

"Have mercy on him. He has done you no wrong."

"I will not spare him. Sacrifice pleases Than, as does battle. It is the will of Than that we sacrifice before battle."

"Will you do nothing for him? You said it does not matter what you do."

"Watch your tongue! You do not speak for Than. If he accepts Than's will, I will cut his throat. He will die faster that way with less pain. But we will make this sacrifice one way or the other."

During all this, the Northman did not cry out or struggle. His breathing became deeper. I think he knew that if he inhaled smoke and hot air, he would pass out.

He moaned. To my horror, his skin sizzled and browned. His training was great indeed.

"Why not cut the artery in his thigh? That is a quicker death. Your god will still be pleased."

"If you want to spare him his fate, will you kill him yourself?"

"If you allow me to, I will show him mercy."

"Mercy? You Freemen are weak! We will easily defeat you in battle. Does nature show mercy? Then neither does Than. And neither do we, the Morifati."

They took me then and tied me to the image of Than. The High Priest ordered a whipping for me. A Morifati warrior came forward with a long bullwhip. The pain was unbearable, but somehow I endured it. Soon my back was bleeding and the High Priest collected my blood in the cup. He sprinkled my blood on the sacrificial fire.

They left me hanging there, and soon I lost consciousness. So they spared me the sight of what happened next to the Northman, but I know they cooked him and ate him.

When I awoke the next day they had taken me down off the image and placed me in a tent by myself, still bound and aching from my wounds. I lay there wondering how long I would have to endure this.

Some warriors came and lifted me up on a pole to carry me to their King. They gave me no food or water and they did not dress my wounds. I blacked out again.

When I came to again, we were on the trail to their village. I don't know how many were in the company, maybe all of them. It seemed that I had held up their attack, or so I hoped. I went back to sleep. They would take me to Blackheart John.

FOURTEEN

BROUGHT BEFORE BLACKHEART JOHN

I have to admit that the only thing I wanted to do was get away. I had never endured such pain, not even during my Order of Manhood. It was not just my stripes from the whip; it was the fact that my muscles were sore and had cramped from dehydration. The way they carried me did not help. There was no way to stretch or relax. They did not offer water or the hope of any comfort. They did not believe in mercy.

I fell asleep. I passed out several times, but I snapped back to consciousness by excruciating cramps in my hips and thighs. I cried out, even screamed. I did not have the Northman's discipline, the ability to endure torture silently. Some of the older Freemen knew these techniques. I had endured the rites of passage from boy to man, during the Order of Manhood, but I had lost that strength now.

I was afraid that I would tell Blackheart John everything. The thought that I would break and tell all filled me with fear. How would I make it through this without dishonoring myself? I tried to call for help with my mind and got no response from anyone. Could they not hear me or did they choose not to respond, or was there in fact nothing they could do?

I had said that I had a message for him, but that was not true. I did not know what I would say to him. I was not even totally sure why I had come here other than that everyone was certain that I would develop the Sight while in captivity and use my powers to defeat the Morifati, and they all claimed that I had to do it. Me alone and no one else.

I was going to have to think of something. If he could look into my mind, then I could hide nothing from him. I only hoped that he would want to keep me alive for some purpose.

Why had he not probed my mind the time before? There must be some technique for it. Something he could not just carry around with him everywhere he went.

#

At last I woke up lying on the ground. I was no longer tied to the pole. They had untied my ankles as well. They tied my wrists in front with a line tied to them so they could lead me forward.

"Get up." One of them said, "On your feet!"

Getting up was difficult in my condition. Everything was sore and cramping. I stood, then my left calf cramped again. I staggered and went down on one knee.

"I said get up! We will not carry you any farther! If you cannot walk, we will leave you here."

"Give me a hand up. I need to walk off a cramp."

"You will walk on your own. Or you will never walk again."

I could see that they meant what they said, so I shifted my weight onto my right leg and stood without putting pressure on the left calf muscle.

"Stand straight."

I slowly extended my left leg and stood on it. I shuffled forward a couple of steps.

"Stand still! You were not told to march."

The Morifati were all sitting around resting, except for my tormenter. He stood a few feet from me, holding the other end of the lead tied to my wrists.

They all got up then, and we moved out. I could not tell how long I had been out. Maybe it had been overnight? If that was the case, then their village was two days' march from the Great River.

A squad of advance scouts ran out ahead of us until they were out of sight. In front of the warriors, I was being pulled along by my personal guard. All the rest of them followed behind us. Despite their threats, they let me set the pace for the march. They were under orders to bring me to Blackheart John. If one of them was a war chief or officer, they didn't show it. They all seemed to know what to do without orders from long practice.

I don't know which was worse, being hung by my wrists and ankles, or being forced to march without food or water and without resting on legs which kept cramping in the calves and hips. A few times I cramped and fell, yelling in pain. That made them angry, and they yelled at me to stand up. One of them gave me some vinegar, eventually. I guess they realized we would never get there if they took the time to torture me.

#

We crossed over a low hill and below us lay a grassland with a little creek running through. The village lay on the other side of a low bridge that crossed the creek. The creek was not wide, and it was shallow, but not so shallow that they could not navigate in it. There were a few boats tied up near the bridge.

They planted the land around the village with crops. They were growing wheat and hay and some other things I could not see well.

We crossed over the bridge, and they opened the gates of the village to us. We formed into a victory parade with me, the prize of conquest, bringing up the rear, lead by my tormenter, who I think was the War Chief of the troop after all.

I saw Morifati women for the first time. They painted themselves all in white except their eyes and mouths and hair were black. They wore red bandeaus across their breasts and red skirts.

No one spoke or made a sound, not even the children, but they all lined the streets to watch us intently. Their streets were narrow and wound a bit. The streets followed no plan I could tell, not until we got close to the village center.

There the street opened into a broad rectangular avenue with Blackheart John's courtroom in the middle of it.

Blackheart John's courtroom was inside a big wooden longhouse they had built for many purposes. The Morifati were excellent carpenters. Their town was an assortment of wooden buildings and a great wooden wall surrounded it, painted black. I could see this village was a fortress. They painted all the buildings white with red trim and black doors. Blackheart John's longhouse was solid black.

His longhouse opened into a long hallway with a stone floor. A floor of flat stones carefully worked and placed together to fit tightly. His throne sat on the other end on a raised platform so he could look down on all who approached him. Guards stood at the ready on both sides of the throne and in two lines, facing each other before the throne.

There were guards standing on both sides of the entrance to the longhouse. Our troop split off to join them on both sides as we approached. When the War Chief and I got close, he signaled them and they silently opened the doors to let us pass in.

He handed my lead off to one guard and walked several paces ahead of us. When he approach the throne he bowed and said, "Hail to you, King John! I bring you a captive from the Free State."

"You're back with a captive? I ordered you to attack the Free State!"

"You also gave orders to report anything unusual immediately, oh King, and having found this intruder, I knew you would want to interrogate him before we proceed with our attack. His presence here is very suspicious. How could he be here unless he crossed the Mountains of the Wolves and the Great River? Is he acting alone? We should know everything he knows before we attack. And he claims to have a message for you alone."

"Bring him forward."

The guards yanked me forward on my lead and shoved me down to my knees at the foot of Blackheart John's throne.

"Who is this upstart who dares to enter my domain and claims to have a message for me? Does he not know where he is and who I am?"

"You have seen me before, O King, in the Forbidden Land."

He recognized me then. "The young hunter! Well, where are your Wolves? Did they leave you to journey alone?"

"They remained in the Forbidden Land. It is their hunting ground."

"You speak too lightly of a Forbidden Land. There is no land that is forbidden to me!"

"I forbid the Free State to you. It is only open to those who believe in peace and freedom. It is forbidden and always will be to all who murder and steal and rape. To those who burn peaceful men alive."

I felt a whip lash me across my back then.

"You insolent young pup. You will learn who has power over this world."

"I wonder why he is here just now, King John. Did he know about our planned attack?"

"What about it, boy? Have you been spying on us? Has someone helped you? Have the Wolves helped you?"

I remained silent. I would not tell them anything. To do so would betray Snake, and Wolf, and Grandfather, and the Free State.

"Nothing to say? I will look inside your mind. No one can hide anything from me."

"When we found him, he was spying on us from the wood next to the Great River. He watched us during our war dance. The High Priest Murdoch saw him so we caught him before he could get away and run back to join his people."

"So he is a spy! Prepare the interrogation room and call the High Priest!"

"As you wish, sir!"

FIFTEEN

INTERROGATION

The interrogation room was a dark place underneath the throne room. It was in a basement area subdivided into a maze of rooms, lit only by firelight and torchlight. It stank of death, burnt flesh, feces, and urine.

I hated the Morifati now; I did not just fear them. Rage welled up within me, frustration at the thought of being held by them and at the long list of atrocities they had committed and intended to go on committing.

They unbound me and threw me into a cell adjoining the room. The interrogation didn't begin immediately. I guess they wanted to think it over or they were waiting for the High Priest to arrive. They wanted me to think it over as well, to let my anxiety build.

They left me in pitch black darkness, taking all the torches with them. It gave me some time to search my memory for what I knew, for what I should not tell them. What if I could not resist the interrogation? What if Blackheart John could see everything? What if he could see into my soul?

I knew I shouldn't tell him about Snake. Then they would know she sent me and that she expected me to defeat them. I knew I shouldn't tell them about the mountain trail, especially how to use it to get to the Free State, but they knew most of that already. I knew I shouldn't let them know the Wolves were waiting to ambuscade them if they made it to the end of the mountain trail. I shouldn't tell them how to find the Wolves sanctuary in the forest in the south of the Forbidden Land, or that Diana was there, or anything about Diana and her powers.

And then it hit me that the worst thing to admit was how little I knew, how little I had accomplished in the development of my powers. I did not have the Sight. I did not know how to gain it. The only thing I knew was that I had to learn the Sight while in captivity. If they knew that, why wouldn't they kill me?

I had to tell them something that would make them want to keep me alive. I had to tell them something that would explain why I was there. But what could I tell them?

While I was trying to think of something, the minutes dragged on. I fell asleep in the cell. I dreamed, I dreamed of Snake. It had been a few days since I had dreamed of her. She had not come to me. I thought she would have contacted me before now. I knew she wanted me to work things out for my-self, but it seemed she had almost abandoned me. I wondered when I would hear from her.

This time, in this dream, she was in the same room with me. I felt as though she was in the cell with me. She was normal size, neither a gigantic anaconda nor a big timber rattler. I guess she was more like a medium size of a species I couldn't identify, white with gold bands.

"You're back!", I said.

"Where are you, Rion?"

"With the Morifati. They have me in a cell. Blackheart John plans to look into my mind. He will return with the High Priest and they will interrogate me. How can I prevent them from seeing what I know? What can I do to keep them from knowing our plans?"

"You must forget. He can only see what you know now."

"But how can I forget?"

And then I woke up when a guard opened the cell door before Snake could answer. How could I forget? When you try to forget something, you remember it. You have it in your mind. The only thing to do is concentrate on something else.

"Get up!"

I staggered.

"Come forward!"

I walked out and after I passed the cell door, two of them grabbed me from both sides. There were torches lit in the center room now. They took me to a post in the middle of the room. They tied me to it by wrapping my arms behind my back and tying them.

They left me and went to stand on either side of the entrance. The interrogation room I could see now was a large room with holding cells all around the sides. There were no torture devices. I guess they didn't need them. A table stood in front of me. I couldn't guess what it was for, but I would find out soon.

How was I going to do this? How could I keep them out of my mind? How do I forget? How do I block out important details? Is it even possible? Can he enter anyone's mind?

#

The High Priest walked in with three servants walking in front of him, holding goblets. They placed the goblets on the table and stood aside. The High priest took up a position behind the table facing me.

He bowed his head and began muttering incantations. When he looked up, he took the goblet on his left and poured the contents into the center goblet, which I guess had been empty. That goblet contained some greenish black fluid. He set it back down, picked up the one on his right and added it to the center goblet. That goblet held some yellow tinted white fluid.

Then he held the goblet up and muttered more incantations. He walked around the table to stand in front of me, his servants came to stand on either side of me.

"You will drink now."

He raised the goblet to my lips. The fluid smelled like rotted plants.

"Drink!"

Were they going to poison me now? It didn't seem likely since they wanted information from me. Still, I knew this potion was not something I was likely to enjoy. I already felt nauseated by the smell.

"You have no choice but to drink. Do not fear. You will have dreams and visions. You will be one with Than."

He gestured to his servants. One grabbed my head and tilted it back, the other held my nose. When at last I gasped for air, he poured some of the noxious fluid into my mouth. It tasted like rotted meat, rotted plants, and dirt would taste mixed together. They forced my mouth shut and held my nose again. I swallowed some of it.

It was not long before I threw up. I could not keep it down. They continued and made me swallow this liquid three times all together. I felt strange then, totally numb, and I blacked out, but before I blacked out, I vomited until I had emptied my guts.

#

When I say I blacked out I am guessing not remembering, because the next thing I remember was being in a completely different place, a place which is difficult to describe. I felt no pain. I have never felt so comfortable, as if I was lying in the most comfortable bed that anyone could ever imagine. I did not want to get up. I could not remember how I got there, but I knew I liked it and didn't want to leave. I wanted this feeling to last.

It was as though I were floating on a cloud. Had I died, I wondered? Is this heaven? Where are my Mother and Father? Will I see angels and saints?

When the High Priest appeared, he no longer seemed evil. He looked down at me and smiled benignly. Soon Blackheart John joined him. They were both grinning. But I didn't sense any menace yet, not like before.

They beckoned me to get up and walk toward them. I obeyed. We all walked to the edge of a high cliff overlooking an enormous valley, a valley which seemed to contain the entire world, all the nations of the world. The world spread out before me was gorgeous with greens and blues, and the sky overhead was the deepest azure, with intricate white cloud patterns and a glorious golden sun.

"You are a very brave man to come to us this way, Rion. Behold, everything you see before you is ours, Than gave it to us to rule over, and we will share it with you if you join with us. Tell us everything there is to know about yourself."

I was slow to respond. I sincerely remembered little about myself at that point. The effect of the potion, the effects of the drugs in the potion, were so strong that I had amnesia. I had to search my mind.

"I, I am not sure. Where are we now? I do not remember how I got here, or who you are, or who I am. Could I not remain here for a while and relax? I need to rest. I feel as though I have been on a long journey."

"Yes, relax. You are among friends. We want you to relax and enjoy yourself, refresh yourself from your long and dangerous travels. You are brave. You were brave to come here. We admire your courage and your bravery. We salute you! Now, tell us who sent you!"

"I don't know."

I wondered then who I was and how I got here wherever here was.

I saw Wolf in my mind's eye. I could not see where he was, though I felt like I was face to face with him. Where were we? I was uncertain who he was, but I was sure that I knew him.

"I can see a wolf."

"Did he send you to us?" said Blackheart John.

"I don't know. He isn't speaking. He is just looking at me."

"Where are you?"

"I don't remember."

"Is anyone else with you? Do you remember a snake?"

"A snake? I know a Snake."

"Do you see her now?"

"No. But I think I, somehow I feel I know a being named Snake."

Blackheart John turned to the High Priest.

"You have given him too much. His mind has gone blank."

"He will remember and tell all, be patient."

"Just let your mind wander over all the world and remember what you can. Do you remember me? Can you remember when you met me?"

I looked out over the view to see if it reminded me of anything. It looked like no world I had ever seen before. There were no landmarks I recognized. Then I saw a long river which stretched from far to the north down past a mountain chain, then into a river delta with the ruins of an old city which it flowed past on its way into the sea.

"I see a big river."

"Do you remember a great river? Have you ever crossed a river?"

"I think so, but I can't say."

"Do you feel pain?"

At that, I felt unbelievable torment. I was back at the totem being whipped mercilessly, then I froze nearly to death on the mountain again, then they suspended me over coals just as the Northman had been, my flesh slowly cooking. I cried out in fright and agony. I did not just see these visions in my mind; I felt them in my body, in my muscles and bones.

The pain was great, and along with the physical pain was an emotional pain. I felt the pain of being totally alone, of being abandoned by everyone, even Grandfather and Wolf and Diana. I could no longer see my new friends, they had left me as well. I wanted to die. How long will I endure this? Will it ever end?

Then suddenly it ended. Blackheart John and the High Priest were back. The glorious vision of the lands of the Morifati was back. I felt no pain, only peace and deep relaxation. They were smiling down at me.

"Where did you go, Rion? We thought we had lost you!"

"I think I was in Hell."

"But you are here with us, among friends."

"A terrible vision appeared to me."

"That was Snake's witchcraft! She is evil. We are your friends. We admire you greatly and invite you to join with us and do as you please, as we do."

I tried to remember who Snake was. I went searching for a memory of her in my mind. She appeared before me.

"Rion! Tell them nothing! Forget!"

"Snake? Is it you Snake?"

"Who are you speaking to! Has she contacted you?" demanded Blackheart John.

"You see she sent him.", the High Priest said to Blackheart John.

"Tell us what she told you, Rion."

"Do not respond Rion! Act as though you have forgotten. Do not try to remember anything!"

"I cannot remember anything about a Snake."

"Then how do you know of whom we speak?"

"I have had dreams of her."

"Rion! Be silent! Tell them only yes or no!"

I was back, suspended over the coals. The pain of being cooked alive added to by the sensation that I felt abandoned by everyone. How could I get them to stop? Was there something I could tell them? Maybe a lie?

"Snake, I have to tell them something."

"Tell them you set out on your own to hunt."

"Blackheart John, where are you? I remember something!"

And I was back in paradise, floating on a cloud. I saw their smiling faces again. They were beaming at me, almost as if they loved me.

"What have you remembered, my son?"

"My Grandfather told me about your lands. He told me that there is an old warpath along the mountain range through the Forbidden Land. He told me you lived on the other side of the Forbidden Land and that the Wolves live in the Forbidden Land. He told me never to enter there, but I had to see for myself."

"Oh? What were you doing with that wolf? Was he guiding you?"

"I met him along the trail. He took me to the Great River, then he turned back. He said he could go no further."

"He can't be telling us everything." The High Priest said.

"Yes. Snake is behind this. I can sense it. Still, he doesn't seem to know very much. I think she is using him as a catspaw."

"Should we continue the questioning?"

"No. He is not going anywhere. Soon, we will all be friends."

Then he turned to me and said, "Rest now my son."

SIXTEEN

THE CELL

When I could no longer see the faces of Blackheart John and the High Priest, it left me to explore the world alone. At first I had no desire to move, I was so comfortable. I had not experienced such pleasure in many days. I had not had it this good in the Free State. There were no cares here and nothing to do. There was nothing to worry about.

At length I got up and looked around. Where was the Free State? Could I see the Forbidden Land? I knew I had seen the Great River before. I turned toward where I thought it had been. I levitated off the ground. I flew a short distance above the ground toward the Great River.

I rose higher as I approached the river and the mountains alongside it. I had no control over my flight. I was simply being carried along.

Though I knew that the river I saw was the Great River, I can't say that I recognized it or recognized any landmarks along it. I just knew it was the Great River. The same was true of the Mountain range alongside it and the land beyond. I knew it was the Forbidden Land.

I floated back toward the Free State, not exactly the way I had come but in that general direction. I stayed about a hundred feet off the ground. I flew over forests and hills. I saw wolves, but they didn't notice me.

Presently I came to the Free State. I saw it from high up, from about the same altitude I had been over the plateau which forms the Forbidden Land. I did not dive immediately, but when I did everyone in my village lay in a slumber, waiting for something to happen.

I went to Grandfather. I found him lying asleep. He woke as I stood there watching him. He looked at me bewildered, as if he were trying to remember who I was and as if to say, 'What are you doing here?'

I said, "I was your grandson, Rion."

At that, a look of recognition appeared on his face. And then I woke up.

I was no longer in the interrogation room. They had taken me to another place. This place was above ground. It was sunlit. There was one high window with bars that let the sunlight through.

I lay in a comfortable bed. Sitting at the foot of the bed was a table. Someone had set food and drink on the table for me. There was one door opposite the table. I felt like staying in bed, but I was hungry, so I slowly got up. I was still a little sore from everything that had happened to me. I didn't feel hung over. I felt stunned. I felt as though a significant change had taken place within me.

There were two chairs at the table opposite each other. I sat. There was sweet wine, roasted meat, and fresh roasted vegetables. There were loaves of bread. As I ate, I felt hunger take over me. I had fasted on the way to the land of the Morifati, and they had fed me not at all until now, only giving me enough water to keep me alive. I stuffed myself. I had to stop and pause and drink deeply from the wine flask to keep from choking.

The roasted meat was delicious, of a quality I had never tasted. They had given me chicken, wild pork, venison, and something else I did not recognize. They had roasted it with care and rubbed it with spices.

I would have eaten anything at this point just to stay alive, so I couldn't help but feel happy. Was the worst over now? Had they decided to make peace? This kind of treatment was the last thing I expected from them.

When at last I was full, I got up and tried the door. They had locked it tight, probably barred it on the outside. They had placed a tub and a chamberpot in one corner of the room. I went over to look. There was no water in the tub. I made use of the chamberpot.

After I had finished, I heard someone opening the door. In came two guards, three young Morifati women, and an elderly lady. The three young women went to clean off the table while the guards stood on either side of the door. The elderly lady approached me.

I say lady, but her face was horrifying. She made me uneasy despite the change in treatment I had received. She smiled at me, a smile which seemed to conceal some malice, although she positively beamed at me and said, "So! You have rested and eaten your fill, young man?"

"Yes. Yes I have. Thanks very much!"

She smiled again. It was definitely a fake smile. Still, I felt relieved that my captivity would not be what I had feared it would be.

SEVENTEEN

THE OLD HAG

The elderly lady looked like a witch, that's why I nicknamed her the Old Hag. She dressed much like the High Priest, with the same color body and face paint and a headdress of black feathers. The feathers shone a little. I realized they were from ravens. Her robe was a finer, more feminine quality than the Priest's, and embroidered in gold.

When I say she looked like a witch, I mean she had a narrow face with a large pointed nose and her skin was a network of wrinkles. The white face paint did not conceal her wrinkles. It seemed to make them easier to see. She painted her eyes and eyebrows dark black.

Her eyes were sky blue and unusual looking. They gave her an intent, piercing expression. Such eyes seemed out of place on her. They were the eyes of a young, beautiful woman. Yet those eyes, when I looked into them for long enough, concealed an icy contempt. It did not matter that she was smiling or what she was saying.

"We want you to be happy here, Rion. You are a brave young man who has traveled on a long, dangerous journey. We welcome such men as you. You will receive all the comforts and the highest honors that we can bestow. The girls will prepare a bath for you now."

The young women carried away the leftover food and returned, bringing pots of water to fill the bath. The guards waited until the girls finished, then they left. That left me alone with the three young women and the Old Hag.

The women had been wearing simple long white robes that covered everything but their faces and hands. They took these off now to reveal that they were naked underneath and they wore no war paint except for their faces and hands. There were washbasins placed on the table with which they washed the paint off of themselves.

"Do you like what you see?" the Old Hag asked me.

I remained quiet. The Morifati kept throwing surprise after surprise at me. I wondered what would happen next. I felt warm and comfortable, probably from the wine. I think from something else they had given me as well.

The three young Morifati women looked very different after they removed their robes and headdresses and their paint. They were slender and fair skinned. They looked like they had never sunburned. I guess they stayed under robes and paint all the time. There were no tan lines from the bandeaus that most of them usually wore.

One was of medium height, one was petite, and one was tall. The tall one had full breasts and blonde hair that she wore up. The other two had small but definitely not flat breasts. The middle one had raven hair and the petite one was blonde. They all wore their hair up. I found out later that was their custom, to always wear their hair up.

They all turned to face me and the Old Hag. They were smiling at me and giving me a good look before we started. One thing more I noticed, which I supposed was a custom of the Morifati, was that they all had shaved off their pubic hair, in fact all their body hair except for head and eyebrows. So their skin was as smooth and hairless as a little girl's.

I looked around at the tub. They had filled it with water. They were obviously ready, so I got up to undress.

"Stop! They will undress you, Rion."

I looked at them. They seemed amused at me and about to laugh.

I said, "I am at your disposal, ladies."

"Silence! Do not speak to them! Do not speak to them and do not touch them!"

"What am I supposed to do?"

"They will show you. They will guide you. If necessary they will tell you what to do, but you must keep your hands off of them. Later, if you answer all our questions, you may select the one you like the most to become your woman."

They came over then and had me undressed in no time. I was not wearing much by that time anyway after whipping and interrogation. Just a robe. They motioned for me to step into the tub. I stepped in and sat down. It was not too cold, but not warm.

They began bathing me then with sponges, scrubbing all the dirt and blood and scabs. My reaction to all this attention from three beautiful women made them giggle at my discomfort. They left no part of my body untouched, which added to my pleasure but also added to my frustration.

"Enough. Stand up now Rion."

I stood up, and they rubbed an ointment all over my wounds. I was still sore, not just on the surface, but deep down in my muscles. Their scrubbing rubbed off the scabs where I had bled, so I bled again. The ointment burned, then I felt no pain at all.

"This poultice will heal you and help you sleep. We have a medicine for you to drink as well."

She motioned for the tallest one to retrieve a flask from the table. She returned and held it up to my lips. It was bitter but not nauseating, not like the High Priest's potion. She beckoned me to step out. The other two rubbed me down with towels, and then the tall one pulled my robe down over my head.

"That's enough girls. Leave us now."

They dressed quickly and left. The Old Hag approached me and looked deeply into my eyes, as if searching for something inside me. I felt drowsy and nodded.

"Pay attention now Rion. When I return, I will have questions for you. Questions you must answer if you want your stay here with us to remain pleasant. You have enjoyed many pleasures today, haven't you? You would like for this treatment to continue, wouldn't you? Which one would you choose? Which one would you like to have as your woman?"

"The tallest one."

"Good! An excellent choice! Sleep now. Take a long slumber and heal. When I return I will bring her along and you and I will have a long talk."

At that, she led me over to the bed where I lay and fell asleep at once. I do not remember her pulling the covers over me or slamming and locking the door.

#

I fell into a truly profound sleep, one with no dreams, not for a long time anyway, but finally, I dreamed about the Old Hag. She faced me; she spoke to me but I could not understand or remember her questions. It was as if she spoke a foreign language that I could not hear clearly.

Then she was showing me the tallest girl again. She presented her to me. The girl was wearing a thin cotton robe, something that she might sleep in. I went over to the girl and kissed her. Her name was Anna.

We were in love. Anna looked deeply into my eyes. I could not look away. It was as though our mutual gaze locked us together. Suddenly we were naked. And then, we were swimming in a pool made by a waterfall that flowed off of a hill.

Then we were back in the bed I was sleeping in. I felt as though I had finally found the love of my life. The emotions were so strong I could feel them in my body.

I slowly woke and realized where I was, still in the cell they had prepared for me. My feelings from the dream remained. I was in love with the tallest girl, the one called Anna. I felt happy and content.

Had they changed their minds about sacrificing me? It seemed to me they were preparing to initiate me into their tribe. As I lay there, I wondered what other rituals I would have to undergo. The Morifati would surely have a difficult rite of initiation into their tribe, and a painful one to endure. Such rituals, kept secret from anyone except the ones who passed through them, would test loyalty and courage. Grandfather told me never to discuss my Order of Manhood. Still, whatever it was, whatever was involved, I would gladly endure it to be with Anna. I was in love with her.

I pictured it in my mind's eye. My life with Anna, the children we would have. I saw three sons, tall like her, strong like me. I would teach them everything that Grandfather taught me. I saw myself making love to her when she returned. Would they let her come back to me alone? Stay here in this cell with me alone, just the two of us?

I wondered if the stories about the Morifati were just that, stories. I knew nothing about them except what I had been told. I knew even less about the Northmen. What had the Northman done before they captured him? Could he have deserved to be cooked alive?

I heard the door opening. The Old Hag came in by herself. She kept her eyes fixed on me the way a cat does when it is watching its prey for signs of movement. Wordlessly, she picked up a chair and set it beside the bed where she could face me.

I tried to sit up. I moved slowly, but I was not sore.

"No, no, lie back, young hero. Rest. I am just here to make sure you are comfortable."

"Where is Anna?"

"Ah! You want to see Anna?"

"There is something I must tell her."

The Old Hag cackled at that. It didn't seem that funny to me. Did I dare to tell her I was in love with Anna already? I had only seen the girl once, had not spoken to her at all. I chose her over the others. Did she have any interest in me?

I wanted to speak. I did not know how to say what I wanted to say. Somehow I just knew that if I confessed to the Old Hag, it would ruin everything between me and my beloved. I could not risk that. Whether I stayed with the Morifati or whether I got Anna to run away with me did not matter to me at that point. I knew I could not live without her.

"Tell me Rion. Do you love her? Are you in love with Anna?"

I wasn't expecting that. I was speechless. I wanted nothing more than to confess my love, but I wanted to make my confession to Anna in person, alone with her. I felt fear, fear that I might lose her, fear that I had already made a fool of myself, and fear that the Morifati would forbid our love.

The Old Hag must have sensed my fear, must have read the expression on my face or the tension in my body, because the next thing she said was, "You do, don't you? You are in love with her. You may admit it to me. I want you to love her. I want the two of you to be happy together."

"I do. I have loved no one as much as I love Anna."

She beamed at that. She was clearly overjoyed, but her blue cat's eyes searched mine intently and I could see not warmth in them but cold malice.

"You want very much to see her again, don't you?"

"I want that more than anything. I want to be with her. Is there any way that she could stay here with me and take care of me while I recover?"

"If you want this girl, you must do exactly what I tell you."

"What do you want? If it is in my power...."

"You must do whatever I say. You must cooperate with us fully. Answer all our questions. Tell us everything you know. Obey orders from King John without hesitation."

It was then that the door opened again, and the High Priest came in with Anna.

EIGHTEEN

THE HIGH PRIEST

Anna walked three paces behind the High Priest, wearing only a simple robe, no paint or headdress. She held a single rose in her hands.

The High Priest dressed in full ceremonial uniform with his paint and robe and headdress, as I described before, but this time he carried a long staff with an ornament on the top of it. He went to the side of the bed opposite the Old Hag and stood. Anna went over to stand behind the Old Hag. Anna smirked at me, like she knew a big secret.

"So, how is our young hero today? Has he answered your questions?"

He looked at me as he spoke, but he was speaking to the Old Hag.

"I have not asked yet Lord, now that you are here, we may ask him together. All his talk, all his thoughts are for our young Anna. He has professed his love for her to me."

At that, I let out a groan. She gave me away before I could speak to Anna privately. It gripped me with a fear that Anna would spurn me out of embarrassment, or that the High Priest would forbid our love.

"Is this true? Are you in love with Anna?" said the High Priest.

I had to admit it now, at the risk of everything.

"I am in love with her."

"How can this be? You have only just met."

"I only know that I do Excellency."

"I cannot allow this union of a Morifati woman with a Freeman. It is not our way. You are not one of us. You are not even our ally."

"Please Excellency, you must. I have never loved a woman as I have loved her. I wish no harm to come to her. If I must join your tribe, I will. If I must go to the Free State and urge them to make peace with the Morifati, I will."

"Would you? Would you even take our side against the Free State in order to protect her?"

He had me at that. I felt torn. How could I fight against Grandfather and my own kin? How could I fight against the people of the Free State? And Diana, did I still feel anything for her? But when I thought about leaving Anna, my chest hurt. It was agony to think that I might never love her. My future, whatever it turned out to be, had to include her.

"Don't ask me to make that choice, Excellency. I can't..."

"Can't what? Can't betray your blessed Free State? Not even for the woman you love? Not even after what they did to you? They sent you here alone, they abandoned you. They will not come for you, they will not rescue you, not even if you die over the coals."

These words were agony for me, more even than the whipping I had endured and the forced march. I had to say yes; I had to have her. I needed more time. Maybe if I helped them, I could still prevent them from attacking the Free State.

"I will take your side. I will take your side for the sake of the woman I love."

"I knew it! I knew he loved me!" said Anna.

She stepped forward and lay the rose across my chest.

"Silence child! Do not interrupt my questions.", said the High Priest.

"Anna, darling, leave us now. Your lover will wait for you to return to him here.", said the Old Hag.

"If you want to see her again, you will answer all my questions with the truth!" said the High Priest.

"Please Rion. Please tell them everything. Don't let them part us forever."

She stared at me intently. It felt like love at first sight. Against all reason, the two of us were deeply in love on first meeting. The High Priest gestured for her to go. So she walked backward a few paces, maintaining her gaze, then turned, then turned back again before exiting the door to look into my eyes one last time.

"I will return, my love. Remember that I love you and answer well."

At those words, I felt my chest contract with pain. I let out a groan.

"It hurts him to see the one he loves leave him Excellency.", said the Old Hag.

"Now tell us why you are here. You did not come here on your own. Our King saw you with a wolf. He thinks it was the Leader of the Wolf Pack."

I had no way out of it now, or so I believed. Nothing they tried before worked, but when they threatened to take my future away from me, the love of my life, I could no longer hold out.

"Snake. Snake came to me in a dream."

"That witch! She has been in contact with him! I knew it! I knew she must be behind this!" said the Old Hag.

"What did she tell you? Tell us everything she said to you.", said the High Priest.

"She said you were planning to attack the Free State. She said that you were looking for the way through the Forbidden Land and that when you found it, you would attack."

"Really? Why would she contact you, a mere boy?" said the Old Hag.

"She said that only I could stop you."

"By yourself? All alone you will defeat the entire Kingdom of the Morifati? What else did she say? There must be more. And why you? Do you have powers?" said the High Priest.

"Snake claims that I have the Sight, but I have no such power. I am not a Psychic. I did not believe that they still existed until Snake came to me and predicted that Wolf would appear to me. I had heard the legends. We teach all the children of the Free State the story of the Great Third War, but these stories do not affect our lives day to day. I no longer believed in Psychics. When Wolf appeared to me, I knew the Psychics were real. He is a living, flesh and blood wolf, but he can speak to me with his mind."

"Why did she send the Leader of the Wolf Pack to you? What did she say? What did he say to you?"

"She said that he would guide me to you. He said that he could guide me through the Forbidden Land as far as the Great River but he would go no further."

"And you, what does she expect you to do here?"

"She claims I will learn the secret of the Sight while I am here. I don't believe it. I know nothing about the Sight. I have no powers. No one one will tell me how I am to perform this thing."

"You dare not oppose us. My powers and those of John our King are greater than yours, greater than those of Snake.

But she is deceitful, she hides from us. Where is she? Do you know?"

"All I know is her domain lies to the south of here. I have never met her. I have never seen her in person. She only comes to me in dreams and only when she wills to do so."

"And Wolf, where is he now?"

"He waits for you in the Forbidden Land with his people. He waits for you to attack them on his home ground. The wolves will protect their land and their holy places. You will have to fight your way through them if you hope to make it to the Free State."

At that point, I felt a deep pang of remorse. I had betrayed my brother Wolf with this information. Wolf who had risked his life for me. I did it because I could not bear to think that they would part me from Anna.

"He is a spy, Excellency. That Snake-witch sent here him to spy on us and report back to her. She may *see* through him as well."

"He is a spy. But he may be more than that. If what he says is true, then she believes he has powers within him waiting to be released."

"I am not a spy."

"Then why are you here?"

"She said I would defeat you. I know not how."

"We cannot trust you now. Not if you are her agent. I am afraid I cannot permit you to marry Anna. We will sacrifice you at the New Moon festival, then we will attack the Free State and those cowardly wolves too if necessary."

"Give me a chance to prove myself to you. I am not a spy and I have no powers. If I had the Sight, then how could I not have foreseen all this would happen to me? Why would I allow myself to be captured, tortured, and interrogated? Let me marry Anna and I will agree not to make war on you. I cannot say what the Freemen or the Wolves might do, but I can speak for myself."

"Are you in communication with Snake? Can she see what you see?"

"She only comes to me in dreams. I know not when or by what means. She cannot see what I see, but she claims to see my future."

"Then there is something you can do for us. Go to her. Pretend that you are fulfilling your mission for her. When you have found her, kill her. This will be a great favor to us. She is our greatest enemy. She has blocked our plans for conquest for too long. She hides from us, whether deep inside her castle or deep underground we know not. Snake has eyes in the sky. The Ravens are her allies, they fly about spying for her. The Wolves spy for her, too, in the Forbidden Land and in the forest. That she has the Sight, we know. How else could she know when we were coming and when to hide? But so far she has not had the strength to attack."

"You would let me go, so I could meet with Snake and kill her?"

"We would."

"And what about Anna? Will I have your blessing to marry her?"

"Only if you perform this task for us first. Until then you may not see her."

"Please, I only want to see her again. What harm can come from that?"

"Absence makes the heart grow fonder young hero.", said the Old Hag.

"You must perform this task for us, you have no choice but this, kill Snake and live happily with the woman you love, refuse, fail and you will roast over the coals at the next New

Moon and feed our warriors before they set out to kill your people."

By that time I was too far gone to know what I was saying. I was no longer myself. They had turned me against everyone, Grandfather, Diana, Snake, and Wolf. The Old Hag had cast a Limerence Spell on me, but I could not see it.

"I will do it. I will do this thing you ask."

"See that you do. We will leave you now so you can rest. If you sleep and the Snake-witch comes to you, tell her nothing about what we have said today."

"Our about your love!" said the Old Hag.

With that, they got up and left me alone. I tried to sleep but my heart was breaking. I tossed and turned. I could tell by the window that it was night now. I had no way to know the time of night, but it felt to me that a long time had passed while I lay thinking about Anna and imagining what she would say and what we would do when she returned.

NINETEEN

RAVEN

After a long while, I grew sleepy but if I slept; it was only a brief nod I didn't remember. My heart ached with love for Anna. I slept again, then woke with a start. I heard my name called softly from the window.

"Rion."

A girl's voice softly croaked a whisper from the high window. I looked up to see a black figure, the outline of a bird.

"Get up, Rion, I must speak to you!"

I got up and stumbled around. It was quite dark, but my captors had left an unlit candle on the table. I felt about for a way to light it.

"I can't see you well. Who are you?"

"I am Raven."

At that, the candle lit itself. I guess Raven knew how to perform such tricks, but without further delay she flew to the table and perched in front of me. She was quite large and had shimmering black feathers. I instantly recognized her as the raven that I had seen before in the Free State and on the Mountain Trail.

"Were you sent to follow me by Snake?"

"Yes, I am to watch over you and report to her and to keep you out of danger. You are in very great danger now!"

"I saw you before, but Snake said nothing about you. She did not tell me you were spying on me."

"I am not spying! A friend does not spy. I am watching over you, making sure you find your way and letting Snake know your whereabouts and telling her whatever befalls you. I am not supposed to interfere, but this is an emergency. You have fallen into the worst potential trap, so I have come here to warn you. Do not believe the Morifati! They lie! They all lie! They fill their hearts with hatred and deceit!"

"But they have offered me friendship! Membership in their tribe and a beautiful maiden who loves me and wants to marry me!"

"It is all a lie! Their friendship is false! Her love is false!"

"I can't believe that. You were not here. You did not hear her speak. How can you know anything about her?"

"It is my job to know. I have watched them for years. I see them come and go. I watch their horrible rituals. They worship death! Their god Than is the god of Death! They will sacrifice you to their god no matter what they say, no matter what you do! Do not believe their lies!"

"I love Anna and I know she loves me!"

"She is acting. She is playing a role. She has done this many times before with other captives. You are not her first, nor will you be her last. She will not remain true to you. They have taught her their ways and brought her up in their ways. She does not fear death, but she fears Blackheart John, the High Priest and that Old Hag. Have you any idea what they would do to her if she disobeyed? It is a fate much worse than being roasted alive!"

At that, the pain of losing her, of being separated from my Anna, struck me like a knife in the chest. I found it difficult to breathe. I had to sit down. Raven hopped over close to me.

"Look at me Rion. Look me in the eye. Tell me what has happened to you while you have been here. What did they say to you? What did they do to you? What did they give you to drink? I know your pain is real, but this love of yours is not real. It is a spell that was cast on you by the Old Hag and her student Anna."

"When they first captured me they did whip me. They made me watch them sacrifice a Northman they had captured. He honored himself and his people in death. He did not cry out or show fear. After that they carried me, then they forced me to march here. They brought me before Blackheart John. They put me in a cell. Snake came to me in a dream, but they woke me up before she could finish telling me her message. They took me to an interrogation room where they forced me to drink a horrible tasting liquid the High Priest prepared. It was then that I had fantastic visions of the entire world laid out before me. Blackheart John and the High Priest became friendly then. They promised me friendship if I would tell them what I knew and why I came here. I did not tell them much. When I woke from the vision, the Old Hag came to me with food and drink and three beautiful young women. They feasted me and healed me and bathed me. The Old Hag promised me I could choose a bride from the three."

"Did the Old Hag give you anything to drink? Did she come to you at night? In a dream perhaps?"

"After I had feasted and bathed, she gave me a drink for my wounds and the pain and told me to sleep. I had a strange dream about her and the girl called Anna, whom I love. I remember little about it now."

"It's just as I feared. The Old Hag has cast a spell on you."

"No! I love...."

"You are under a Limerence Spell, Rion. She gave you a love potion."

"That cannot be!"

"Did you tell them anything?"

I felt a deep sinking feeling now. I no longer knew what was real. I had told the Morifati everything I knew. I still loved Anna. I still hoped to be reunited with her, but now Raven was telling me it was all a lie, that everything I feared most was true. The Morifati had given me a deep delusion with their potions and their talk of friendship and love.

"I told them everything I know, Raven. I did it for the woman I love."

"The woman you love does not love you, but there is another who loves you and you have forgotten her."

"Who is that?"

"You see. You are under a deep spell now. You have forgotten that Snake is your ally, and she cares for you. You have forgotten Diana, the one who loves you more than anyone. Do you not remember how Diana saved you and Wolf from the blizzard? How she led you to the mountain peak?"

I had to admit I had forgotten. I remembered now, but the memory of it seemed like a dream. A dream that I could not be certain was real.

"Did that really happen? On the Mountain Trail?"

"Yes, it did. I saw it. Do you not remember when I flew over?"

"Who is Diana? How could she do what she did for me and Wolf?"

"Only she can explain her true nature to you. Keep her in your mind. Remember the beautiful maiden that used to follow you around when you hunted. Keep her fixed in your mind. She can come to you, she will come to you, but you have to call to her like you did before. She can restore your memory and remove the Limerence Spell."

"How can she come to me here? They will capture her and kill her."

"How did she come to you before? As a dove!"

"Snake said that I would defeat the Morifati. She said I have the Sight, but I don't. I don't know how to do anything. I have no powers at all."

"You have powers, Rion, but you do not recognize them for what they are."

I understood what Raven was saying, but I could not feel it. All I could feel was my love for Anna. The only future I could imagine was with Anna. The thought of living without her broke my heart.

I had not told Raven that the High Priest wanted me to kill Snake. Should I confess it? Should I trust her? She would surely warn Snake that I was coming. That I planned to kill her. I felt torn. Torn between my memories of who I was and everything that had gone on before I met Anna, and the certain knowledge that if I could not do what the Morifati required of me, then I would never see my love again.

But everything Raven said rang true. Maybe Diana could explain. If only there were a way to speak to her, or Grandfather. I wished I could speak to him now. He always gave sound advice.

"Have you told me everything, Rion?"

"I have told you all that I remember."

"You seem deeply troubled. I can sense that thoughts of this Morifati girl still torment you."

I couldn't tell her. Not until I decided who I was and what I wanted. I felt as though my world and everything I thought I knew about it had been a lie.

"I can see that this Limerence Spell you are under is a deep one, Rion. We will have to remove it before you can go much farther. It will have to be removed soon."

I thought I ought to change the subject if I could. I said, "How were you able to get here without being seen?"

"I can see around the corner."

"What is that? They told me I would have that power, but I don't have it."

Now Raven, as I mentioned before, was a large bird with black feathers that shimmered and glistened. There was a little iridescence in her feathers the way there is in the feathers of a golden eagle. When she spoke to me, she spoke with her mind as Wolf did, but she could also speak to me with her voice, since ravens can mimic human speech. When she walked and hopped back and forth on the table, she gave an impression of being happy and confident, like a little girl who was playing a game she could not lose. When she looked at me, her eyes were bright. She would cock her head back and forth.

She started doing all those things now in response to my question. She went over to the end of the table and paused for a few seconds. Then she came back over to me, looked me directly in the eyes, turned her head sideways and said, "I will have to leave soon, the Morifati will return."

"How do you know that?"

"I can see what they are going to do, before they do it. I can also see what they see through their own eyes. That is how we ravens can spy on them so well. That is why Snake can hide from them and stay hidden long before they can get anywhere near her. It makes them furiously angry. Sometimes they will kill a raven who is not a Psychic and then they wear the feathers to show off. They are so stupid, so blinded by evil that they want to kill all the Snakes, Wolves, and Ravens, not just the ones who are Psychics."

I could swear she was smiling at me. But how do you smile with a beak?

"Then why does Snake fear them?"

"She is an Empath. She cannot bear to be near them, to feel their evil. Also, just because they have failed before does not mean they will not eventually succeed. They keep trying, they have tried for three hundred years to take everything they can seize and kill anyone who opposes them. Snake is afraid that they will spread their evil cult, this worship of Death, to all the Tribes and Nations and put to death anyone who does not join them."

"That is why she wants me to defeat them. Not some other man but me, and not any of the Psychics."

"Exactly! We Psychics can defend ourselves, but we have no way to launch a successful attack."

She straightened up then and turned about, remaining perfectly still for a second. Turning quickly back around to me, she said, "They are coming back here now. In a few minutes. You must blow out the candle and get back into bed. They will probably question you again after they have fed you breakfast. As soon as you can go to sleep and contact Snake!"

"How do I do that?"

"Don't you know?"

"She has always contacted me."

At that Raven laughed out loud, a silly cackling laugh.

"Do you not realize that you have been going to her in your mind?"

"What?"

"You have always gone to her! She has never come to you! You see! You do have powers!"

"But how can I .....?"

"Quiet now! They come! I must fly. Goodbye for now, remember all that I told you!"

And with that, she flew up to the window ledge, then flew away. I blew out the candle and quickly got into bed. While I waited for the Old Hag to arrive, it occurred to me I should not go to Snake until I had decided what to do. I had thought that Snake would come to me and she would discover everything. It seemed now that I had been going to her, but could I control it?

I hoped Anna would be with the Morifati who were coming.

TWENTY

FATTENED UP FOR THAN

I did not have long to wait. The door opened and the Old Hag and the other two maidens entered. But Anna was not with them. They carried food and drink with them and they set the table for me.

"Where is Anna? Will she not come?"

At that, the girls laughed. The Old Hag walked over next to the bed and gave me another one of her penetrating stares. She gestured for me to get up.

"You have not performed your task yet, Rion. I fear that you never will."

"May I not at least see her in the meantime? Everyone knows how much I love her, and that I am sincere. Even the High Priest must believe that."

"Come to breakfast now. No more thoughts of your beloved just yet. You must regain your strength."

So I got up, went over to the table, and sat. They laid it out, much as it had been before. I did not feel like eating, so disappointed was I that my beloved had not come.

"I am not that hungry as I was before."

"Eat young hero. You must eat to regain your strength. Here, drink!"

She took a small flask of something and poured it into my cup. Then one maiden added some wine. The Old Hag set it before me.

"Drink deeply Rion. It will restore your appetite and heal a broken heart. We can't have you pining away now. That will not do, you have labors to perform."

I looked at it dubiously. I knew intellectually that they had been giving me potions daily, Raven had said as much. I struggled to believe that they would give me something that would poison me. I had that lump in my throat that someone gets when they feel lost. I drank it down in a gulp.

"Good! Good! Have some roast and bread!"

Then they piled food on my plate for me and filled my cup. My appetite returned at once, a little at first, then it grew until I felt as though I were starving. I craved the dishes they had spread before me. I began stuffing it down, and they kept handing it to me.

While I feasted, I felt better. That is less heartbroken. I had been so much in love with Anna that I could not think straight. I had betrayed Wolf. I was planning to betray Snake, not just planning to betray her, but to kill her. So while I was eating, the effects of this potion cleared my head well enough that I got an idea.

Maybe if I could get the Morifati to set me free to go to Snake's domain to kill her, I could instead come back here to their village, find Anna and persuade her to run away with me? It could work, but only if Anna really loved me. I could see it all unfolding in my mind's eye, our life together after I escaped. It would help if I could learn to 'see around the corner' the way Raven could. That would make it easier to find my way in and

117

out. But what if they would not let me go? Or what if Anna did not return my love?

I pushed back from the table to relax and let my food settle.

"That's the best meal I have had in a long time."

"Good. Have some more, what would you like?"

The Old Hag was smiling at me again, practically beaming, but her eyes continued to be cold and menacing. I always felt she could turn in an instant and stab me with a stiletto.

The maidens just sat there, smiling at me expectantly, like they were expecting me to do something hilarious at any second. They spoke not a word, nor was I allowed to speak to them, but they hung on every word that the Old Hag and I said to each other and they rushed to refill my plate and my cup as soon as they became empty. It became clear their goal was to make sure I ate as much as I could eat.

"When will you send me out to perform my task?"

"You ask that question of Blackheart John."

"Will he come here soon? Or will they bring me before him?"

"We will take you to him in time, but you do not want to be brought to him now. As for whether he will come here, I cannot say. He will do as he wills. He is our King."

"What about the High Priest? When will he return?"

"I can send for him, but what will you tell him? Have you been in contact with the Snake-witch? Did she come to you?"

"No, she has not come to me."

I did not tell her I had been going to Snake in my dreams. That would make her suspicious of me if she knew I could contact Snake on my own.

"If she comes to you, tell her nothing about our plans. It will go hard for you if you turn against us. We can devise a death and tortures even more horrible than what you have seen so far. And your Anna, you want to see her again, don't you?"

She watched for reactions while she told me all this. She reached out and held my chin so she could look into my eyes. Her eyes told me she enjoyed my pain. She could not disguise it or did not bother.

"I want to see Anna again more than anything else you can offer me. I do not fear torture or death as much as I fear the thought of losing her forever."

"Well, thanks for the information, young hero. But I believe you have already lost Anna."

At that I felt a sharp pain in my breast and I suddenly lost my appetite. I am ashamed to admit now that tears flowed down my cheeks. The Limerence Spell was so powerful I could think of nothing else but the love of my life. I could imagine nothing other than that, something destined us to be together.

"Why? Why do you say that I have lost her?"

She smiled a knowing smile then. Those evil blue eyes pierced into mine.

"You have stopped eating, Rion. Have you lost your appetite?"

The maidens burst into laughter at those words. The Old Hag looked amused herself, then her expression turned angry.

"Silence! Prepare another cup of wine for our hero, Anna's hero."

The maidens snickered, but did as they were told. When they poured a cup of wine for me, the Old Hag added some of the same potion she had given me before to help me eat.

"What have I done to be parted from her?"

"Relax, relax, eat. Eat and drink your fill. We want you to feast. Be content."

Just at that time, the door opened again, and the High Priest entered. He looked as friendly as he could look, dressed as he was, but he beamed at me as well.

"So, is our young hero eating well this morning? Has he told you anything more about himself and his mission?"

"He is eating well, excellency. He speaks only about his love for young Anna."

The maidens snickered once more until the High Priest glanced at them, then they straightened up quickly.

"When will I have leave to go hunt Snake, your Excellency? How long before you give me a chance to prove myself?"

That really made him grin.

"So you are ready to go hunt snakes then? Has Snake come to you? Have you told her anything?"

"She has not come. I would not tell her about our bargain, her life for my love. She has not come to me in days now, maybe she will not come to me again."

"Is that so? She has given up on her hero? The one she hopes will become a great wizard, the one who will attain the Sight, the one sent to defeat the Morifati?"

"I don't know. I never know what she is doing or why. She tells me nothing. Just go there and wait for inspiration is all she said."

"You are not going anywhere. We cannot trust you now."

"But you know I love Anna!"

"Oh yes, you love Anna."

He snorted with laughter. They all laughed at me like it was the funniest thing they ever heard.

"Snake is no fool. She chose you for a reason. We are certain of that, but exactly who you are and why she would send you here alone... You must tell us more!"

"But I have told you everything I know!"

"Then tell us what you do not know! Do you still hope to see Anna again?"

Had I known then what I know now, had I truly understood what was happening to me, I would have known that Anna was not in love with me, not only that, but pure evil, and she hated me. All the Morifati hated me. This offer of friendship and love followed by ridicule and hatred, they kept changing what they said back and forth. It was just a technique to break me down. The Limerence Spell the Old Hag cast on me was so strong I forgot who I was. I was in love beyond all hope and reason with a woman who would enjoy watching me die.

"Can't I just see her? Even if you do not let me go?"

"We must be certain that you do not communicate with Snake. If she contacts you, if we find out that you have told her anything about us, about our new friendship, you will never see Anna again."

"But you already said I could not see her."

"As long as you cooperate, there is hope for you. But if you talk, there is no hope. And if we find out you have helped Snake, you will suffer worse tortures than you have imagined."

"What can I do now?"

"Your only hope is to do whatever we tell you, and answer every question put to you."

"Maybe I can lead you to Snake."

I spoke the thought as soon as it popped into my mind. It was a rash and dangerous proposition, but I was desperate. One side of me hoped they would send me on ahead as a scout and I could then give them the slip. But how would I find Anna after that?

"We already know where she is, or at least, where her castle is, but she always escapes before we arrive. We always find the place deserted."

"Then take me there and leave me there. She will find me when she returns."

"Nice try. We cannot risk having the two of you join up. You might learn these powers she expects you to gain. But keep thinking about how you can help."

"Now you must stop talking and continue eating.", said the Old Hag.

She showed another plateful of food at me. One of the Maidens refilled my cup. I tried, but I could not continue.

"I can't go on eating. I'm full."

"Nonsense!" said the Old Hag.

She glanced at the High Priest. He nodded, so she gestured to one of the maidens, who then left.

"Why is it so important for me to stuff myself full?"

The High Priest snorted and laughed again.

"Our concern is about your health Rion.", said the Old Hag.

The two of them exchanged a knowing look and started laughing again.

It was then that the maiden who left returned, and with her was Anna! My heart lept, it overjoyed me to see her again. I started to get up.

"Keep your seat!" said the High Priest.

Anna seemed to be as happy as I was. She smiled at me and rushed to stand by my side, where she could attend to me personally. She had bathed and perfumed herself and changed into beautiful clothes. Her hair was up as it usually was, but this time in an elaborate pile of braids and jewelry. She placed her hand on my cheek.

"Rion my love, do everything they say, tell them everything they want to know, answer every question with the truth, so that we may never be parted.", said Anna

"He has not cooperated.", said the High Priest.

"And he has stopped eating.", said the Old Hag.

"Rion, you must eat to regain your strength, my love. You have a long journey with much fighting ahead of you if you will join us in our fight against the wolves and Snake."

"I can't eat Anna. The thought that we would become parted has choked me."

"We will never part, my love! Not if you do as they say and fight bravely for the Morifati."

"I am afraid that it is too late for you two, I cannot allow this union.", said the High Priest.

"But your Excellency! I love him!" said Anna.

"And I love her! Can't you see we are sincere? Can't you see Than meant us to be?"

"I will tell you what Than meant to be Freeman! We are preparing you for sacrifice to Than at the next New Moon. You will be the guest of honor at our King's dinner table, and the main course."

"We will fatten you up like a goose, then we will sacrifice you to our God!" said the Old Hag.

"Our King John will feast on your liver, as is his right!" said the High Priest.

"And our children will feed on the soup from your bones. You must die, so that we may live!" said the Old Hag.

"Oh Rion! You have failed me! Why didn't you tell them everything? How could you?"

Anna then burst into tears.

"Anna, I have cooperated with them! I told them everything!"

"You couldn't have!" she said.

Then she turned and fled the room, slamming the door behind her. I turned to look at the High Priest.

"Have I not done and offered to do everything you asked?"

"You have done enough. Don't be afraid, it is a great honor to die this way. You will feast with King John and then feast with Than in the afterlife."

TWENTY-ONE

SNAKE APPEARS

They spent the rest of the day feasting me like it was Thanksgiving, like the Prodigal Son had returned. They would leave me alone for a while, leaving the table full of food and wine bottles, then come back in at mealtimes bearing more dishes. They pushed these at me, and if I couldn't eat the Old Hag would give me another dose of her potion.

When I say "they" I mean the Old Hag and the two maidens. The High Priest left after he made certain that I was miserable. Anna did not return. I felt the pain of knowing that she might really have left for good this time. I spent the time alone, dreaming about how I could reconcile with her. I knew it was crazy, but I could not stop doing it.

I couldn't make sense of what was happening to me, of everything that had happened to me. The appetite-restoring potion helped a little. But the Old Hag was careful to only give me enough to make me hungry. And when it wore off, the Limerence Spell returned.

They kept this up for three days, never letting me go outside or exercise. In fact, they had kept me locked up with little sunlight and no exercise the entire time I was in captivity. I gained weight. I don't think they were joking about fattening me up or fattening up my liver. They were treating me like a prize goose.

The Morifati didn't plan to eat me because they were hungry though. They had plenty of food. They thought that there was some kind of magic to be gained from eating their victims, or maybe they just enjoyed it. Most of all, I think they just enjoyed having power over other human beings. They claimed they didn't fear Than, but I think that death is the thing that they feared the most.

And Snake? What about Snake? What could she do to them? What had she done to them to become such an enemy for them? I was going to have to have a long talk with her. I had come to my senses on the question of killing her. I don't know if I ever really meant it, or whether the power of the Old Hag's spell was enough to make someone kill a friend or a loved one. Could that old witch make someone act against their own will? The Morifati had tried to make me believe that the world that I knew was completely different from the one I thought I lived in. They tried to change reality for me!

When I could think, I knew the Morifati were my enemies, and they planned to kill me no matter what I did for them. I knew that Grandfather and Diana loved me. I knew that Snake and Wolf and Raven were my friends. But when I thought of Anna, my heart broke. How could I change her into the woman of my dreams? How could I ever reconcile with her?

On the third night, before I fell asleep, I told myself that I had to reach out to Snake finally. I knew I could not go on like this. But how do you intentionally dream about someone?

The only thing I knew to do was to lie in bed, picturing Snake in my mind. I tried to remember and visualize the dreams of her I had in the past. Maybe if I thought of her the way I had thought of Diana on the mountainside, she would appear to me?

"I will go to Snake tonight.", I said aloud.

I kept repeating that thought over and over. I stopped doing it, though, when I realized I was keeping myself awake. I switched to consciously relaxing my body and my breathing while keeping an image of Snake in my mind. Presently, I fell asleep.

I had some crazy dreams, nightmares really, about the Morifati. I had one where Anna was grinning at me wickedly, all the love gone out of her eyes. Diana was there in the dream. Anna went after her with a knife! Diana turned into a dove and flew away just in time. The Morifati started shooting arrows at the dove. I felt a knife in my back. I turned to see Anna there, then she turned into the Old Hag. I woke up yelling.

I fell back asleep again after lying awake for quite a while after. This time I dreamed of Snake. She was small again, this time small enough to crawl in under the door. She had the same coloration as in the last dream, white with gold banding. She came into the room with me as in the previous dream, we were not in her castle or far away somewhere I didn't recognize. She illuminated the room with a soft golden glow, just as if someone had lit a single candle.

"Wake up Rion.", she said.

"How will we speak if I am awake?"

"I have come to you. I am in the room with you now. Wake up and get out of bed so we can talk."

I thought to myself; I am dreaming. Can I make myself wake up? If I wake up, won't that break the connection with her?

"Come on Rion."

So I tried hard. I had that feeling of being paralyzed at first, but I came to. I sat up. To my astonishment, lying on the floor was a small white snake with gold bands around it, and the room was illuminated, just as it had been in the dream.

"Is it really you?"

"Yes, it's me.", she said. "Get up."

So I got out of bed and went over and picked her up carefully.

"Allow me.", I said.

Then I went over to the table and placed her on it and sat down, looking at her.

"I did not know you would come here in person, or that I had been going to you in my mind while I slept."

"I know. Raven told me everything you said to her. I knew that with the spell that you are under you might never contact me again so I came to you in person."

Her coloration in this form was beautiful. The colors were bright and contrasted well. Her scales were shiny. She had bright little yellow eyes that held no sinister intent, but a little merriment or mischief. I could tell I amused her.

She looked right at me, but of course she spoke with her mind.

"Is it safe for you to be here? Aren't you taking an enormous risk coming here?" I said.

"I could ask you the same question, Rion."

"No, really, how did you get here in this form?"

"That will be my secret for now. I know many things and have more than one way to travel. The Ravens are my eyes and ears. They are watching out for us both even now as we are speaking."

"But why did you come here in person?"

"Like I said, I had reason to doubt that you would come to me again. It is also time for you to learn the things you must learn. You must pass these tests now. The longer you remain here as their prize goose, the harder it will be for you to succeed."

"I no longer understand why it is necessary to defeat the Morifati. There is a young maiden that they have introduced to me. I am in love with her and she is in love with me. They have offered to let me marry her and they have offered to make peace with the Free State."

"You are under a Limerence Spell Rion."

"That's what Raven said."

"She has seen it in you and in them. She watches over this little shack where they are keeping you. She sees them come and go, she knows what they are going to do before they do it. She knows their actions, she knows their intentions. They will not let you touch this girl. Anna does not love you, and she is no maiden. The Morifati do not want peace with you or the Free State or with me or the Wolves. They believe the entire world is theirs. They believe they have a right to take anything they desire, to control, to possess everything and to do their own will without restraint."

"Why are you their enemy?"

"Because I lie between them and what they want!"

"Is there no hope for peace?"

"Not as long as they follow Blackheart John and obey his commandments!"

I fell silent then. I wanted to confess to her, but I feared the consequence of saying anything. I couldn't think straight. I kept changing my mind about what I wanted and what I ought to do. I had lost my grip on what was real.

"I can remove the Limerence Spell you are under, but I can't do it here. In the meantime, no matter how much it hurts, you must realize that this girl has betrayed you."

"What can I do?"

"Learn the Sight. Learn how to 'see around the corner' as Raven does."

"But no one will teach me anything! No one will tell me any-thing!"

"Diana will come to you and she will help. There is still much you must do on your own, but as long as you have hope of loving this Anna, you will not try. You will lie here and get fat and wait for them to kill you!"

"I can't conceive of life without Anna! I want to love her and be with her so badly that I agreed to...."

"What did you agree to?"

"To kill you."

"I am here in front of you now. Do you think you can do it?"

I had not thought of that. I got up and paced the floor. My imaginations of the future and my memories of the past were at war within me. I knew killing Snake would be wrong and crazy, that everyone would think I had lost my mind. Yet, I couldn't shake this dream of a life with my love, of a future with this girl, the girl of my dreams.

"You have lost her, Rion. You never had her. She planned to betray you from the start. She is the Old Hag's apprentice. Her heart is as cold as the grave."

I had to lie down.

I was in agony. My head told me that there was no way to change Anna into someone who could love me, into someone I could trust and love, but my heart kept trying to find some way to get to her and change her, but to kill Snake, how could I do that and then face Grandfather?

"I can't. I can't kill you. I can't do all the things they are asking me to do. But I can't stop loving that girl. There must be some way I can help her."

"You can't help her. There is nothing and no one there to help! She is evil. They have all been playing a mind game with you to confuse you and make you believe in their friendship and the truth of their religion. They have used both psychic power and psychology on you. Have you not noticed that they change back and forth? First, they are your friends and then

129

they are your enemies? First you can marry and then you can never see her again? First Anna loves you and then she hates you?"

"I had noticed, but I still hope that.... Is there nothing I can do?"

"Why would you want to do anything when you have Diana's love? She has loved you since she was a child. The marriage between you and Diana has already been foreseen. It is your destiny."

"I can't explain Snake. I understand what you say though."

"This Limerence Spell must be removed. It will take both Diana and I to remove it. We must act now. Diana will have to risk coming here to teach you some things. Then you will have to come to my castle before so we can remove the spell."

"I thought I had to learn on my own."

"You do. But you have already learned some things. You know how to call to Diana and bring her to you when you are in danger. And you know how to go to me in your dreams. You always knew how to do that, but you didn't realize you were doing it! You thought I was coming to you!"

She laughed at me then.

"Am I that stupid?"

"No Rion. Your gifts are much greater than you realize. That is why I chose you. When you came to me the first time, I knew you were no ordinary man. Only a very few receive gifts like yours."

"What gifts do I have?"

"You already know you have at least two, but you have not learned how to control them yet. You can reach out to someone in your dreams and speak to them. For now, you can only do this while asleep, but soon you will do it when awake. You have only just realized that it was you who was performing this. You acted involuntarily, but you can perform this type of telepathy at will."

"How do you know all these things? Will I gain this power?"

"I know many things. I can see many things. There are some things which I cannot describe with words. There are some things that you can only know through experience. That is why no one has told you much, it is a waste of breath to do so."

"Is that how I will learn to 'see around the corner'?"

"Yes. Find out the secret yourself. I cannot teach it directly. There is another gift that we can teach you. Diana will come and teach you this gift. It is the ability to see through the eyes of another and feel what they feel. It is a gift we call, Telempathy."

"That's what Raven was talking about!"

"Right. Diana and Raven are masters of this gift. All the Ravens are. Few master this gift completely. We dared not to teach it to you beforehand because we were afraid that Blackheart John would see into your mind and gain it."

"The Morifati looked into my mind. Why do they not have these powers?"

"They cannot feel what another feels. They are incapable of any kind of empathy."

"But they showed me a future with Anna."

"All dreams, illusions. They cannot see the future. They do not have the Sight. If they did, they would not live as they do, as if there were no consequences for what they do. They think that nothing they do matters. They stubbornly refuse to do anything else, to live any other way."

"Why are they attacking the Free State now? What do they have to gain by attacking the surrounding tribes?"

"Greed. It's all motivated by greed. They have enough and to spare but they want more. If someone else has anything, they have to have it. And they enjoy it, they enjoy having control over other people. Their hearts became corrupted long ago, during the Great Third War and the years that followed. They survived by stealing, and killing, and by the capture and rape of women. They believe it is natural, that is the will of their god Than."

"So that's all they know and there is no hope for them?"

"It would take a miracle to change any of them."

"So what can I do to stop them? Do I have to act all by myself? Will I have to kill them all?"

"The answer to that question must be kept secret still. They will interrogate you some more before we can get you out of here, and they will promise you that girl. We must keep your true nature hidden from them. We would lose everything if they knew. They wouldn't wait till the new moon. They would kill you now."

"I didn't do a wonderful job of keeping quiet. I betrayed everyone. Wolf, Diana, Grandfather, and you."

"Do not suffer because of it, Rion. No one can withstand prolonged torture without breaking. The Morifati are masters of these techniques. It does not matter to them if you tell them anything or not. They enjoy torture."

"They suspect me. I think they suspect there is more to my story. They don't understand why I came here."

"Keep them confused. They are not in a hurry, such is their arrogance."

"That won't be too hard, I guess. I am confused myself."

Just then Raven perched on the windowsill, high up.

"You must leave now, your Majesty. They will come soon!"

Then Raven flew off as rapidly as she had appeared. I turned back around to look at Snake.

"Place me on the ground near the door."

"Will you be alright? What if they see you?"

"I'll be fine. I can move quickly when I need to, much quicker than they can react. Raven watches over me, too. She will distract anyone she sees coming."

"What shall I do now?"

"Practice calling others with your mind in your daydreams. Especially Diana. Go to Diana and call her here."

I put her down near the door as she requested. She slipped underneath the doorframe, slowly at first, then suddenly she was gone.

TWENTY-TWO

DESPAIR

As soon as Snake left, my heart sank. I knew what I had to do, but I dreaded doing any of it. I still felt torn, despite understanding everything she had said. And now I had to face Diana. What would I tell her? If they brought Anna to me again, I would have to play their game, or else they would realize that something had happened.

Luckily, I was still under the Limerence Spell. If anyone had removed it, surely the Morifati would notice. The Morifati must be certain that I was an idiot by now. I don't see how they could have been afraid of me at that point. That was probably a good thing, since if they believed I could do what Snake predicted I could do, they would have to kill me right away.

The room was dark now that Snake had left. I stumbled back over to the bed and threw myself down. I didn't want to talk to the Morifati now; I didn't want to talk to anybody or do anything. I felt tired.

I dozed off, but I jerked back to consciousness when the door opened. It was the Old Hag coming back with my breakfast and with her were the two maidens and Anna was with her! My heart leaped in spite of my head.

"Anna! You've come back!"

"Yes, I am back, my love. They tell me you will not eat for wont of love for me. It is important that you eat! You must eat a proper meal at least three times a day. We have brought food, specially prepared for you. You must stay on a special diet."

At that, they busied themselves preparing the table. I thought that under the circumstances, I ought to play my role to the hilt. So I got up and walked over to embrace her.

"Stop! Do not touch her! I forbid you to touch any of them!" said the Old Hag.

"You must not keep me from my love!"

I advanced with my arms spread wide.

"Stop Rion! No! It is not time!", said Anna and she backed away. The other two got in front of her and in between us quickly. Then the Old Hag grabbed me and spun me around.

"You can't keep me from her! Why do you keep us apart when I have done everything you have asked?"

"You are not to ask questions! Your task is to do as you are told! You have not killed Snake yet and you will not get the chance if we cannot trust you."

I stood facing the Old Hag. What should I do next? They were already convinced that the Limerence Spell was working, so I had accomplished little. They were determined to keep me captive, getting fat and out of shape. They would not let me leave, and they would never let me so much as touch Anna. I had to escape if I wanted to live, and that meant learning to 'see around the corner' and some other tricks as well.

I turned back around to face Anna and the two maidens standing in front of her.

"I love you Anna, can I not at least greet you with a kiss?"

She motioned for the two girls to step aside then, and she stood in front of them. I felt a pinprick on my left shoulder. The Old Hag had stuck me with something! I dropped to my knees, staggered by whatever it was she had poisoned me with.

Emotion gripped me again. The Limerence Spell grew over-whelming. I felt like I was going to die if I could not have Anna! I lost my balance and fell forward on my hands and knees.

Anna stood directly in front of me. I wanted to get up but could not move. It took all my strength just to keep from lying flat.

"Rion, if you love me, then you must obey me. You must do as you are told while you are our guest here. Everything that we do for you is done for your own good. We are honoring you. We are going to honor you still further at the Feast of the New Moon. Do you not feel honored in my presence?"

I have to admit, in that state of mind I felt honored, al-though I wasn't thinking straight enough to know what any of that meant.

"Yes Anna! It is an honor to be with you!"

"And you will continue to love me and do whatever I say, for your own good and for the sake of our love?"

It's hard to describe what I felt at that point. What had brought me to behave in a manner so out of character for me? I had never felt this way about any woman ever before. I didn't really understand why I felt that way about Anna. There really was no reason for it, unless you believe in soulmates, or love at first sight, or that kind of thing. I had not gotten to know her at all. I did not really know her. The Old Hag had used a combi-nation of drugs, and psychology, and psychic powers to bring me to the point where I was desperately in love with a woman I did not really know, and groveling on my hands and knees in front of her.

"Yes, I want nothing more than to make you happy!"

"And anything that displeases me makes me unhappy and drives us apart from each other."

"Yes."

"Can you live knowing that you lost me by making me un-happy?"

"No. No, I can't bear the thought of that."

"You may rise then, and take your seat at the table, but do not attempt to touch me again."

So I got up and meekly went to sit down. I felt frustrated, my heart was breaking, and yet at the same time I was happy to be with her. The power of the Limerence Spell was such that I was happy just to be with her. I clung to the possibility that she would change her mind and let me show her my love.

They shoved plates of food and a cup of wine at me. There was nothing to do but shove it down. Their eyes were on me the whole time. I'm not sure what they were watching for, but they reacted to everything I did, every move I made.

After some time had passed, when they had finished feed-ing me, the Old Hag turned to look at Anna. They exchanged a knowing glance, and Anna nodded to her.

Everyone got up and cleaned off the table except for the food they always left behind for me to snack on. Then, without a word, the Old Hag and the two maidens walked out of the door.

At last they left me alone with Anna! To my delight, she went and sat on the edge of the bed. She raised her gown to show her legs from the knees down. She kicked off her shoes. She gestured for me to approach her and pointed to a spot in front of her.

"You may kneel here.", she said.

I rushed over and knelt, hoping that at last she would offer greater favors than that. Would she at last give herself to me now that we were alone? I could feel my entire body burn with excitement. My heart ached. Somehow, I felt choked with cau-tion still. I couldn't approach her boldly. I couldn't just take her, even though we were alone together. I was afraid. Afraid that any wrong step, any wrong word and I would lose her for-ever.

"Do you love me? Do you love me more than you have ever loved anyone?"

"Yes."

"Are you prepared to do anything I ask?"

"Yes."

"Are you willing to make any sacrifice, no matter how great?"

"Yes."

"Will you forsake all others, and remain loyal only to me?"

"Yes."

"Will you answer all questions put to you with the absolute truth?"

"Yes."

"Will you offer your life if that is what I ask?"

"Yes."

"Then you may kiss my hand."

She extended her left hand then, fingers pointed down. I leaned forward and took it gently in my hand, and kissed it. I know that I should have felt humiliation and anger at these words and gestures, but the Limerence Spell also made me feel joy and love for her and gratitude at finally being allowed to express my love, and to in some way receive some token of af-fection from her.

"Enough. And now, my feet. On your hands and knees."

I sat back, and she extended her feet together. I leaned for-ward, bowed down before her on my hands and knees, and kissed each of her feet. Then she withdrew them quickly.

"I love you Anna, I swear my loyalty to you alone.", I said.

"Now you must tell me everything you know about Snake!"

"But I have told you everything I know about Snake already! There is nothing more to tell!"

"You liar! Do you love me? Do you want to make love to me? Then tell!"

"I have told you everything! I swear it!"

How I could find the strength to lie in this situation I will never know. Somehow, even as strong as the Limerence Spell was, I knew that everything we were saying and doing was a game, an act. She was pretending to love me. She felt no more love for me than a predator has for its prey.

"Who are you? What powers do you possess?"

"I am just a simple hunter from the Free State. I am not a Psychic. I have no powers."

"More lies. Snake would not have sent you here for no reason. I will give you one last chance to tell the truth."

I was left speechless at that. I did not want her to go. The thought of her leaving me now was excruciating, especially since we had come so close to making love and fulfilling my dreams about her and our future life together. I knew better than to tell her the whole truth about everything Snake had asked me to do, however. I knew in my heart that Raven and Snake had not lied to me.

"I have told everything. Forgive me if it is not what you seek."

At that, she quickly stood up. She started abruptly to leave. I grabbed her around the knees.

"You will never see me again, Rion! Let me go at once or I will call the High Priest in here and let him deal with you!"

"Please Anna! I'm begging you not to go!"

She struggled against my grip, but I held on.

"Let me go at once! It will go badly for you if you do not do as I say. The High Priest will have you whipped!"

"If you must punish me, punish me yourself!"

"You pathetic coward. Did you imagine I loved you? Did you dream about living happily ever after with me?"

At that, she laughed and kicked herself free of my arms. I let go of her. The whole thing had gotten completely out of my control. There was no hope of loving her now. She rushed over to the door and slammed it behind her, and I heard the bolt slam on the outside.

I was in agony, but I had accomplished one thing. I had told her nothing that I knew about my mission there among the Morifati.

What would she do now, I thought? Surely she would report everything to them. The Limerence Spell made me feel devastated at the thought that I had lost her for good. I mourned losing her. It was as if my life was over. The critical part of my brain kept telling me it had all been an act, but it was still unendurable to "lose her."

I actually imagined that things were not as they were. I dreamed about a past where everything had turned out differently and we had wound up together. I racked my brain for any way to reconcile with her. Was there anything I could say to any of them to get another chance with her?

And what would the Morifati do now? Would they kill me? Surely not. They wanted to sacrifice me. They had said it before. The Morifati were confident of their power over me. There was no doubting that. There was no way to escape from them. There was no doubting that, not unless I learned the Sight.

I knew then that I had to find a way to learn to 'see around the corner'. Everyone had told me that before, and I understood what they said, but I could not feel it. I did not believe it, because I doubted myself or because of the hope of loving Anna that the Limerence Spell had produced in me.

I lay down then, closed my eyes and tried to see. I said nothing, not even in my mind. I just tried to imagine what was going on around me.

TWENTY-THREE

I LEARN TO SEE

I noticed through my closed lids that Anna had rushed out, leaving three candles lit. I opened my eyes. Should I try to burn the cabin down? That probably would not work out. That could easily backfire on me and leave me trapped in a burning building.

I sat up and looked at the three candles. Maybe if I extinguished two of them and concentrated on the third, it would help. I got up and did just that and sat at the table staring into the remaining candle. It seemed to help a bit, but it hurt my eyes so I closed them. What should I try to see? Who should I try to contact?

I let my mind wander. Images floated through of everyone I knew. I would have to pick one of them, but how do you see through another's eyes? I tried to imagine where they all were now, Snake, Grandfather, Wolf, Diana, Raven, even the Old Hag, the High Priest, Blackheart John, and Anna.

It was more difficult than I thought. I had no way of knowing whether what I saw was real, or something I was imagining about them. I thought I better not concentrate on any of the Morifati just now. It might summon them back and I was tired of them all and their questions and their games.

I tried not to think at all. The light from the single candle made a rosy glow as it shone through my eyelids. Snake said that I had gone to her in my mind before in my dreams, and that I had called to Diana on the mountainside. Could I go to them in a daydream? I had to find out!

I daydreamed about Diana, to let my mind wander over my memories of her. I pictured her in my mind with the wolves, with Lara, Wolf's mate. Where was Diana now? What had I done before that made her come to us on the mountainside?

She had appeared as a dove. How did she do that? She claimed she wasn't a Psychic. Then what was she? Could she appear to me now? Was it too dangerous? Maybe I could go to her and speak to her, as I had with Snake.

I relaxed and continued to picture her in my mind. I saw her as I had seen her the last time we were together. The two of us alone with the wolves on the other side of the Forbidden Land. There we were, with Wolf and Lara and the others. I remembered the scene clearly, but somehow I felt it wasn't enough.

What about the dream I had in which we were about to be married? That might have been a vision of a time when I had gone to her in my dream. I had gone to Snake in the same dream, so my mind must have been active.

That felt better. I was on to something. I tried to imagine the wedding between the two of us, at the wolves sacred place, the Forest Chapel. I remembered it as I had dreamt it, but was it like that now? How could I picture it as it was right now?

And where was Diana? I couldn't imagine it, to daydream about a place I had never seen. It occurred to me I should try to say something, that I should try to imagine the priest speaking to us.

Wait! Who was the priest? When I dreamt the complete scene before, all I saw was Diana at the altar with the Wolves on either side. Shouldn't there be more there than that? The people of the Free State, Snake, or Raven, maybe an entire flock of ravens?

Then I imagined Grandfather was there presiding over the whole thing. That made sense. That way we would marry in the eyes of the Free State.

Still, nothing happened. She did not speak to me, and I did not go to her in my mind. What had I done before on the mountainside? What had I seen then?

I searched back through my memory. It was harder to do than I had hoped. The Morifati had done so much to me since then. They had given me so many potions and warped my view of reality. It was difficult to know what was real, what was really a memory. My memories, my hallucinations, and my dreams about the future were all wrapped up together. They had made me see the world and the people I knew in it differently than I knew them before. Each memory had to compete with what I knew was real.

I knew it all started with a picture of Diana in my mind. And what else? A longing to go to her, to be with her, to see her again. Then she transformed in my mind's eye into a radiant dove and then she appeared to us in that form.

The Morifati had made me forget about her. They had made me forget about all women except for Anna, who had to be a witch. I understood why now. They did not want me to summon up Snake or Raven or Diana or anyone else they knew of or did not know about.

So how could I picture her? The candle still glowed behind my eyelids. I concentrated on it. Would it assume the shape of a dove, I wondered? I could imagine any shape I supposed. But to start with, I should imagine Diana's face over the image of the candle.

So I started that way, imagining Diana's face in the candle's image on my eyelids. After some minutes, I gave it up; it wasn't working. I opened my eyes and looked at the flame. I stopped trying. I just let my mind wander. I relaxed.

My mind drifted back to memories of life in the Free State before all this trouble began. I thought about Diana as a child. I had watched her grow up. When she was old enough, she began following me around. She would follow me on a hunt. She wasn't strong enough to use a bow well, but she was great at finding game. I know why now, but at the time I didn't suspect the Sight. I just thought that she was good at reading structure and sensing patterns. Some people are good at that and they are not Psychics.

At the time she was a little pest, but I tolerated her because of this ability of hers to find game. As she got older, she grew into a beautiful young girl and people teased us about it. Some of the old people warned us not to stay out on a hunt too long or get lost. If a couple lived by themselves for three days, we considered them married by law. Sometimes a man would kidnap his lover if her parents didn't approve of him. When the couple got back, if she claimed he had taken her away by force, they would charge him with kidnaping, but if she agreed, then they were man and wife.

I pictured her face again in my mind's eye. I thought of the dream when she came to me as I slept. In the dream she said, "I love you Rion."

I pictured that clearly in my mind. Suddenly she said, "That's good, keep trying."

It startled me so I lost my concentration. I regained the image.

"Can you hear me now, Diana? Can we speak?", I said.

She said nothing. I didn't know whether to relax or to call out to her in desperation. When she came to us before, it was when Wolf and I were in danger of freezing to death. I was in danger now, just not immediate danger, or so I supposed.

144

"Keep thinking about me. Reach out to me, Rion. Let me know where you are."

"I am being held captive in the Morifati village. In an old shack with only one window and one door. I am never taken outside. They come to me and feed me well and ask me questions, they promise friendship and love and then take it away just as quickly."

"How can I find you?" said Diana.

"Raven came to me here and so did Snake. Maybe they can tell you."

"But I asked you to tell me. Show me what you see around you."

So I turned and looked around the room. I picked up the candle and held it aloft. I walked around, illuminating every corner.

"Can you see now Diana?"

"Yes. I can see what you see, my love. Behold!"

Then the room glowed with a light that came not from the candle.

High up in the middle of the room, at the center of the ceiling, the glow brightened and formed a center. The image of a dove formed in the center of this glowing orb, just as it had on the mountainside.

TWENTY-FOUR

THE DOVE

I watched as the image grew brighter and more distinct. It appeared as a golden dove at first, then as it took shape the outlines of a real dove appeared, then suddenly the glow disappeared, the dove turned white and materialized into a real dove which fluttered down to the table. We were back to only the light from my single candle.

"You did it Rion!", said Diana.

"I guess so, but I don't understand exactly what it was I just did."

"That's okay. It's okay to learn things a little at a time. There is so much to teach you it will take a little while no matter what we do, but we must hurry now. You have to escape soon. We will not break the Limerence Spell easily. We have to get you out of here first."

"Who are you Diana? How can you say you are not a Psychic?"

"I am something much more powerful than a Psychic. You are not ready for the explanation yet, but soon you will understand. Soon you will be like me and we will be together forever."

"I'm getting tired of everyone withholding information from me. If my actions are so important, then tell me what I need to know."

"Be patient, my love. We just don't want to overwhelm you with it all. Here, watch this."

And then the white dove that had fluttered down to the tabletop and walked over to face me, transformed before my eyes into Diana herself. She smiled at me mischievously.

"Now I'm back the way you remember me."

She walked over to me, embraced me, and kissed my cheek. Then she offered me her mouth, which I accepted. I don't think I had ever kissed her properly before then. The degree of passion I felt surprised us both. I felt a combination of relief at seeing someone I knew again and a release of all the frustration the Morifati women had caused me to feel.

I felt a twinge when I remembered Anna, but I could see the way to forget all about Anna. We broke our kiss. She smiled at me and looked deeply into my eyes. I thought I could fall into her eyes like they were a deep well.

"I'll make you forget all about that Morifati witch!" said Diana.

"So you are going to save me?"

"No! I am not! You are going to save yourself using the techniques I will teach you."

"Why couldn't you teach me before?"

"You weren't ready. Everyone has to endure a trial first, or it just doesn't work."

"How did you learn?"

"I was lucky. I am gifted."

"So you've been living a double life in the Free State. How long has this gone on?"

"Since I was nine. But I didn't know then what I know now. I have learned some things recently as well, from the Wolves."

"How long have you known about Snake?"

"Since I was nine. She contacted me then. She contacted me just before you went out on your mission. You've been in contact with Snake for much longer than I knew about."

I couldn't be sure, but I thought I saw a brief flash of jealousy then. What was there to be jealous about? My relationship with Snake was not romantic that I was aware of. I was dealing with two females here, though. The greatest mystery I have ever faced. Much harder to understand than the Morifati or Psychics or world history.

"Doesn't anyone in the Free State know about you? You must feel all alone."

"Grandfather knows."

"He does? I wonder why he didn't tell me?"

"There's a lot he hasn't told you. He knows many secrets. Things he has to keep secret from everyone. Things he hasn't told me. Things he refuses to discuss!"

"He knew all about the Psychics and the history of the Great Third War when I talked to him last. This all started with a dream I had about Snake. I thought she was just a dream, and in the dream it felt like she had come to me. Now I know I had gone to her, had been going to her. I didn't understand the dream, I couldn't believe it was real, so I went to him for an explanation."

"So what did he say?"

"He told me that if a wolf came to me and spoke to me with its mind, I would know that the dream was true. So when I met Wolf, I knew what I had to do. But what about you? What did you know?"

Diana just smiled at me.

"Cat got your tongue?"

"I knew I better follow along, make sure you were okay. I do have the Sight, remember. I see glimpses of the future. Not

148

anything set in stone but possibilities based on the way things are going now. You and I have a future together, and I want to make sure it comes true."

"Don't I have a choice in any of this?"

"No, you don't!"

"But you can't make things turn out the way you want all by yourself, can you?"

"No, none of us can, but I can influence the outcome, and so can you. I am here to teach you how."

"But everyone keeps saying I have to learn on my own."

"That's still true, but there are ways I can help, techniques I can show you. The first thing you've got to learn is how to 'see around the corner', but there are a couple of other things first."

"I just want to know how to get out of here!"

"You can get out of here any time you want Rion." said Diana.

"How can that be true?"

"It is, you just haven't been trying. They were successful at seducing you with that girl. If I can make you see how important it is to defeat them, you'll try harder."

I had lost myself after being captured by them. It was true, but Snake had never explained how I was supposed to defeat them, only that I had the power within me to do it. And why me? What is so special about me?

"What is so special about me, Diana? Why me?"

"Just shut up! You are too deep into this now to quit. The first thing I am going to teach you is how to see through another's eyes and feel what they feel. It's a technique we call telempathy."

She looked around, studying the room. She took the two chairs and set them directly across from each other, so we could face each other across the width rather than the length. She moved the candle to one side and sat, trying to see how to position the two of us across from each other, with the candle just off to one side.

When she got everything just right, she motioned for me to sit.

"Get comfortable. This will have to take as long as it takes."

"That's going to be tough in these old wooden chairs. They have hurt my backside."

She laughed and said, "Stop whining! Sit up straight and look into my eyes. We are going to look directly into each other's eyes until we can see into each other, and then, we will see through each other's eyes."

I adjusted myself; it seemed that it helped to lean forward a little. Then I looked directly into Diana's eyes. It was much more intimate than I expected. It startled me. I looked away.

"What's the matter Rion?"

"It's stronger than I thought it would be, more intimate."

"Don't be afraid to reveal yourself to me. You can't reveal anything I haven't seen already, anyway. I know much more about you than you realize, my love. Just know that I love you. Let me show my love with just my eyes."

I tried again. This time it was easier. I was enjoying it.

"When you are completely relaxed, enter my mind. Don't try hard, just let it happen."

"Okay, but how do I .....?"

"Just be quiet and relax. Look at me, gaze into my eyes, enter my mind until you can see yourself. You will see yourself through me."

Now when someone tells me to relax I find it hard to relax, so I kept quiet and while I maintained eye contact with her, I practiced the breathing techniques and relaxation techniques that Grandfather taught me before. I reached out to place my hands on top of hers without breaking eye contact.

I was feeling her love for me, no doubt about it. I was also feeling love for her myself. I forgot about Anna completely for a while. I thought maybe I should use my imagination. Maybe I should try to imagine what she is seeing now. I let my mind wander a little.

I caught a brief glance of myself, then I pulled back.

"Just relax. Keep trying."

I tried again, just letting it happen, until suddenly I was looking at myself.

"I can see myself.", I said.

"Good. Just keep it up for a while. Get used to it."

It was almost like holding a mirror up to a mirror. I could see myself looking directly into Diana's eyes. Should I risk breaking contact and look around? I turned, but I turned my own head, not hers. That broke contact.

"Keep looking into my eyes until you get the hang of it.", she said. "Try again."

So I straightened back up and looked into her eyes. It didn't take long to reestablish seeing through her eyes. But how to see without looking directly at someone? I tried closing my eyes slowly. I found I was still looking at myself through her eyes, but this time my eyes were closed. I opened them back up.

"Should we try it with you looking away? Or walking around the room?"

"Yes, that's next, I guess. Eventually you will have to learn to cast your mind about to find people who are close by but outside your line of sight. This can be difficult with the Morifati. Not because it is so hard to do but because their hearts and minds are so evil that many cannot bear it. To see what they see and feel what they feel. Snake took an enormous risk coming here, she usually has to hide from them and their grotesque thoughts."

"But seeing around the corner isn't just about the here and now, is it? I thought it also involved the Sight?"

"It does, but first things first."

We resumed eye contact. This time it took no time at all to see me through her eyes. She pushed back her chair and got up, watching me the entire time. Then she took a walk around me. I maintained telempathic contact with her as she walked around behind me and returned to look directly at me.

She turned then abruptly and walked over toward the high window and looked up at it. She turned back and looked over her shoulder. I could see myself turn to look at her with my own eyes, and that broke the contact.

"You discovered how to break contact. Don't use your own eyes. Maintain the focus of your attention on my focus of attention. Your mind will go on automatic, just like it does when you are deep in thought and you suddenly discover you have been walking along noticing nothing."

"So I should concentrate on your thoughts and feelings and forget myself?"

"That's right. Just relax and let yourself see whatever your target sees and flow along with whatever they are doing. It can be difficult, even revolting when you are seeing through a Morifati's eyes."

"I see that now. Like when one of them is eating human flesh."

"Ugh. Too much information! But yes, you will see whatever they focus their attention on, even if it is something imaginary. That is one way to use the Sight with them. You can see what they are imagining will happen next."

"How can I see what will actually happen?"

"No one ever sees the actual. Only the possible future. But when the time is short, what you see is almost certain. But of course your knowledge, and your reaction to that knowledge, can change it."

"How will I be able to see through another when I cannot look into their eyes?"

"You will learn to cast around and search for them with your mind. We'll try that next. I will look around and find a Morifati to see through, and you can see through them by seeing through me. That's the best way to start. Some things are better experienced than explained."

So we started over. Soon I was seeing myself through her eyes again. Then she closed her eyes and let her mind wander. I could see everything Diana imagined or saw. There were no Morifati nearby that I knew of, but it turned out there were two guards outside watching the door across a little alleyway.

Diana entered the mind of one of them, and I could see him regarding the door and window of the shack with boredom. Then, turning to look at his companion, he resumed his conversation with him. The conversation was about as crude and vile as you might expect, so I will not relate it here. They argued, and then they gambled by throwing a die against the wall of another building. So that was how Raven, and Snake, and Diana had entered the room. The Morifati was barely paying attention. I sensed some overconfidence in them then. That was good. It would make it easier for me.

"Should I try to see ahead? To see around the corner?"

"These two are going to stay put for a while. Let's look for someone who is walking around or just about to."

So Diana began casting about again. Just a little further away, she found the two maidens walking along with trays of food. She entered the first one's mind. I could see the direction the girl was walking in.

"Now try to see ahead, Rion."

I relaxed, concentrated, let my imagination flow and I could see the girl walking up to the shack, speaking to the guards. The guards crudely propositioned her and the other girl. The maidens angrily brushed them off and entered the room to find me alone with Diana.

"They're coming here! They're close!"

"Don't worry. I can stop that. I can control people's actions to a limited degree."

Diana did something to the girl that made her trip over her own feet and spill the tray she carried. The other girl fell over the top of her. The meal ruined and their clothes needed to be changed, so they cursed each other, gathered everything up and turned around and went back toward the kitchen they had come from.

"That was a neat trick Diana. How much time do you suppose we have now?"

"Let me see."

She paused for a minute and let her mind flow around the surrounding space. I could see what she saw. She went back along the way the maidens had come and there was the High Priest. We entered his mind.

"Now see around the corner, Rion."

I looked out and saw through the High Priest's mind. I projected the path of his thoughts and his temporal path out ahead of him. He was coming here. I followed along through his future as he walked up to the shack and the guards and let himself in. I saw his astonishment as he found Diana here, talking to me. Then he yelled out.

"He is coming here, Diana. We have to change this."

"Oh, we will. Grab a chair, and go stand behind the door."

I quickly did just that.

"Now reach out in your own mind, Rion, without my help."

So I let myself dream back to where I was before. I found the High Priest, and I entered his mind. I projected his path out ahead of him and I saw him enter the shack. As soon as he entered the room, he saw Diana and then, pain and blackness.

"Now I've got him!"

"Good. Keep watching. It shouldn't be long now."

We waited for the High Priest, neither one of us moving, but we prepared ourselves to take action. Diana remained where she was and watched with me.

"Are you not going to leave now, Diana?"

"I will wait here and draw his attention when he enters the room. It will be easier for you that way."

"What will you do after that?"

"I'll have to leave you here. You know enough now to get out of the village. When you get out, follow the stream down to the Great River, steal a boat if you can. After you are well clear of them, call to me and I will return to you."

"Shouldn't I go to where you are, with the Wolves?"

"No, we need to go pay a visit to Snake. I don't think you are completely over the Limerence Spell yet. Snake and I will have to work on you some more."

"Do you know how to find her?"

"The Ravens will guide us."

"Won't the Morifati try to follow?"

"They will. But you know how to see out ahead of them now, and the Ravens will be our eyes in the sky."

It was then that the door opened. I heard the High Priest gasp when he saw Diana standing behind the table. She immediately transformed into a dove and shone with a nearly blinding light. I sprung at the High Priest and brought the chair down hard over his head.

"Good bye Rion, I must go. Remember, I love you and remember all you have learned."

And with that she flew away, leaving me standing over the High Priest.

TWENTY-FIVE

THE SIGHT

After I knocked the High Priest unconscious, I closed the door quickly so the guards could not see in. I would have to hope for them to look away or for something else to happen. Could I make them think I was him? Maybe if I put on his robe and headdress and went out while they were looking the other way at the same time. I quickly took his headdress and robe and the amulet he wore and put them on. Then I went back to the door and looked into their minds.

Soon I had my chance. The two maidens came back toward us carrying trays of food, and the guards looked over at them and started toward them. When they got close enough to the girls to keep them distracted, I just opened the door and walked out and around the side of the building, with none of them seeing me.

I paused and crouched down. I was in the clear for now, but I had to see what was out ahead of me. I daydreamed. I projected my path in my mind out ahead of me toward the stream which ran down toward the Great River. Was there a boat I could steal? Would I encounter anyone along the way?

I saw myself running into the Morifati if I took the most direct route. I would have to meander around, but there was a way out. Incredibly, the gate to the city was open. I guess they left it open all the time, such was their overconfidence. I would have to time my exit again, catch them off guard.

I saw a way through that involved heading away from the shack, but not toward the gate. If I traveled sideways to over toward the wall of the village at a point perpendicular to the path to the main gate, I would avoid most foot traffic. I would not have to get creative until I got close to the gate.

I set off as rapidly as I could go. I had to focus my attention on what the Sight, on what 'seeing around the corner' revealed to me and not on my senses. My body flowed between the buildings on its own with no problems, like bumping into someone. I could maintain the focus of my attention on the immediate future, on the actions and intentions of the Morifati who were close by.

None of them got anywhere close to me or threatened to cross my path until I was over near the far wall. It looked as if it was going to be easy. All I would have to do is weave my way over to the gate and then sneak through. But then I noticed a commotion.

Out ahead of me, in the immediate future, my path got crowded. They were searching for me! An alarm sounded. The guards and the two girls must have found the High Priest!

Which way should I go now? I let my mind drift around. Should I move further away from the gate? Was there another way out? Would the Morifati close the gate in a situation like this, or just block it with men to prevent me from leaving?

I tried one path after another, all leading to "dead ends." At least in the sense that I would eventually run into a Morifati along that path and have to come up with a way to divert him. I had no weapons, but I could not fight them all, even if I had a bow and a machete.

Something told me I should kill none of them. The best thing to do would be to pass through them unseen if I could. That would shake them up more than anything else I could do. If I could pass among them at will, into their midst or out of their midst without being seen. That would instill fear. They had to feel some fear, despite all their talk about being "fated to die."

I looked down one path, and suddenly I came upon Anna and the Old Hag walking together. That was a possibility I had forgotten about. What could I do then? Could I resist the Limerence Spell?

I let them see me. They thought I was the High Priest until I got close and they could see I was not wearing war paint. The problem was as soon as I locked eyes with Anna; the Limerence Spell kicked in again.

I had to find a way around them. I quickly backed away from them in my mind. I had to resist temptation then. It was crazy but instead of thinking about how to escape; I wondered if I could find a way to be alone with Anna in all the confusion.

I reached out and put myself into her mind. I saw what she saw and I could sense what she felt. I ran her path forward. When she realized that the man she thought was the High Priest was me, I felt her hatred and disgust, and her fear. What had I done to the High Priest?

That burst my bubble for the moment. I could see her for who she really was. I knew how she really felt about me. The force of her contempt staggered me with remorse in my lovesick state of mind. I found a spot to hide against a building while I composed myself.

There had to be a way out still. I searched along the wall in my mind. Was there another gate? Was there some kind of parapet? Could I climb over with a ladder or a rope?

I found a set of stairs leading to a guard post. There was only one guard inside, and he had his back to me. That gave me an idea. I started out for the guard post physically.

When I got there, I climbed up quietly. He was still standing his watch, looking out over the wall at the fields beyond. He didn't hear me walk up to the doorway. I stood to one side where he could not see and knocked.

"Who goes there?"

I paused, then knocked again.

"Stop playing games, show yourself!"

I had already seen that he would walk out to inspect the landing and turn to his right. I waited on his left. He did just as I had seen. I grabbed him and put him in a choke hold. I dragged him back inside the guard shack.

He was strong, he struggled, but he could not get out of the hold I had him in. Seeing around the corner gave me an enormous advantage. I put him in the hold without him even sensing that anyone was behind him. I caught him completely off guard!

He was big. I don't know if I could have beaten him in the ring, but taken at a disadvantage like this, I soon had him unconscious. Now what to do?

I had to change clothes with him. The High Priest's robe, headdress, and medallion made me too conspicuous. A warriors' uniform and weapons could allow me to pass unnoticed if I timed my exit. Where could I get a hold of some of their war paint? Did he have any on him? In his pack?

I dug around in his possessions and sure enough; he carried his war paint around with him. The Morifati typically armed themselves with bows and machetes, so I took those from him. I needed to change into their warrior dress, so I got out of the High Priest's robe and headdress and smeared myself with their war paint. I started with my face, painting it black, then painting the red stripe across my eyes and the red stripe across my mouth. I rubbed the white paint across everything else that would show.

I quickly put his clothes and weapons on and stuffed the amulet into the warrior's pack and shouldered it. I had no way to check my reflection, but it would have to do. I would make sure that no one got a good look at me.

I threw the robe and headdress out over the wall. What should I do with the guard? Should I throw him out too? Should I kill him?

Somehow, the thought of killing him repulsed me. I should have killed him, I suppose, since they were planning to attack the Free State, but I had the felt sense that there was another way.

I took off his pack and rummaged around. He had some rope and some bindings I could use. I quickly tied his hands and feet. I dragged him over to a corner of the room where no one would see him until they entered the room. Then I made a gag and wrapped it around his mouth.

I looked out ahead to see if anyone was coming and if there was a way clear to the gate. I saw a way through that would take me to the gate if I cut back just in time twice, so I set out toward it.

Walking down the streets and alleyways of the village was not too hard. It was just a matter of seeing them coming and stepping out of their sight or waiting for them to pass while they crossed in front of me. But what would I do when I got near the gate?.

A bunch of them had gathered near the gate, not blocking it so much as standing so that there was no way past. Could I walk up and join them?

I got as close to the gate as I dared without being seen. I looked around in my mind and through the eyes of the ones near me. I saw a small party of Morifati walking down the street around the corner from me. They were going to the gate to join the others. I took a chance then. When they walked past me, I quietly joined in behind them. They did not notice me following them. They were rushing along in a hurry to join the others and not stopping to look around.

That worked. I followed along in behind them and we all joined the crowd and no one noticed anything about me dressed as I was with war paint all over me and everything. What to do now?

I milled around through the crowd, which was loosely organized, not military ranks or anything. I could see ahead with the Sight that if I just wandered my way to the back of the pack, I could turn and walk out the gate with no one noticing me.

They were not expecting anyone to come up behind them or expecting me to be outside the gate. I don't think they were expecting to see me at all. They probably thought I was hiding somewhere in their village, still walking around in the High Priest's robes.

So I did just what I had foreseen. Suddenly, I was standing outside the gate. No one had turned to notice me. I had to control my excitement at having pulled this off. I casually walked away along the side of the wall and got out of sight, just in case any of them turned around.

I checked around for patrols outside the village. I went into their minds and eavesdropped on their conversations. They thought I was still inside their village and dressed like the High Priest.

All I had to do now was cross a field to their boat dock along the stream. Was anyone down there? It was completely unguarded. Would anyone see me if I walked down the road that led to the little bridge? Yes, they would. The gate gave an unobstructed view of the road, and so did guard towers next to the gate.

Luckily, the Morifati war paint was the perfect camouflage for low light. The sun had been setting and had now set during all the commotion. I could see that if I strolled across the field, none of the guard towers would notice the motion. If they had seen me, they probably would have thought I was a Morifati going to check on the boats.

Soon I was standing on the dock where they kept their fishing boats. Which one should I take? Did it matter? I gave them a quick once over. They were all the same, but one had some extra bows and arrows stashed in it, plus some fishing equipment. It looked like someone was preparing to leave in it, maybe just before dawn.

I untied it, stowed the lines, and jumped in. I pushed it away from the dock. I thought it best to just let it drift out to midstream and then downstream with the current until I was out of sight of the Morifati village.

I lay down low in the boat to stay out of sight. I searched in my mind to see if they noticed. To my astonishment one of the guard towers had noticed, but they thought I was a Morifati leaving early on a fishing trip. This was too good to be true!

I sat up then and looked for the oars. I found them and slowly paddled out to midstream and then downstream as fast as I could. Soon the Morifati village was out of sight as the stream entered a wood. I would need to travel as far and as fast as I could while it was still night, in case they tried to pursue me.

I looked out ahead. The stream got wider and deeper, with no rocks or logs, but it meandered a bit. I made good time just keeping it flowing along in midstream, avoiding the shallows. I continued like that until morning.

TWENTY-SIX

DIANA REAPPEARS

The sun rose on the most beautiful day I had seen in a very long time. I had forgotten what it was like to be outdoors after my captivity. My muscles ached as well. All that inactivity had made me soft.

I didn't care about my soreness and fatigue; I filled my lungs with fresh air. I could smell the stream, I could smell the fish spawning and see the ripples they made as they surfaced to feed on minnows and insects.

I felt calm. It was tempting to take the time to just relax and fish. I knew I had no time for that, though. At most, I could take a brief nap and then continue on my way. I was not far enough away to outrun the Morifati yet. I needed to go as far as the Great River, at least.

Still, I needed to rest. Should I find a spot against the shore to nap or should I risk just letting the current float me along?

I looked ahead. The stream wound around enough that it would ground me against the shore whether or not I steered, so I decided just to pick a spot with a little sandy beach. I pulled up there and then got comfortable. I dozed off at once.

I sank into a deep sleep. I don't remember dreaming at all. Fatigue had piled up on me so I had no trouble falling off to sleep, or staying asleep for hours. I'm not sure how long I was out, but after a few hours I gently woke up.

Someone was calling my name. I felt relaxed and peaceful, so it didn't bother me or anything, but I would have been just as happy to continue sleeping.

"Rion!", it was Diana.

"How did you get here?"

"How indeed? How did *you* get here?"

"I escaped. I used the trick you taught me."

"So I see. We need to get moving, darling. They will come after you as soon as they realize you stole their boat."

"Where are we going?"

"To see Snake. Don't pretend you don't remember. Get up and man those oars!"

I felt a little groggy when I sat up, but I felt better just the same. I stood up and stretched and went and put my arms around her.

"I missed you too let's get going.", she said.

I took an oar and pushed us away from the bank.

The current was strong, but not so strong as to create a problem. We moved along quickly, flowing along with the stream. The Morifati boat had a shallow draft and a fairly wide beam. They had built it for shallow water. You could stand up in it and fish if you wanted. Now that it was daylight, I could see that the boat had a pole for polling your way through shallows and marches. How well would it do in the Great River? We were going to find out.

Diana was quiet for the moment. She sat forward of me, facing forward. I think she must have been meditating, or maybe looking out ahead of us. Not literally ahead of us, but into our future, trying to see any future threat on our trip.

I noticed a flock of birds flying over and circling around, calling to each other. They were big birds with shiny black feathers. A flock of ravens. They landed in the branches of the trees that lined the bank ahead of us. From their perches they kept croaking back and forth to each other. I got the feeling they were waiting there for us.

When we got a little closer, one raven flew out of the trees and landed on the bow of our boat. It was Raven. I recognized her now that I could see her up close again.

"Hello again! What brings you back to us, Raven?" I said.

"I'm here to warn you, the Morifati are after you! You must hurry now!"

"How far behind are they?"

"Not far enough. They will be upon you before you can get to the Great River."

"What can we do then? I can't let them capture Diana."

"Raven and I can fly away, Rion. It's you we should worry about.", said Diana.

"Is that so? Well, what would you suggest?"

"You must abandon the boat and let it float downstream. They will not expect you to set off on foot.", said Raven.

"Then how will we find our way to Snake's domain? Don't we need to follow the Great River?"

"Follow along the stream and then the Great River on foot. At least until you can find or steal another boat."

"And the Morifati? What will we do about them?"

"They will not give up the pursuit until you are in Snake's domain. They may not quit even then. We may have to kill them all."

"I will not abandon this boat. Scout ahead and see if there is some place we can hide it."

"You need to do something quickly. They are not far behind."

"Then have your flock scout ahead at once. Look for smaller streams flowing into this one. Look for marshes."

So the Ravens all took flight to scout downstream. I joined with Raven in my mind so I could see what she saw. There was a little branch that joined the stream a couple of hours ahead of us. Heavily wooded on both sides and just deep enough to pole into. It would have to do as a place to stash the boat and then walk. Or maybe, what if I just let the Morifati go past us and then continued in the boat?

"That will have to do.", I said to Raven in my mind.

"You do not have time! They will be upon you by then!"

"Will they? Let me look."

I looked ahead as far as I could, but I could see no encounter with the Morifati. I could not see all the way to the branch though. I would have to keep 'seeing around the corner' until we were safely out of their sight.

"I can't see them catching up to us, Raven. Bring your Ravens back and keep watch for us. When the Morifati appear, harass them as much as you can and if possible slow them down. I have a plan for what Diana and I should do."

"Aren't you going to abandon the boat?" said Diana.

"No, I can save it. There is a branch up ahead. I can pole us up that branch far enough that the Morifati will not see. I can hide the boat in there and so can we."

"Then we will set off on foot from there?"

"I have a plan. We will hide in there and wait for the Morifati to pass by. When they have gotten far enough ahead of us, we can come back out and follow behind them. They will not know we are there. They will expect us to be ahead of them."

"That is dangerous Rion. I see them catching up to us just as we reach that branch."

"I can't see that far, but I know how to outmaneuver them. The Ravens can distract them just before the Morifati see us."

"But what if they search the branch? How will you get out of that? You will trap us in there!"

"Raven and her flock will keep them so busy they won't notice the branch or have the time to investigate it."

"I hope you are right."

"If I am not right, then I will think of something else. Don't worry. I can see what they are going to do before they do it."

"They outnumber us, Rion."

"That's right. How many of them are there?"

"Three boats, each with three oarsmen and three more crew, plus one skipper each. So twenty-one Morifati in all."

"That many Morifati for little old me? Are they scared I'll get away?"

"Don't be sarcastic. You know what they will do with you if they capture you, don't you?"

"Yes, I have seen what they do."

She had reminded me of what they did to the Northman. I wondered if I should tell her about that, but then I thought, what was the point? No sense in that kind of story just now when all it would likely do is just increase anxiety for both of us.

"They can row faster than I can with three oarsmen each.", I said.

"That's why I want you to hurry. I see them catching up just before we get to the little branch off the stream."

"Are you getting all this, Raven?"

"Yes Rion, I have seen it and heard it."

"I'm counting on you to slow them down for long enough for us to hide in that branch."

"You can rely on us. We love to torment them. They are so slow they can never hit us with their arrows. It makes them furious. We will strike at just the right time and make them chase us downstream."

#

I could see the Morifati approaching us from behind now, catching up to us just before we got to the branch. If the Ravens were going to save us, it had to be now.

"Raven! It's time to attack!"

She called out something to them I couldn't understand, and they all took off together. They circled around the Morifati and dove low in front of their boats. They dove on the skippers who were standing up in the boats, barking orders to the men, and struck the Morifati on their heads from behind. The Morifati became furious and the ones who were not rowing took up bows and fired arrows, but the Ravens could see where the Morifati were aiming and where the arrows would fly before the Morifati could adjust so they just scattered their arrows around and got madder at the Ravens who kept weaving around them. The Ravens flew in a pattern that kept changing faster than the Morifati could predict.

"Hold your fire! Hold your fire!" the skipper called out.

He gestured wildly to the other boats. The oarsmen had unconsciously slowed their rowing during the melee. I could see now that they would not catch up to us. We had just enough time to get out of sight.

The branch was just around the bend from us now. I doubled my pace to get there as fast as I could. The boat I had stolen was smaller than the ones they were chasing us in. Small enough for one man to row by himself and steer at the same time. I made for the entrance to the branch as soon as it came into view.

"There it is Rion! Hurry!"

"I see it! We have time now. The Ravens have stalled them!"

"I hope you are right about this."

"Why do you doubt me?"

"Because I can see another possibility. They may come looking for you."

It was much shallower and contained quite a few weeds and lily pads. Trees overhung it on both sides, which kept it shaded, and I wouldn't have to go very far to get us out of sight of the stream. I would have to pole us through the entrance though as it was thick with weeds except for a small trail. I jumped up and got the pole and started pushing us in.

Behind us, the Ravens were keeping up their harassment of the Morifati. The Morifati had stopped firing arrows at them and were angrily planning some other strategy. They had dug up some fishing nets on poles for landing big fish. Some of them argued it would not work, others claimed they could catch a raven with one.

The Ravens kept circling downstream from the Morifati, leading them on farther and faster. In the meantime I polled us up into the branch, out of sight of the stream. The Morifati would not see us when they passed the entrance. That's what I thought, but when I looked ahead I saw the last Morifati boat turn and look at the entrance to the branch. The skipper had noticed something.

I had disturbed the weeds in a way that could only have been caused by a boat. He steered his boat over to investigate. The Morifati in the last boat called out to the other two boats, but they were so intent on catching up to the Ravens that they didn't hear and continued headlong down the stream.

"They are in there, I know!" the skipper barked out to his men. "Row! Row hard!"

The Morifati boat immediately got stuck in the weeds, which were too thick to row through. They got out a couple of poles and began polling their way in.

"We've got trouble Diana. They are following us!"

I had paused to rest. We were still out of sight, but would not be for much longer. Maybe I could take us deeper than they could follow. If not, I would have to get out and flee on foot.

While I was doing this, I noticed a motion up ahead in the branch. A snake was swimming toward us! An anaconda! A normal sized one but still a big one.

"Diana look! Snake, is that you?"

I called out, but it was not her. It was one of her servants though, because it swam past us and went for the Morifati boat. I entered the minds of the Morifati. They were terrified now because, in addition to the big anaconda, water moccasins crawled out onto the trees overhanging their boat.

They tried to retreat out of the branch, but it was too late. Moccasins began falling out of the trees into their boat. The anaconda struck their skipper and pulled him into the water and wrapped itself around him. He disappeared struggling under water.

The Morifati tried in vain to kill the moccasins in the boat with them, but they were all struck and poisoned. Some of the Morifati panicked and jumped out of the boat. That was a mistake, because there were moccasins waiting for them in the water as well.

The attack took only a couple of minutes. The Morifati remaining in the boat got themselves free and started downriver, but they couldn't kill the moccasins in time to keep from getting bitten. The Morifati had to treat their snake bites as best they could.

"Did you see that Diana? Snake attacked them!"

But she was not there. I looked around and Diana was not in the boat. I looked into the trees but I could see no dove. I closed my eyes and went to her in my mind. She had transformed into a dove and flew ahead downstream to spy on the situation.

The Ravens were leading the Morifati on a merry chase. The third boat floated downstream, unguided, with Morifati lying dead and dying in it.

"My plan worked Diana."

"You were lucky. Snake was looking out for you. She saved you this time."

"So you still want to walk?"

"You've got to hide that Morifati boat and their dead. If the others find it, they will know something happened."

"I can catch up to it. It is just drifting."

I polled my way out of the branch and set about the oars. I didn't have to go far before I found the Morifati boat grounded on a shoreline covered with stones. It occurred to me to burn it, but that would send up smoke. I could sink it, but that would mean having to find a deep enough bend in the river. If I tow it out to the Great River and scuttle it there, that could work, but the Morifati would need to be too far downriver to return easily.

I called out to Raven. "How are you doing?"

"We are having fun, Rion. Did you escape from them?"

"With a little help from Snake. I need you to lead them downriver. Can you do that?"

"We are almost there now. Keep coming. We will not let them out of sight."

TWENTY-SEVEN

DOWNRIVER

So with the Morifati boat in tow, I rowed down to where the stream flowed into the Great River. It had not taken long. I just jumped out and grabbed one of their mooring lines from the bow of the boat and tied it to my boat.

It was sometimes hard to row both boats, but the current was strong there, so I let the stream take both boats along. I could afford the time, since I wanted the ravens to lead the Morifati far ahead of me.

Diana had gone quiet on me, so I took the time to think things over. I had no idea what to expect from Snake's domain. I knew she lived in an old castle. It didn't seem possible to me that it could be an actual castle, but that's how everyone described it. It must be some gigantic building left over from the Great Third War.

I don't think anyone from the Free State had ever been this far in their travels before. If they had, no one ever spoke of it.

I needed to decide how I was going to do this, scuttling the Morifati boat, I mean, and dumping the bodies. Should I weight the bodies or just dump them over the side? What are the chances that anyone would find them or know what happened to them now?

While I thought this over, I saw a dove flying toward me. It landed on the bow of the boat. The dove transformed back into Diana. It glowed with the same light that I had seen each time before. The body of the dove turned gold, then it changed its form into hers. Raven colored hair put into a warrior's braid, snow white skin, and sky-blue eyes.

"Why did you fly off like that Diana?"

"Like what?"

I had to think about that. I had meant to tease her about flying away when the fight broke out, but her mind was on other things.

"Someone has to look out for you, Rion. To make sure you don't get into any trouble. That's my job, watching over you."

"So that's why you took off when the Morifati came after us?"

I was trying to make a dig at her, but without skipping a beat, she said. "I knew that Snake and Raven would keep you safe. I thought I better get an aerial view and a picture of our future trip down to Snake's castle. It's easier to do that from up high."

She had me there. Better not to pursue it anymore. I had fallen in love with her. Not like in a Limerence Spell, but genuine love. I had not felt this way about her back in the Free State. I liked her; I tolerated her, but she just seemed to me to be a pesky kid. I did not know of her true nature or her inner beauty. That was now being revealed to me. In all that previous time, I did not know who I really was or who I would become, and I did not know who she really was. Diana apparently knew more about my future and her future and our future together than I could even guess.

"What do you think we should do about these stiffs?" I said.

"I would just capsize the boat. If the Morifati downstream or any other war party come along and find it, they will just think that they capsized and drowned. They might waste time trying to find survivors."

"That's a great idea. I want to see if they've got anything in that boat I can use first."

There was a small island with trees on it nearby so I rowed over to it. I wanted to get out and stretch my legs a bit as well. The sun was getting low by that time, and I had endured a long day. We probably needed to get out and make camp.

"It's getting late Diana. Let's make camp on this island. We have the time, don't we?"

"If you say so."

I wasn't sure what she meant by that, but if she wasn't raising alarms or making objections, then I was going to act on the assumption that it was okay to rest, make a fire, and get some sleep. The Morifati boat I had stolen didn't have any food in it, but it had fishing equipment. I might catch some supper.

I grounded our boat and got out and pulled it up on the beach. Then I pulled the Morifati boat around lengthwise to the shore. They were stinking. I think they must have stunk to begin with, and now they were dead.

There were only three Morifati left. They looked like the three oarsmen. Unable to get away when the moccasins dropped on them from the trees. Their bodies lay there, contorted from the venom.

I picked them up one by one and rolled them over the side. They floated off downstream. I turned and searched the boat. I found an unexpected treasure. The Morifati had caught some bait fish and placed them in a live well. I could use them to catch something to eat.

There wasn't much else in the larger boat except some bows, arrows, machetes, tools, and so forth. I already had most of those things in large enough quantities to get us to Snake's domain so I only transferred what I thought I could use.

What to do about their boat now that I had emptied it? I searched around the stern and sure enough, there was a drain plug. I untied the boat, pulled the drain plug, then shoved the boat out into the river. It floated off with the current. It would swamp now, maybe sink entirely.

"Should we risk building a fire Diana?"

"Yes. They are far downstream now and there are no more after us for the present time."

"I'm going to fish as well. I'm starving. Are you hungry?"

"No, but I'll eat when you catch something."

I went after catfish since the sun was setting. I had more than one rod and the Morifati had caught just the right type of baitfish. The Morifati knew how to make crude reels that worked well for the job. They also knew how to make simple hooks of the right size and shape.

I set up three rods by picking out some driftwood to use as rod holders and driving the ends of the rods into the sand. After I got everything baited and cast out into the deeper part of the river, I set the rods in their holders and waited.

I went out and gathered some more driftwood for a fire and discovered that Diana had already done that job for me, so we had plenty of wood now.

I had to get the fire started the old-fashioned way by striking quartz stones together over some pine straw I found. Soon I had a blaze going and Diana sat in front of it. I went and sat next to her and put my arm around her. The sun had gone down now, but a red sky remained. A red sky at night is always a good omen.

"All we have to do now is wait and relax.", I said.

"I see a big catfish in your future Rion."

"Hey! I hadn't thought of that!"

I looked ahead to see if I was about to get a bite. In just a few minutes, the rod on the left would start twitching and then bowed hard over with the weight of a fish.

#

After I caught and cleaned the first catfish, I staked it out over the fire, which had burned down enough to make coals. It smelled wonderful.

"That's what the Morifati had planned for you, isn't it?"

"Thanks for reminding me."

That reminded me of the Northman again. I wondered if I should tell her about that. I didn't feel much like talking about it, but maybe I should tell her a little, just skip the gory details.

"I had to watch them sacrifice a Northman Diana."

"I'm sorry. They are so evil and cruel. To have to witness that and not be able to do anything to stop it. It must have been terrible."

"He died bravely. He didn't cry out. He knew techniques."

"That shouldn't happen to you now. Now that you can 'see around the corner' you should be able to get the best of them the way the Ravens do."

"I didn't do so well in captivity. They pumped me full of their potions. They cast spells on me. I answered all their questions. I told them everything. Most of what I know. And they put a Limerence Spell on me. I made a fool out of myself over that girl."

"To learn what you had to learn and to become who you will become, you had to be tested and tried. There is no other way. You have done well. But still ...."

"But still what?"

"I don't think Snake is satisfied. I think she wanted you to do more. I think she still expects you to do more. And the Limerence Spell, it still has to be removed."

"I'm not under the Limerence Spell any more."

"You say that now, but it can come back when you least expect it. It affects people on a deep level. It tests your concept of reality and your memory. It makes you believe a lie. A Limerence Spell is very hard to break but we must break it."

"I think I'm over it."

"You say that but all it could take is one sight of that witch and you would go back to wanting to die rather than part with her."

"I disagree. There's something else though. You said I didn't do everything that Snake expected. What else did she expect?"

"She expects you to defeat the Morifati."

"To defeat the Morifati? Single-handed? The whole village? What makes her think I can do that?"

"She knows you have powers beyond just seeing around the corner. Powers like her's. Powers beyond her's. She can't attack them on her own or she would. They are the primary source of evil in our world. Everyone would live in peace were it not for them. Their King Blackheart John is plotting greater conquests. He envies the prosperity of the Northmen and the Free State. He can't stand to see people happy. It makes him doubt his faith in Than."

"But she snuck into their camp and spoke to me. Can't she launch an attack of Snakes and Ravens that would defeat the Morifati?"

"She visited you only with great difficulty and at significant risk to herself. If they had found her, they would have killed her. She is an Empath. She feels their thoughts and feelings too strongly. It's overwhelming for her. And besides that, the Snakes and the Ravens do not have the physical strength to defeat men. They can only attack when they have an advantage, just as they did when we were in the stream. There was surprise and camouflage there, not so at the walls of the Morifati village."

"So she is relying on me. Why isn't she afraid of me if she believes I am that powerful?"

"She has seen inside your mind and your heart. She has seen your future. She has waited for you for a long time. Snake is ancient by our standards."

"As old as the Great Third War?"

"I think so, maybe."

Just then I heard some Ravens call to each other in their normal cackling speech. I looked up to see them silhouetted against the night sky. They circled around a bit and then landed within the ring of firelight. Raven landed and then hopped over to us.

"So where are the Morifati now, Raven?"

"Far to the south. They think you are ahead of them and that the other boat is behind them. They are waiting for that third boat to catch up to them."

"It might. I tossed the bodies over the side and swamped the boat. They might see something float by."

"Then again, they may not.", said Diana. "I wonder how long they will wait."

"Not too long Highness. Their first priority is to catch Rion at all costs.", said Raven.

"So you will let us know when they are on the move again?"

"You will know as soon as we know. Did you discard the Morifati long ago?"

"A couple of hours ago. Why?"

"We are getting hungry."

I had forgotten that ravens often feed on carrion, but Morifati corpses? Disgusting!

"You can have some catfish. I threw the head and guts and skin of this one on the beach over there. I will catch some more soon."

I looked ahead at my three rods. Two of them would start bending with fish at the same time in the next few minutes. Since we had guests now, I thought I better put some more rods out. I started to set up another three rods down the bank, but I was interrupted by the two fish on the other rods.

"Diana, grab one of those rods, will you?"

"Sure thing. This is starting to get fun!"

We wrestled our catches in. One was pan size and the other too big to taste good. I gave the big one to the ravens who had made quick work of the entrails of the first one by that time.

I set the next three rods out quickly and baited and recast the two that had caught fish. I looked ahead to see what was coming and I could see that soon we would have our hands full. The catfish would soon start feeding and taking our bait.

The Great River was wild and hardly ever fished, at least down this way. No one came down here much, not even the Morifati. Catfish feed more at night and the sky was dark and moonless. The stars came out and shone brightly.

I looked for all the familiar constellations and the milky way and the north star. I found the constellation of Orion and pointed toward it.

"There's my namesake Diana."

"Orion the Hunter! You should have been named after the fisherman!"

"I don't know if there is a fisherman. Aquarius?"

The ravens made quick work of the catfish I gave them. I soon caught enough that I had too many to clean and more than Diana and I could eat. I just started tossing them to the ravens. More of them arrived to help the others eat.

"My flock thanks you, Rion." said Raven.

I put a blanket down on the beach that the Morifati had stowed on their boat. I piled a tent still rolled up, some blankets and so forth at one end to make myself a backrest so I could sit and watch the fire. I motioned for Diana to come over and join me.

She sat next to me and cuddled up to me. We had never been this close before. I was letting my guard down with her. I had considered her too young before, but that time had passed. She was a different person than I had imagined. I was a different person than I imagined, but that gave us something special in common. It made us different from everyone else in the Free State.

"Can you see what will happen tomorrow?" I asked.

"I'll try. It might be best to sleep on it."

I felt tired. It had been a long one. We sat there watching the fire and the rods. The Ravens caught up on eating the catfish and flew into the trees. I thought about kissing her, but I nodded instead.

She fell asleep before I did. I dreamed before I even realized I had fallen asleep. I had a nightmare about the Morifati. I dreamed I was back in their village. I had gone back for some reason or they had captured me. They were furious. They kept demanding that I tell them about something, but I wouldn't talk. They brought me to an enormous bonfire. They were getting ready to roast me alive.

I woke up with a start. Only a short time had passed. I could tell it was still midnight or early morning. Two of the rods were loaded down with fish. Diana was stirring. I guess I woke her up.

"Let me up Diana. I need to get to the rods."

"I had a dream, Rion."

"Me too. About the Morifati. I dreamed I was back in their camp and they were going to barbeque me."

"I saw what will happen tomorrow. We do not need to hurry. They will look for us between where they are now and Snake's castle. If they do not find us, they will lay siege to her castle and wait for us to arrive, or for her to come out."

"In that case, we better get some sleep. I'll pack away they fishing equipment."

I straightened up the camp and threw the two catfish out on the beach where the ravens could get them. Diana made us a pillow out of the rolled up tent. I lay down next to her and held her. Presently we started kissing, but we were both so sleepy we passed out soon after.

TWENTY-EIGHT

SNAKE'S DOMAIN

The Great River, as it flows south, reaches a point where it spreads out into a broad delta with multiple streams and a dense swamp. When we drew close to that point, it was time to get out of the boat and walk the rest of the way. Snake's domain lies to the east of there inside a dense forest with large trees, live oaks and so forth. The trees create a rain forest canopy which lets in some light but is dark in places, too dark for much to grow underneath.

Diana knew the way. I had never been there, of course. I wondered how we would find our way through and back out again without leaving signs for the Morifati to follow. The Morifati knew how to find Snake's castle of course, but I didn't want them to find us.

"We're getting close now, Rion. Take us closer to the bank."

I maneuvered us over to the east bank, which was mostly over hung by trees with no obvious places to ground the boat and tie up.

"What are you looking for?"

"There is a gap in the trees with a little space to pull the boat into. Not unlike the branch off the stream we entered before."

I soon found it after a few minutes search and began rowing into it.

"This is it isn't it Diana."

She nodded.

I lodged the bow of the boat against a good spot on the bank. I hopped out quickly and tied the bow and stern to a couple of trees.

"So what do you think we should take with us?" I said aloud as much to myself as to her.

There wasn't too much we would need other than the weapons I had taken off the guard and the tools and weapons from out of the boat and of course the High Priest's amulet. I would make a gift of that to Snake when we arrived.

I wasn't sure what she would do with it, but I suspected it would be of great value to Snake.

"Do you know the way from here, Diana?"

"Not entirely, Rion. I usually fly over it. I know the general direction and some landmarks."

I helped her out, and we turned and entered a deeply shaded clearing underneath the forest canopy. Nothing grew there except for the trees. The forest floor was covered with leaves.

I saw motion ahead of us. A snake was crawling toward us. It did not speak. It was a rattlesnake about six feet long, but it did not rattle or make any threatening gestures. When it got close to us it stopped, turned back around, crawled away, then turned to look at us again.

"I think it wants us to follow Rion."

"I think you're right."

We walked toward it and it turned and crawled away from us, guiding us through the forest. I looked ahead along our path. I did not see the Morifati. They were well ahead of us by that time.

The snake was some sort of ordinary snake that was under Snake's control. It was not a human Psychic that had transformed itself into a snake. It communicated mostly by movements, by body language, if you will. There was, of course, nothing to be said. Its job was to lead us to Snake's castle through this dark wood and forest canopy.

There was nothing too eventful about that. Just a long trek through a dark humid forest, with little to eat or drink. It was pretty humid in there. I was getting tired when we came to a muddied out trail. A large group of men had walked through the forest there leaving footprints upon footprints and they didn't care who found their trail.

"This has got to be where the Morifati came through Diana."

I stopped to look at their tracks. The rattlesnake waited patiently up the trail for me.

"The snake seems to have brought us here on purpose, Rion."

"I think you are right. Now we know where the Morifati are and where they are going."

I looked ahead along the trail to see if we would bump into them if we followed it in behind them, but they had already gone too far down it for us to catch up.

"We should follow it. The rattlesnake looks like he is waiting for us to follow him, and the Morifati know how to find Snake's castle somehow. This trail should lead us straight to her, and to them."

"Then lead on."

I walked toward the rattlesnake and it turned and crawled down the trail over the Morifati footprints. We added our own footprints to theirs.

At last, we came into a clearing in the forest. Across a grassy plain, a half a mile away from us, stood a mediaeval castle. I couldn't believe what I was seeing. I had expected the stories to be exaggerations. I thought she would live in some old concrete and steel building from before the Great Third War. An abandoned factory or something like that. Our rattlesnake guide slithered off toward the castle and disappeared into the grass.

"That's got to be Snake's castle.", I joked.

"You are a genius, Rion."

"I've got the Sight too.", I said.

I looked ahead of us. There were the Morifati waiting near the forest on the other side where they could watch the entrance. They waited and watched, either for us to arrive or for Snake to come out. The Morifati were persistent; you had to give them that. They stood little chance against enemies who could see their future movements, but that did not stop them from trying to win. Death really meant nothing to them. Their own deaths, I mean. All these Morifati would die down here in Snake's domain and they knew that, but they would still attempt to capture me or kill Snake or Raven or Diana.

The outcome meant nothing to any of them personally. The only thing that mattered was the will of Than. I looked ahead at our future as we approached the castle.

We could sneak up only a short way without being seen. The grassy plain offered no cover for us. What if we ran for it? That worked fairly well until we got halfway there. Then they saw us and rushed out to capture us.

"So how do you think we can get in?"

"All I have to do is fly in and land. The question is how do we get you in?"

"So how do we get *me* in? I've tried looking ahead but whether I walk or run, they see me in time to rush out and capture me."

"Let's wait. Let's wait for dusk. It will be easier for you to pass unseen then. And the Ravens can come and help by providing another distraction."

"That's good thinking."

"It's not thinking. I saw it."

"So when were you planning to tell me?"

"Just before you did something foolish. Like running across open ground."

"You should have more faith in me, Diana. I wonder if I shouldn't try to sneak up on them. I can see what they are going to do before they do it."

"It's not worth the chance. Besides, you don't really want to kill any of them, do you?"

How did she know that? Somehow, despite their nature, even though they were our enemies and they had to be stopped, I had resisted killing any of the Morifati, even when I had the chance.

"Somehow, I feel as though I should defeat them another way."

"What other way?"

"I don't know yet. But a war, an enormous battle, somehow I just don't think it would be the right thing to do. I feel like there is some other way to prevent them from killing. I don't know what it is yet, but I know I have to find it."

"Snake expects you to kill them, Rion. She expected you to kill them before. At least to kill Blackheart John and the High Priest. This mission of yours is not over yet, as far as she is concerned. And there is still the Limerence Spell. She will want you to deal with the Old Hag and that apprentice witch of hers, Anna."

"Who made Snake the leader of us? We are both citizens of the Free State. I think I should do what I know is right, or obey the decisions of Grandfather and the Elders. She is our ally, but she doesn't get to give the orders."

"You are going to get to tell her all those things in person soon. Don't expect her to like it. I can't say that I trust her one hundred percent. I think she has an agenda, an agenda all her own. She will help us, and she will help the Wolves, but only so long as she is helping herself."

So we waited for the sun to set. We stayed down low, just at the edge of the woods. We lay close to each other, close enough to cuddle. I was tired and I know Diana was, so we fell off to sleep.

I woke to the sounds of Ravens calling to each other. Diana had already gotten up, but she still crouched low. I couldn't see the Ravens. It sounded like they were above us and behind us. Were they flying or just perched on the treetops?

I looked for them in my mind's eye. They were flying over the forest, circling around a little before they went after the Morifati. I spoke to Raven in my mind.

"What are you doing now, Raven? Are you preparing to attack them?"

"We are waiting for you two to wake up and let us know when you want to try it."

"Do you think it's time yet, Diana?"

"You tell me. Look ahead."

So I looked around the corner at what would happen if we tried it now, as opposed to a little later when it was darker. Darker was better than right now.

"We should wait until the sun sets a little more. If we go now we will make it, but they will see us. With just a few minutes more they won't be able to see across the field."

"We await your signal, Rion.", said Raven.

"I'm going to go ahead then Rion.", said Diana.

"What for?"

"It will be easier for you to pass unseen by yourself."

"If that's what you want then."

She walked back into the shade of the trees where the Morifati could not see her. Then she shone with the light of transformation and morphed into a golden dove and then a normal dove and then flew high into the trees. I watched her fly overhead to Snake's castle.

I hunkered down and waited. I didn't think about too much or try to look ahead. That was a mistake. I should have looked ahead the whole time. I should have kept a lookout in my situation. That way, I might have seen what was going to happen next.

As I sat there watching the field, I heard nothing and no one behind me, then I felt a spear tip at my back.

"No sudden moves Rion of the Free State!"

So I froze.

"Put your hands behind your head."

I did as they ordered. How was I going to get out of this? I had come this far. I was just outside Snake's castle, and now they were going to capture me? I better look ahead to find an opportunity. Before I could do that, one of them grabbed my wrists and bound them behind my back.

"Now stand up slowly and turn around. No sudden moves."

It was the Morifati captain that had taken me to their village before. He was grinning at me.

"So, we meet again.", I said.

"Happy to see me then?"

"No. No, I can't say I'm happy."

"Well, I'm happy. Not happy to see you, but happy to see you in bonds again. I'll be happier still when I see you roasting over a spit."

"You lack imagination."

"Shut up! I only have to bring you back alive. No one said I couldn't bring you back half dead."

"You've got a long dangerous trip ahead of you. Are you sure you can make it?"

"We're not afraid of that Snake-witch, or your little girl-friend, or those damn black birds! Than will win in the end. Than always wins. No one can escape Than!"

"You're going to meet him long before I do."

I couldn't look too far ahead in that circumstance. Looking ahead involves concentrating on things that are not directly in front of you. I couldn't afford to take my eyes off them. All I could do was cry out to Raven in a semiarticulate way. She heard me.

As I stood there facing the two of them, all the Ravens attacked. I had never seen them attack like this before. Usually they stayed well out of reach. This time they struck in a black cloud of flapping feathers and beaks.

They went for the heads and eyes of the Morifati. One raven gouged an eye out of the captain's man even as he held his spear on me.

"Run Rion! Run for the castle!"

I turned and ran toward the castle and almost immediately fell down. Running with my hands tied behind my back threw me off balance. I pulled my knees up and rolled over on them. I couldn't see anybody around me. I looked ahead to see how I ought to do this. The best thing to do was walk as quickly as I could until I was about five hundred feet away from the castle and then run for it. I would just make it.

The captain and his man had taken off running for their company with the Ravens still swarming them. The Raven's beaks cut them up pretty bad. They were both missing an eye. They weren't moving too quickly, since they had to fight the

Ravens off of themselves as they ran. I wondered if they would make it. I hoped not.

What would I do when I got to the castle gate? I looked ahead at that. Diana was waiting there for me! She would let me in.

I got up and started trotting as fast as I could with my hands tied. It was dusky now. It would be hard for the Morifati to see me until I got close. I needed for the Ravens to swarm them.

"Raven, can you cover me?"

"Sure thing. We are through with these two now."

The Morifati captain and his man had collapsed. They were both wounded now. The captain missing an eye, his man with his eyes gouged out, their heads and faces were bleeding profusely.

TWENTY-NINE

HER THRONE ROOM

Diana and I stood facing each other just inside the gate-house. I wondered if the Morifati would try to get in. I looked outside with the Sight. The Ravens had abandoned their pursuit and flew away to their regular perches and nests on the battlements and the towers of the castle. The Morifati stood looking at each other. They realized that I had gotten past them. They turned and went back to their camp, where they could watch the gate.

I looked around at the bailey within the walls, and the keep, and walls, and battlements, and towers. Everything was made of stone and looked old and weathered. Grass grew up through the stones of the bailey, and vines grew on everything all around. There were bushes and trees that looked like they had never been trimmed or kept. Snake's castle looked like it had been abandoned long ago. It looked like the perfect environment for snakes.

"Watch out for snakes.", I said.

"Oh, there are snakes here, Rion. Some big ones."

"Shall we?" I pointed to the door of the castle keep.

"We must."

I opened it up easily. Inside, as you might expect, it was un-lit.

"We are going to have to find ourselves a torch.", I said.

I set about looking for a large enough stick and something to wrap the end with. I found a suitable stick soon enough, and I had a flint and steel already, but I had nothing to wrap the end with. Diana emerged from inside the keep, holding an unlit torch.

"Is this what you were looking for?"

"You are so resourceful, Diana. What made you think of that?"

"Well, who ever heard of a castle without torches?"

"Yeah, but what would a snake do with a torch?"

"Maybe she keeps them for guests."

"Or maybe she assumes human form sometimes?"

She shrugged that one off. I set about making sparks with my flint and steel. Soon I had the thing just barely lit. I picked it up and blew gently on it. It glowed and burned brightly then, so I held it aloft in the entrance. It revealed a dusty old en-trance hall, which led to a grand staircase.

"I didn't think to ask if you could shine and show us the way Diana."

"I can, smarty, but I save that for special occasions. Plus, it's rude to display your powers like that when you come visiting a Psychic like her. It can be interpreted as a challenge."

"You are no threat to her, are you?"

"Now that you mention it, I might be."

"How so?"

"You'll see. I've said before that I don't trust her fully. We'll find out if we can trust her now. Now that we are at the seat of her power."

"But what would she do? She needs us to defeat the Mori-fati, doesn't she?"

"She needs *you* to defeat the Morifati."

"So what are you here for?"

"To keep you out of trouble."

I thought of making an answer to that one but she had taught me how to 'see around the corner' even though that was not her gift. Who was she? What was she? What were we both fated to do? It seemed our fate was to do a lot more than just defeat the Morifati. No one would tell me anything, though. It made me angry, the way they all kept me in the dark while I was learning. They only told me just enough at each stage.

"Are you afraid to tell me my future, Diana?"

"Not afraid. But is best not to know everything about the future. What someone sees can change based on what they know. If that knowledge can lead to an action, a decision can change everything. We have to be very deliberate about what we do with the knowledge we have. Remember the Great Third War started because Psychics were greedy and used their knowledge for whatever purpose they desired."

That was a good answer. I had not thought about it like that before. The Sight could pose a great temptation in the hands of someone with an evil character. The Morifati, for example, what did they know about the future?

"What about Blackheart John? What does he know?"

"His powers are limited, but he can teleport, as you saw. The High Priest has the Sight, but he has no telempathy. That prevents him from being more powerful than he would otherwise be. We can't count on their lack of knowledge, though. We need to stop them, and soon. The real reason they wanted you in love with that witch is so you would work with them, become one of them."

"But they claimed I failed them and had to die."

"They will say one thing one time and something else another time. That's how they brainwash someone. They use magic, psychology, psychic power, anything they can to fulfill their desires."

I looked down the long hallway toward the staircase. Shadows flickered everywhere from the torch. There were no rats or vermin, though. They would stay well away from all these snakes.

"I thought the bailey looked snaky, this place looks like a snake pit. Something tells me we are going to find a big one in here."

"Not here Rion. Up high. We will have to climb the staircase all the way to the top."

I failed to describe the keep while we were still outside, so I will tell you about it now. It was rectangular, nearly square, and it appeared to be about nine stories high. The three upper floors would have magnificent views of the surrounding countryside, as they had large picture windows. The lower floors only had the kind of windows that archers could use. The roof had a wall around it, and there were square watchtowers in each of the four corners. The front of the keep faced north. The whole upper part of the keep was designed to give its occupants a three hundred sixty degree panoramic view of the grasslands and the forest beyond. Someone had built a perfect replica of a medieval keep with just a few modern embellishments.

"Nine floors up?", I said.

"Yep, nine."

I led the way, holding the torch aloft so we could both see where we were going. I got the impression that she received few visitors or that her visitors flew or slithered in some other way because we kicked up a considerable amount of dust climbing those stairs. Not enough dust to be a problem, mind you, but it told me of a staircase long abandoned and never cleaned. We were leaving a trail behind us that anyone could follow. I got the impression that a Morifati attack was not something she worried about. I wondered why she didn't just go ahead and deal with them instead of letting them loiter outside, "laying siege" to us. Maybe it amused her.

"I wonder how she does it?"

"Does what?"

"Goes up and down. No one has used the stairs or cleaned this place in a very long time."

"She is a different kind of being than you are used to, Rion. You can't apply human standards to someone like her."

That was right, I had never met a Psychic before she came to me in my dream and told me that Wolf would appear to me. Later she claimed I had been coming to her in my dreams and not the other way around. Why would I do that? What did that say about me? Was she telling the truth?

I had never seen or met a Psychic before then; I had only heard the stories that people told. Stories about the Psychics and the Great Third War. The Psychics left us alone in the Free State. As far as we knew, they were a myth.

Until she came to me to warn me about the Morifati, and Grandfather told me the truth about the Psychics, and then Wolf appeared I had no reason to believe in any of the stories. As far as I knew Diana was an ordinary girl, and I never had any idea that I would develop powers or that I held the key to defeating the Morifati.

Even the Morifati were a legend to me. They had not attacked us in so long. But I knew Grandfather had fought with them, as had many of the elders. They had always seemed more real and more frightening than any Psychic. Especially since so many in the Free State fought with them in the past or were killed or captured by them in the past. I had no trouble believing they existed.

And then there were the stories about my father and my mother. I don't want to go into that now. It's too painful to recall and beside the point for now, but I know it's related to everything else somehow.

The Psychics hid themselves away all the time. They hid not just from the Morifati but from all men, the Free State, the Northmen, all the tribes. That's one of the primary reasons they assumed animal forms, so they could live well away from people and hide from us until such time as they chose to contact us. If Snake was contacting me now, there was no doubt that she wanted something from me, and she had a compelling reason to take the risk.

It suddenly occurred to me that I dreaded meeting Snake again. I was not afraid of it, not afraid of seeing her again here in her domain. I just dreaded doing it. I wanted to be somewhere else. I wanted to go back to the river and fish. I wanted to go back to the Free State and tell Grandfather everything that had happened to me. What did I need to meet with her for? What could she do for me?

I looked ahead to see what would happen on the way up. Nothing yet, we just went by floor after empty floor until when we got to the ninth there was a great doorway. I guessed it was the entrance to her throne room since it could be nothing else, really, but I could not see beyond. I could not see us pass into it. We just seemed to get there and pause.

So we made our uneventful way to the ninth floor and stood in front of the door to her throne room. I went over to open it, but it wouldn't budge.

"You'll have to wait for her to open it.", said Diana.

"So it's a magic door?"

"Not exactly, but she keeps it locked to all who she wants kept outside, or who she wants to keep waiting."

"I guess we are the latter. Is there no way to let her know we are out here?"

"You are a little slow, aren't you, darling? You have been going to her in your dreams and in your mind all this time and you still don't know how to communicate with her!"

That stung a little. It seemed like an innocent enough question to me with a straightforward answer. I expected a riddle or something or a secret latch. I guess I did dread this visit. I knew I could go to her in my mind, but I had not tried the entire trip downriver. Raven, yes, and Diana, but not her. I closed my eyes and tried now. I daydreamed about Snake.

As soon as I could picture her in my mind's eye, I heard the doors fling themselves open wide. I opened my eyes then and held my torch aloft. I looked down the length of her throne room to see a large rattlesnake, impossibly large really, the biggest rattlesnake you have ever seen sitting coiled up on a throne. It was exactly like the dream I had on the Mountain Trail in the Forbidden Land. Was that dream then an instance of the Sight, or had I actually come here before in my dream?

"Welcome! Come in! Come in at once, both of you!"

"Yes, Highness!" we said in unison.

We strode in together side by side until we stood at the base of her throne. Then Diana bowed to her and gestured to me. I didn't know what she meant.

"Take a knee.", she said sotto voce.

I knelt on one knee and bowed a little.

"Thank you for admitting us. We came as you requested, Highness.", I said.

I wasn't quite sure how to address her other than that. I found out later that she had a name and a title other than "Snake" but she kept it a secret. Names, it seems, can be used against you if someone with certain types of powers knows your name. So she kept hers private and secret. She could not afford to let the Morifati or some kind of evil Psychic, there were some of those around, find out what her actual name was.

"I am thrilled to see you here in person at last. Here, where you live and not whereever I was in my dream. I confess I have been and remain a little confused at to what this is all about and what you expect from me."

"Well, I am not happy to see you, Rion! You have failed!"

THIRTY

RECEIVED UNHAPPILY

"Failed? How have I failed?"

"You did not kill Blackheart John! You did not defeat the Morifati!"

"Was that what you sent me to do?"

"How can you say such a thing! You know they were preparing to attack the Free State. You know I sent you there to stop them!"

"Yes, I guess that's what you told me to begin with, but events changed once I got there. I guess I've had a change of heart."

"A change of heart? Really? Don't you care about your people? Are you still under that Limerence Spell?"

"Well, it just seemed to me while I was in captivity, and it seems to me now that the point of all this was for me to learn to 'see around the corner', and to develop telempathy. And now that I have, I don't see the necessity for killing. As evil as the Morifati are, I think there is still another way. I think I may yet be able to reach them. I feel I can persuade them to have a change of heart."

"You are talking like a fool, Rion. They gave you potions. They cast a Limerence Spell on you. I know now that you are still under it. You still hope that you can love that girl, that little Morifati witch called Anna! I will have to remove that spell from you before we can proceed any further."

"It will probably take both of us working together to accomplish that Highness.", said Diana.

"There is something else. Something that I accomplished, that you didn't ask for. It was by accident I guess, but I seized the opportunity when it presented itself."

At that point I reached into my pack and brought out the High Priest's amulet. I held it up so Snake could see it.

"Rion! Why did you not tell me you had that?" said Diana.

"I was going to. I did not mean it to be a secret from you."

"You should have told me at once!" said Diana.

"Bring it to me! Bring it here so I can see!" said Snake.

"Rion, she does not have the right to ask you for that. It is not hers to possess."

"Silence Diana! He must do my bidding here in my castle, and so must you."

"It is not yours to possess, Snake. You cannot control its power. Only someone like Grandfather or I can control it properly."

I felt torn at that point. I had planned to give it to Snake all along, but I didn't really know what it was other than it belonged to the High Priest. I did not know what it would mean to Diana or that she would react this way.

"It is too late for him to give it to you, Diana, not now that you are here in my castle, here in my domain. If he gives it to you, I will simply seize it from you, or my Snakes will."

I turned round and looked at Diana.

"I'm sorry Diana. I didn't know what it meant."

"No, I'm sorry. I should have kept you out of trouble like I said."

So I stepped forward and approached Snake's throne, where she lay coiled up. I slipped the amulet over her head and let it fall to lie on the cushion of her throne.

I stood back and resumed my previous place, this time standing facing her. Snake transformed herself. It differed from Diana's transformations. She glowed with a soft light that filled the room, her body slowly metamorphosed into that of a woman.

She sprouted arms and legs, much as a tadpole does. Her tail shrank and the shape of her body and head changed. When her legs grew out enough, she stood. There before us stood a tall, slender woman with golden hair and piercing brown eyes. She was completely nude.

"Avert your eyes now, Rion, don't gawk!" said Diana.

"Diana, darling, bring me my robe from the closet behind the throne."

We both did as we were told. I have to admit a little embarrassment that I completely forgot to look away at first. I felt taken by the sight of her. I had never seen a blonde with brown eyes, although now I understand it happens.

Diana helped her into her robe, then walked over to me. She stood in front of me and whispered.

"You can open your eyes now, but don't let them fall out of your head."

I opened my eyes and looked into Diana's eyes. Her cheeks were burning. She was jealous! I had stepped into it again. She turned and stood beside me, both of us facing Snake, who stood before her throne wearing her robe and the amulet.

"Did the amulet do that? Does it have the power to transform you?" I asked.

"No, I had that power already. Do you remember when you were under the spell of the High Priest's potion? How they came to you and spoke to you as you dreamed?"

"The High Priest and Blackheart John appeared to me and questioned me. They sent me to different places, and I felt different things, they promised me a paradise and then they tortured me."

"That's what the amulet does, among other things."

"So now they don't just want to find you, they have to find it.", Diana said.

"Wait. What you are telling me is that the amulet allows someone who knows how to use it the ability to enter someone's mind and see everything they see, whether they are awake or asleep?"

"More than that. It allows you to create what they see. It allows you to create the world they live in inside their mind.", said Snake.

"So it's a magic object? I thought there was no magic, really."

"No. The potion they gave you is not magic. It is a mixture of hallucinogenic drugs. A drug the ancients called DMT. The amulet, on the other hand, helps those with psychic powers to focus those psychic powers, but it is not magic. We have known now since the Great Emergence of the Sight that psychic powers are real. They manifest in the physical, spiritual, and psychological dimensions."

"The amulet greatly amplifies the Sight and any other powers that a Psychic possesses, Rion. It can be very dangerous in the wrong hands. It was good that you stole it from their High Priest, but you should have told me immediately so that I could safeguard it properly.", said Diana.

"Don't you trust me, Diana darling? What have you to fear from me?" said Snake.

I could feel Diana tensing beside me. She was holding something back. I had unknowingly put her in a tight spot. I thought that I might have gotten a fight started between them, or created a rivalry, or reawakened an old one. Before I could say anything, Diana spoke.

"I don't believe we can put complete trust in you now, Snake. By we I mean the Free State. Not now that you have that amulet in your possession. You should give it to me, as a token of good will, for safekeeping, until Grandfather decides what is to be done with it."

"Why, you impertinent little bitch! How dare you command me in my domain in my throne room! I will keep the amulet. Only I can use it properly against the Morifati. You Freemen are too compassionate, too forgiving, too good to understand the true nature of evil and the corruption in the hearts of the Morifati. They must be utterly destroyed! I have the power to do that now."

"You see what you have done, Rion. Snake wants the amulet for herself, only for her own purposes.", said Diana.

"Now you know that's not true! How will Rion defeat them without my aide, and me without his. You, on the other hand, I'm not sure I need you."

They stood glaring at each other. I thought I better interrupt before things got out of hand. But what should I do next? What could I say next? Everyone knew more about what was going on and what had gone on before than me. It was difficult for me to understand it all.

"I'm going to need you both if I am going to defeat them.", I said.

"I need for you to finish what you started for me, Rion." said Snake.

"Do you mean I will have to go back? That I will have to face them again on my own?"

"Not totally on your own. I can watch you. I can help you, but you must find a way to kill them. Blackheart John, the High

Priest, the Old Hag, and even that lover of yours, Anna. They all must die if the world is to be free of the Morifati."

"Will the Morifati never stop? Will they never cease to do evil?"

"No, they will not. Not until you stop them, Rion."

I didn't have the Sight. I couldn't see how this would play out, but I had a gut feeling that there was another way. I didn't know what it was then. I felt convinced that the idea of having power over the Morifati had seduced Snake.

Massacre an entire tribe? Was it possible? How could it be the right thing to do?. The Free State didn't believe in it. We considered massacre to be one of the evils of the past. I knew Grandfather wouldn't consent to any of this if he knew.

I was going to find my own way out of this situation. Whatever she had in mind, I would have to turn it around into something I knew was the right thing to do.

THIRTY-ONE

JEALOUSY

"Diana, will you leave us now?" said Snake.

"I don't think I should. I will though. Rion has many decisions to make for himself if he is to succeed. I can't choose for him."

At that Diana turned to go and quickly got halfway down the room before I thought to ask where.

"Diana, where are you going?" I said.

"I have some apartments here, Rion, which I have used in the past. I will be there when her Highness has finished with you."

So I turned back around to Snake. She stood before her throne in her robe, smiling at me knowingly. Her human form was quite beautiful, her blonde hair and her brown eyes. Was I feeling limerence again?

"Come here to me, Rion. We have much to talk about now that we are alone. Diana has a conflict. Her personal feelings for you prevent her from seeing what is best for you and for the Free State, and they prevent her from understanding my interests in defeating the Morifati."

I went to her, and she stepped down off the dias. She took my left arm in her right and guided me across the room.

"Come with me. We need to have a long talk and a walk around the keep. I will give you the grand tour. Lets go up to the roof first so you can see the observation towers."

Snake was very much a woman now, totally feminine, and yet regal, powerful. There was nothing at all reptilian about her. I thought this must be her true form, that the body and the person called Snake was a persona she assumed for protection and to project her power. Her skin was soft, her eyes held no menace.

"Do you have a name?" I asked.

"I will tell you, but you must first swear to tell no one or repeat it aloud to anyone but me. The consequences of revealing it to enemies could be grave, even fatal."

"I swear. I swear on my honor as a Freeman."

"My name is Dorothea."

"Were you a human before? Is this your true form?"

"Yes, I was born a human, of course. All the Psychics are truly humans. I am over three hundred years old. I am the only one who can say that now, all the others my age have died. I am the only one who remembers the Great Third War and the Emergence of the Sight."

"So, how did you build this old castle? How old is it?"

"I had some help. I persuaded a tribe of men to bring in the stone by boat from the mountains. The design is my own from old documents. The Morifati had not settled to the north of here then. They were still south of here looting the ruins of the old city."

"Wasn't there radioactivity? How could they survive down there?"

"They weren't afraid of the radioactivity. They lived off the remains of the old world. They stole food or whatever they needed from the free groups of people they found living in the ruins. They killed when they needed to, or for fun, or to appease their god. They raped, took captives, they took whatever they wanted. They made their captives join them and serve Than or they would sacrifice them to him."

"Who were these people who helped you build your castle? Where are they now?"

"They are the ancestors of the Northmen. Some of them stayed behind and became Ravens. A few of them went into the mountains and became Wolves."

"Were any of them Freemen?"

"Your people have a unique history. I am surprised Grandfather has not told you."

"He has told me some things. He does not like to teach a student until he believes that student is ready to receive the information."

"He is wise. I will defer to his judgement and let him explain how the Free State came to be to you when he is ready."

We went back out into the entryway and went through another door which led to a flight of stairs that led up to a covered space in the center of the roof of the keep. From up there we could see the entire roof with its guard towers in the four corners and a glimpse of the lands beyond. Ravens were roosting in each of the guard towers.

"Are they keeping watch for you?"

"Yes, they are. They are the best guards I could hope for, they are my eyes and ears."

We walked over to the north wall and looked out. The grassland spread out beneath us. To our right the forest had grown close, the closest the forest came to the castle wall. The Morifati were hiding in there, keeping watch on the castle. I looked but I could not see them with my eyes, so I looked with my mind's eye.

They were there all right. About a half dozen were watching the castle even now. They could see us. I suppressed the urge to wave at them.

"The Morifati are watching us Dorothea."

"Yes, they are. They will do nothing yet. They just want to make sure you don't leave without being seen."

I turned to look at her. She had turned to face me and brought her face in close to mine. Her eyes gazed into mine. It was not unlike the dream I had of her before, only instead of holding me in the grip of her vision, her expression was softer. She was offering her mouth to be kissed.

I wanted to; I was ready to, but I thought I better not, not when Diana and I had just become lovers. Diana claimed we would marry as well, that she saw it with the Sight in her visions of the future.

Why had Snake chosen to seduce me at this point? Surely she knew about Diana and me. She must have seen the same future events.

It was difficult for me to be angry with her, though. In fact, I felt love for her. Was she putting a Limerence Spell on me? What was she up to? I had not known there was any rivalry between Dorothea and Diana. As far as I knew, until now we were all allies out to defeat the Morifati, our common enemy.

There was another agenda here. I seemed to be the focus of it.

"Can you see the Old City from up here?"

"You can just barely see some of the tallest towers from the south wall."

She said that with indifference and made no move to walk in that direction. In fact, she held her gaze on me, still waiting to be kissed.

"I'd like to see. And the Morifati are creeping me out. I can watch them watching us with my mind's eye. Surely their thoughts are disturbing to you."

"I've learned how to put them out of my mind at times like this. I rely on Raven to warn me of their actions. She can stand their presence better than I."

"Let's go to the south parapet now."

She didn't budge. So I broke our embrace and pulled her toward the south wall by her arm.

She stayed put. She did not yield to me.

"Rion, why are you in a hurry? We can discuss anything we need to right here."

"Look, I think you want something from me that I can't give to you."

"Oh? What is that?"

"Love. I already love another."

"You don't know what love is. You don't know what the purpose of any of this is, or who you are, or who you will become."

"So why don't you explain all those things to me, Dorothea. I have been trying to get someone to explain all this to me all along but everyone keeps saying 'wait, you must learn the answers on your own'."

"This is love."

She stepped toward me, maintaining eye contact. I froze, just as I had in the dream. I wanted to hold her back, to keep my distance without hurting her, to remain faithful to Diana, but I could not move or look away. She pressed her lips to mine. They were sweet, gentle, so I kissed back. I could not pretend to be repulsed by her, but if anything happened between us, I did not want it to be like this.

I had to do something, so I tried to enter her mind. She was already in my mind! She blocked me from entering hers. Just before she pushed me out, I glimpsed what she was doing. She had the power to enter someone's mind and to force them to move and to speak and to act as she willed! She could control another human being! Even remotely!

I tried to speak aloud, but I couldn't. So in my mind I said, "I don't want you like this Dorothea. Let me go. Let it be my choice."

"Who is it? That little bitch Diana? Or does Anna still hold you with her Limerence Spell? Both?"

To tell the truth in my heart of hearts, I guess both were true. I loved Diana, but I still had the occasional dream or daydream about Anna. I would not know how I would react if I went back to the Morifati. I was determined to resist them. But how was one problem I would have to figure out on my own.

What did Dorothea want with me? Why was she doing this? What was she after?

"Why do you pursue me knowing what you know, Dorothea?"

She broke away finally and walked away from me for a few steps, thinking. Then she turned and walked back to me, looking at me intently again. Though she held me in her eyes intently, she made no more effort to control my movements. She paused, just looking at me closely, then she spoke.

"I have never had any children, Rion."

Then she let that sink in. Was it difficult for her, somehow? Could she mate as a snake? Did she have to assume human form?

"I don't understand. Do you have to be in human form?"

"I do if I want the child to be human and to be a Psychic."

"But you have had so much time. Was it never possible?"

"Alas no. Oh, there have been those who would comply, but they were not acceptable. Either they had no powers, or they were evil like the Morifati, or stupid, or someone who would want to challenge my power here, to rule over me and my kingdom. I want a husband, not a King."

"Why me?"

"You are very special, Rion. You are unique. You were foreseen by many. You may come to rule this world. You will if you choose to rule this world with me beside you. There is no necessity that you marry Diana. You can even give me the child I seek, then marry her. I think something destined you for greater things than that, however."

She fell silent and stood smiling at me knowingly. I could feel myself falling under a spell. I wasn't being controlled like I had been before. She was inside my head, though. That was the purpose of the eye contact. You could look into someone's mind and soul that way. That's how Diana had taught me telempathy and 'seeing around the corner'.

What was real? What should I do? Who was I supposed to love? I longed to talk to Grandfather about all this in the hope he could give me a reality check. I was beginning to understand what everyone meant when they said I would have to figure it out by myself.

I needed time to sort it all through. Between the drugs, and people entering my mind, and all the hardships I had endured, it was hard to know which way was up.

"Alright now come along Rion."

She began leading me to the south tower. The Ravens all scattered when we got close. We went inside the watchtower and she brought me over to a corner wall where we could not be seen from the keep. She stood with her back to the wall and drew me in close to her.

"Don't be afraid Rion. Don't be afraid to love me."

She drew me in for an embrace and a long kiss. I didn't even think about whether it was her controlling me or whether I had given in of my own free will. All I know is I had gone too far.

I had let things go too far. I enjoyed it and I wouldn't stop, couldn't stop at that point.

"So, this is what you want? You want me here and now?"

"Yes. I've waited a long time for you, Rion. For years I have waited for you to come here. I saw this with the Sight long ago. You are the hero this world has waited for, the lover I have waited for, the father of my child."

We kissed deeply again. Whether it was love or limerence, I did not know and did not care any longer. Who was the most beautiful? Dorothea or Diana or Anna? It did not matter to me at that point. Her brown eyes and her blond hair and her face they captivated me. I held her as tightly as I could.

#

I woke later on in her bedchamber. I could not tell if it was day or night. I looked around. She lay beside me, asleep. We were both naked. I slipped out of bed and got up to look for the chamberpot. I found instead a bathroom and toilet.

When I finished I went back to her but I didn't get into bed. I stood there watching her, wondering what to do. Her sheets draped her as she lay, like one of those classic statues from before the Great Third War. She looked like one of those goddesses from the ancient world, from long ago. Who had Grandfather told me about? The Greeks?

She stirred and rolled over and looked at me, smiled victoriously, and stretched.

"Come back to bed, sweetheart."

I went back over and sat on the edge.

"You look very pleased with yourself. Are you satisfied by what happened?"

"You were wonderful Rion. Better than I had hoped. It's been ages, literal ages since anyone made love to me, and never like you did. I wonder if you are aware of what you can do for a woman. You are still a boy in so many ways. Still a baby."

"I don't think I am a baby at all. I passed my order of Manhood two years ago. You should not talk down to me."

"I'm not. Not at all. I'm ready to surrender to you completely, Rion."

"But not to share your Domain. You said you weren't looking for a King."

"I can teach you things, Rion. I can teach you powers that no one else can teach you. That no one else will share with you. You can become invincible through me. Diana will not teach you what I will teach you."

"I need to go find her. It's time I went to check on her."

"There's no need to worry about her. Why concern yourself with her? She's perfectly safe. What really do you know about her, anyway? Hasn't she concealed her true nature from you?"

"I know she is loyal to me!"

"Really? And what if I am pregnant now? You, the father of my heir, with the innocent little dove waiting for you to fulfill her prophecy about the two of you?"

That startled me a little. I had forgotten in the heat of passion that Dorothea wanted a child by me. Was it already too late? What had I gotten myself into?

"Are you pregnant now, Dorothea?"

She just reclined in bed, smiling at me dreamily.

"Time will tell, lover. Time will tell."

THIRTY-TWO

A HOSTAGE TAKEN

I needed to talk to Diana right away, to tell her what was going on, to find out what she thought we should do. I had gone too far with Dorothea. The thought of admitting it mortified me, but I needed to let Diana know Snake was plotting against her, and that she had plans for me.

Should I go back to the Morifati now? Did I need to? Or could we escape and go back to the Free State and unite with the Wolves against any attack? Did we need Dorothea at all? It didn't appear we could trust her to do anything more than look out for herself. She would only help us if it helped her.

Dorothea didn't seem to want me to leave. It occurred to me I would probably need to 'see around the corner' to get away from her. Should I just wait for her to fall asleep?

"Dorothea, I need to walk around for a bit. Get some fresh air and some exercise. Think things over. This is a lot to take in all at once."

"And go visit your little sweetheart in her apartments?"

"Yes, I need to do that, too. It's only fair for me to speak to her, to let her know what's going on. After all, I have decisions to make and decisions to announce don't I."

"You do. Go to her. But when you have finished speaking to each other, I want both of you to come right back here. I have some announcements for the two of you. And some predictions about your future!"

So I left the room at once. What had I gotten myself into? I can't say I didn't enjoy what had happened, but it wasn't like the Limerence Spell. I did not feel like I couldn't live without Dorothea. In fact, I wondered how I could ever live with her. How could I explain to her that it would not work out for us? She didn't seem to care. All she cared about was what she wanted. I was only a means to an end.

Now how could I find Diana? I searched with my mind. Her apartments were on the north side of the top floor of the keep. I could see what she was doing through her eyes. She was looking out of one of the tall picture windows on that side, gazing out far to the north, lost in thought. I had the feeling that she wanted to fly away, that she was sad. Did she know I had disappointed her, that I had loved another? Perhaps.

What should I do? Should I tell her? Would Dorothea tell her? How was she going to take this? Would she no longer want me?

I had to find a way to tell her. I had to find a way to convince her I wanted her and not Dorothea and not Anna. Would she understand? All I could do is open my mind and heart to her when I got there, let her use telempathy and see inside me so she would know my intentions. Dorothea didn't seem to want that. She didn't care what I felt, only what she wanted.

I wove my way through the dimly lit hallways until I arrived at an enormous set of double doors. I knew this was the entrance. I knocked. The doors swung open and there she stood, tears gently flowing down her cheeks.

She turned and walked away. She went back over to the window. Her shoulders slumped. I could tell that she already knew what had happened.

"Diana...", I began.

"Say nothing Rion. I already know."

So I went over to her and put my arms around her. She started sobbing harder. I wasn't sure what to say at that point. Best not to say anything, I thought.

We stood like that for a while. The view from up there was panoramic. I could see far out over the forest. I could see flocks of ravens on patrol out over Snake's domain.

"We've got to get out of here. We'll leave. I'll pretend that I am going back to the Morifati, but we will go to the Wolves instead."

"It won't work. She'll know. The Ravens will find us and follow us."

"We got to do something. She used her mind to control me."

"That's right. Now that she has that amulet, she can control others with her mind. Oh, why didn't you tell me?"

She sighed and began sobbing again. But this time she turned to bury her head in my chest. There wasn't much else to do but hold her tightly. We were going to have to go back to face Dorothea, and I was going to confront her. I had decided about that. I was not going back to the Morifati.

"Look at me Diana. Look into my eyes."

She slowly lifted up her head, but she didn't look at me right away. Diana had taken down her hair, which was long and raven colored, and now much of it was hanging down in front of her face. Her eyes were still closed and her nose was red and her cheeks were wet.

I brushed her hair back out of her face with my fingers. She opened her eyes and glanced at me. And then resumed her downcast stare. I tilted up her chin.

"You must use telempathy now. Look deeply into my eyes. Look into my heart, my mind, and my soul. See what is there."

She complied. Her eyes flashed a little anger at first. I could feel her entering my mind, so I relaxed as much as possible and let her examine whatever she wanted. Wordlessly she guided the focus of my attention to my memories of what had happened, to my dreams about the future, to my thoughts and intentions.

"You do love me.", she said at last. "But you must learn to be stronger. You do not have enough integrity yet to resist a Limerence Spell."

"Snake claims she can teach me greater powers."

"She can, but she will not unless she thinks she has got you under her power. Dorothea does not share power. She will only coexist when it benefits her."

So I held her tight then and lifted her chin up and kissed her. She tried to pull back, so I grabbed her head in both my hands and devoured her mouth.

"Believe me now?", I said.

"We don't have time for this now, Rion."

"We've got as much time as I care to take."

"Look behind me, at the window."

I looked, and sure enough, one of the Ravens sat perched on the windowsill, watching us. So Dorothea knew what was going on, she probably knew already. I didn't like that, the constant surveillance. I was going to have to figure out a way for both of us to escape. Going back to the Morifati village was no longer an option. Neither was staying here and being Snake's consort.

"Come on then. Make yourself ready to appear before her."

I let her go and wash her face and put her hair up and all the things that a beautiful young woman would do. I paced the floor a bit. I was angry now and anxious to get things settled. More ravens were collecting on the windowsill. I strode over to them and banged on the glass suddenly. They didn't move. I had forgotten that they could 'see around the corner' as I could. They would not be surprised or scared by anything I did.

Before we went to Dorothea, I thought we ought to get our story straight. But how could I tell her that we planned to leave? She wouldn't just let us walk out, I was certain of that. Diana could transform into a dove and fly away, I suppose, but wouldn't the Ravens follow her, maybe attack her?

And as for me, I could only escape if an opportunity presented itself. I would have to choose my battles and wait for opportunities. I don't think I could disguise my motives very well at this point. This was going to be a confrontation, one we might not win, not at first.

When Diana came back out, she was radiant. She wore a simple silver robe and her hair was up in a classic chignon on the back of her head. My first impulse was to embrace her, but instead I said.

"What are we going to tell her? She is certain not to like it. Can you escape on your own if she refuses to accept my decision?"

"Those Ravens of hers can follow me and kill me, so you need a better plan than that. If we escape at all, it will have to be together."

"If we can distract her, then I can find a path through her sentries."

"Yes, if you can. But I doubt it now that she has the amulet. You must go back to the Morifati Rion. I don't think we are going to be given another choice."

"I am free to make my own choices, aren't I? Doesn't the success of this whole thing depend upon me?"

"That's right. Now you know what to tell her."

"If defeating the Morifati depends on what I do, then I get to decide what needs to be done."

"Agreed."

I took her hand and led her out then. We went back through the dimly lit hallways to Dorothea's boudoir, or should I say lair? I wondered why I had not seen any of her servants the entire time I had been in the keep. Were her snakes there but hiding from us? Maybe they had some secret passageways or rooms that they preferred.

I knocked on the doors of Dorothea's apartments.

"Enter!" she said.

Dorothea stood in the center of the room wearing her robes and a crown, the amulet around her neck. She had piled her hair up into a chignon, as Diana had. That seemed like a curious coincidence to me.

"So here is the little couple from the Free State, come to me hand in hand."

"How else were you expecting us to be?" I said.

"Defiant as always. You still have so much to learn."

"He still loves me, Dorothea. Your magic has not worked."

"So I see. It's very touching how loyal he is when it suits him to be."

"Can you afford to be jealous now, Dorothea? Doesn't the success of our campaign against the Morifati all depend on me? On what I do? Why risk my anger?"

At that Dorothea laughed, a high shrill laugh. You would have thought it was the funniest thing she had ever heard. She turned from us abruptly and walked over to her throne and sat. She motioned for us to follow like she had expected us to know and respond to her lead. That left us standing in front of her as she sat with her legs crossed, regarding us with a triumphant smile.

"Do you know what a catspaw is, my young hero?"

"No, I guess not."

She chuckled some more.

"You are right, though, Rion. I simply cannot defeat them without you, and you are useful in so many other ways!"

"I am free to make my own decisions."

"Yes, you are! You are a Freeman from the Free State. But there are consequences to everything we do. So you had better choose wisely. The welfare of others depends on what you do!"

"I don't see why I should go back to the Morifati, Dorothea. Not now that I have successfully escaped. Not since we know they plan to roast me alive as soon as the New Moon."

"You will go back as I have asked you to! You can only defeat them in this way! Do not think that the Free State and the Wolves can defeat them without me! Do not make an enemy of me or betray me!"

"We are not your enemies, but neither are we your servants!", said Diana.

"She's right. How can you expect me to do anything that is not of my own free will? Am I to face death just because you order me to? Where is my cause in all this?"

"You want me to give you a cause?"

"I'd like you to answer my question."

"Suppose I told you that you are free to leave, but Diana must stay here."

"What do you mean by that?"

"Exactly what I said!"

She was wearing the amulet around her neck. Dorothea grasped it in both hands and closed her eyes. Diana walked toward her and knelt in front of her.

"Diana, you will leave your apartments and go to the east tower. You will confine yourself there and you will not leave until Rion has returned victorious over the Morifati."

"Yes Highness.", said Diana.

Diana got up and began walking out of the room. I ran over and grasped her shoulders. She pulled away from me, or tried to, I held on to her.

"Let her go Rion! I command it!"

I felt Dorothea take command over me through my mind, using the amulet. I let go of Diana and watched her walk out of the room. Then Dorothea turned me around to face her again.

"Does that help? Will you decide now? Diana will remain my prisoner here until you return."

"Suppose I return with an army."

"Then you will never see her again. You must do what I command if you will ever see her again. You will go to the Morifati waiting outside. They will take you back to their village. In a few more days, in about a week, they will try to sacrifice you to Than. You will not allow it. You will escape from them and kill Blackheart John. You will bring his head back to me here. You will not be alone. I will send word to Wolf and Grandfather to bring their warriors to the Morifati village and lay siege to it."

"So just like that, you expect me to leave Diana behind, walk out of here, and hand myself over to them?"

"Rion, remember how I said that I have things to teach you, powers to teach you how to use? And there is much more you need to know about yourself and the history of the world you are living in, and about who you will become in the future. I will teach you all these things before you leave. And remember, you go to gain a glorious victory for me, and for yourself, and you will free your beloved, but only if you do everything I command."

"I will do what I think is best, or nothing at all!"

"You had better listen to me now, Rion. You are not prepared to defeat them yet. You have not learned enough. The most you can hope for is to escape from them like you did before.

That will not stop them from attacking the Free State and killing your people. You must learn what only I can teach you!"

She stood up at that point and walked over to me. She put her arms around my shoulders. Her eyes sought mine and looked deep inside me.

"Don't be difficult."

We kissed again for a long time.

"Diana isn't the only one who loves you, Rion."

THIRTY-THREE

THE HISTORY OF THE PSYCHICS

When we had finished in her boudoir, Dorothea led me to a dining room with a long candlelit dining table. On one end of it, her servants had prepared a feast for us. I could finally see the answer to my question about her Snakes. There were servants standing by who had prepared the meal and set the table, who were waiting for us to arrive and served us wordlessly unless a question needed to be asked. They avoided eye contact and kept their heads down.

I found out later they were snakes transformed into human form. When their services were no longer needed, they transformed back into snakes and they slithered off into the dark recesses of the castle keep. There were tunnels and dens built into the structure just for them. That's why the Morifati never found them before. They had only to retreat into their dens, and then sneak out into the darkness to attack.

I was starving by then, but still determined to get away. If I did, I would have to find a way to free Diana. That was a conundrum. Should I try to free her and then escape? Should I escape on my own and then come back and free her? By myself, or with an army?

The techniques Dorothea was using on me were not too different from the ones the Morifati used. First love me, then hate me. Give me pleasure and then give me pain. But never at any time acknowledge me as a free, separate individual with free moral agency.

"Here we are Rion. They prepared dinner for us."

The servants rushed to seat us, Dorothea at the head of the table and me on her right. They filled crystal goblets for us, one with sweet red wine and one with mineral water for each of us. They took our plates and sliced meat onto them and heaped on vegetables.

"Enjoy yourself Rion darling. You are going to need all your physical and mental strength for the labors ahead of you."

I drank deeply of the wine. It was the most delicious vintage I ever tasted. I could say that, not just because it had been so long for me, but because it was true. I had never tasted such wine. The water tasted like it had flowed from out of a spring high in the Forbidden Land.

"Where did you get such refreshing drink, Dorothea?"

"I have many secret talents, my love. You are just now learning. Taste the roast."

The meat and vegetables were as wonderful and well prepared as the drink had been. The Morifati had fed me well, but they had not fed me like this.

Dorothea had let her hair down from the way she wore it when she received us. Now she let it flow down her shoulders on the sides, with one slender pony tail running from the crown of her head. She wore a little tiara; I guess to remind me I was in her domain, and she wore the amulet over her heart, just beneath her cleavage. She had changed out of her royal robe into something which was no more substantial than a night-gown.

When we finished our meal after dinner, her snakes brought drinks. A flask of some sort of liqueur that tasted like liquorice. Dorothea began eyeing me silently, as if she was looking for something or expecting something to happen. Was she waiting for me to say something?

I proposed a toast. We had not toasted at all before the meal began. I had forgotten. I was a little groggy before and more than a little preoccupied. I lifted a small glass of the digestif.

"I would like to propose a toast. To us, and to the success of our war on the Morifati!"

"To you and the success of your mission, Rion!"

We emptied our little glasses. The servants quickly refilled them. I looked around at her servants. None of them would look me in the eye. They all avoided my gaze. Dorothea, on the other hand, never stopped looking deeply into my eyes. Her own eyes dilated wide, full of sexual interest and love. I would say she was trying to cast a spell, but it was clear she already had me under a spell.

What type of spell? Clearly a Limerence Spell, but her method differed from that of the Morifati. They had lain a powerful spell all at once, quickly overpowering me. Dorothea, on the other hand, had been slowly seducing me ever since she first set eyes on me.

Her method was the more powerful. Even when I made a fool of myself with Anna, some part of my mind knew I was behaving out of character. With Dorothea, I could feel the beginnings of genuine care and concern for her even though I knew she was on some level insincere. It was difficult not to think of her as both a lover and an ally. To feel about her the way I thought of Diana.

"Did you enjoy your meal? Are you quite satisfied now, Rion?"

"It was wonderful. The Morifati feasted me. They tried to fatten me up for sacrifice to Than. But their cooks cannot compete with yours."

"No, I don't imagine they can. I can provide you with anything and everything you could desire here in my castle. I have the power to do so."

"So what shall we do now? Despite everything I am a bit bored."

She laughed at that remark. It occurred to me she was quite a solitary figure. How did she amuse herself? What did she consider to be her avocation? I imagined she spent long hours remotely viewing friends and enemies alike. Did she ever go outside?

"There is something important to discuss. Something of the utmost urgency."

"I don't know if I can deal with serious matters now. The liquor and the food have left me totally relaxed."

"Good! That's what I intended. We have to settle some things, though. There are things you must be told."

"Can we not take a walk? I wish we could walk through the wood. I'd like to breathe some fresh air."

"We can walk the parapets again if you like, or I can take you on a tour of the castle, but now, we need to go and have a talk in my salon."

At that, the servants rushed over to take our chairs. Dorothea extended her hand to me and I guided her out of the dining room. Next to the dining room was a large open door that served as the entrance to the salon. A salon furnished with chairs and couches and a chaise lounge as a centerpiece. The chaise lounge served as an informal throne from the look of things. All around on the walls were bookshelves filled with

227

old books. They looked ancient and rare. They were, of course, priceless and irreplaceable.

Dorothea indicated I should guide her over to the chaise lounge. She let go of my hand, then turned to speak.

"Rion, one way or the other, you want to defeat the Morifati, don't you?"

"Yes, I do."

"And wouldn't you like a little revenge on them for the way they whipped you? The way they tortured you? The way they made a fool out of you with that girl?"

"Yes."

"They even had you promising to take their side against the Free State, didn't they?"

"You know all these things are true. Why do you ask these questions when you already know the answers?"

"Because I have the solution to your problems. I have all the knowledge you need not just to defeat them but to establish yourself over all the world."

"And you plan to simply hand it over to me. Why?"

"There is one condition."

She walked over to a chaise lounge and sat, removing her shoes and spreading her robe open to reveal the entire length of her slender legs.

"You must pledge your loyalty to me, Rion. I demand total loyalty from you and a committed devotion to my welfare."

This was reminding me of what happened between me and Anna. It convinced me all the more, not that I needed more convincing, that she had placed me under a Limerence Spell. Still, her hands were not touching the amulet and I could not feel myself being physically controlled against my will as I had been before.

"So what exactly, are you asking me to do?"

"You will kneel and pledge your devotion and in return I will present you with 'The History of the Psychics'."

"What? You are going to bestow the entire history of the Psychics on me at one go? What will that do for me?"

"The History of the Psychics is a book Rion. It contains the entire story of how the Psychics came into being and what happened to them after they attained their powers. But it contains much more than that. It lists all the known Psychic abilities and how to go about acquiring them."

"And you are going to give it to me provided I pledge my devotion."

"It will not be yours to keep. You must leave it here in my castle where it belongs, but you must study it while you are here so that you can prepare for the trials ahead of you. I will teach you everything I know that is in it but there is much still that I do not know. You may learn some of those things. That is why you must swear an oath of loyalty and devotion to me and you must recognize me as your Queen."

"So that's all? That seems like a lot to ask considering."

"You have little choice, all things considered. Remember, Diana will be my captive until you return triumphant. But keep in mind. You cannot violate this kind of oath once made. You are bound to it forever."

"Why is it so necessary to control me this way?"

"It's for your own good. Believe me, I feel nothing but love for you and for Diana. Nevertheless, my very existence depends on the outcome of this war with the Morifati. So I will leave nothing to chance."

I had some idea of what she was expecting from me. It really wasn't want I wanted or how I wanted things to go. I couldn't see any way around it, though. I would have to agree and then work things around to my advantage later on. To have any hope of freeing myself or Diana I would have to gain Dorothea's confidence.

"So how do I make my pledge, Highness?"

"Walk over here and take a knee."

She was pointing to the foot of the chaise lounge. I could guess what was coming next. I obeyed.

"Repeat after me. Upon my life and my sacred honor, I pledge my lifelong loyalty and devotion to Dorothea, Queen of the Snakes, and I recognize her as my sovereign, and my Queen."

I spoke the oath just as she pronounced it to me.

"Now you may kiss my feet in token of our bond."

I bent over and kissed each foot once. Suddenly, I felt compelled to kiss them more passionately, so I covered them with kisses.

"That's enough Rion darling. I don't expect you to grovel, quite the opposite. Do you love me?"

"Yes, Highness!"

"And you will execute my strategy against the Morifati?"

"I will follow your plan to the letter!"

I'd like to say that she compelled me to do all these things with the amulet, but that would be lying. She had somehow seduced me into a passionate love affair where I had given up the normal male role of leadership and had behaved like a devoted servant.

She pointed to the center of the far wall.

"You will find it over there! Go and get it and treat it with all modesty and respect. Let no harm come to it!"

"The History of the Psychics?"

"Yes, of course, darling. Go and get it and bring it to me!"

I went over to the area she indicated and found a thick manuscript. It must have been six inches thick and eighteen inches tall, bound in leather. I drew it out. It had no title printed on the front or the spine or anything else written on it except for an engraving on the front depicting a snake coiled with its head raised and a single eye in the middle of its head with rays emanating out of it like the rays of the sun. I turned.

"Is this it Highness?"

"Yes. Bring it to me and come and sit with me."

It was quite heavy and smelled old, but there was no dust on it. She must have consulted it frequently. Some of her other books looked like they had not been touched in a hundred years.

I did as I was told and brought it over. She had sat up on the chaise lounge and pointed to a low table nearby.

"Set it there. Bring the table over and we will examine it together."

After I arranged the book on the little table in front of her, I sat next to her. Dorothea placed her left hand on the book and her right hand over the amulet and quietly muttered something to herself. Then she opened it up.

It contained the most beautiful and detailed illustrations I have ever seen before or since. There were far too many illustrations in far too much detail for me to describe them here. She turned through the pages slowly, but she was looking for a precise spot. I guess she wanted me to see how complicated it all was.

"You are still studying this yourself, aren't you, Majesty?"

"Yes, I am. Someone could study this work for a lifetime. I contributed to parts of it but many others did as well. It contains the collected knowledge of Psychic Power. Oh, and by the way, you can drop the formal titles when we are alone together, we are lovers after all."

"So what did you want to show me?"

"The different sections of the book. There isn't time just now to go into great detail. Devote yourself to studying it over the next few days. You must learn a couple of things before you go back. Without these skills you cannot defeat them."

"Go on then."

"I divided the book into two sections. The first is all history. The period before the Great Third War. The events that lead to the Great Third War and the war itself. The aftermath and the Chaos that ensued. The formation of the Morifati and the Free State and the other tribes, and most important of all, where did all the Psychics go and what did they do and where are they now?"

"That sounds like a lot."

"It's about two-thirds of the book. I don't expect you to learn it all in a short time."

"I don't think I can."

"You will need to, eventually. To understand the world we live in now, you must study this book."

"So what's the second part, then?"

"It is a description of all the known psychic powers and how to attain them. It is crucial you study it in the time you have left. You must learn how to survive your captivity and win a victory against the Morifati or else you will wind up being burned alive."

THIRTY-FOUR

REVELATIONS

Dorothea flipped through the pages to show me where the table of contents was and where each section was that she wanted me to read. It contained a summary of each period in the history of the Psychics and then detailed sections on each period. The whole thing was far too much to read in the time I had before I had to go back.

"Just read the summary of each period.", she said.

We spent a long time looking at the illustrations which were in fact exquisite works of art. There were drawings depicting major events and there were maps of the world the way it is now, including lands I had not heard of beyond our own. There were maps of the World the way it had been in the past, in the time of the Great Nations before the Great Third War. Also, there were maps of the old cities before their destruction by the Nukes.

And then there were sections on the natural world and on people. I found drawings of all the plants and it described the ones with medicinal properties. The animals were all depicted along with their known habits and behaviors. The tribes and nations of men listed and portrayed. There were portraits of people who were important figures in the past.

I relaxed as we leafed through the book. I suppose because she was finally relaxing. She had seemed tense to me the entire time I had been there, even before and after we made love. It was as if she was afraid to let her guard down with me. It dawned on me that she wanted to trust me, and she wanted me to trust her, but she had no idea how to establish trust.

Had someone or something betrayed her in the past? I understood that despite her powers and her wealth; she found happiness elusive. It could be that she was unhappy and felt totally alone.

When she finally came to the part of the book that taught psychic powers, she gave me a warning.

"Do not wander around in these pages trying things. Stick to the attainment of the powers I tell you to study. Those who linger in this book become lost. This book will change you. Its purpose is to change you through the attainment of new powers. You can become corrupted by delusions of grandeur. No one has all these gifts. You can only learn what you have been gifted beforehand. The most anyone can accomplish is to fulfil their fate. No one can become anything other than what they are fated to become."

That was a good and kind thing for her to say, and it appeared at the time to be a lesson intended for my benefit alone. I learned later, not long afterward in fact, that she had a motive for not wanting me to study some specific techniques. She knew without a doubt that I could surpass her, that I would surpass her in the strength of my powers. She wanted to postpone that time for as long as she could. Not that I posed a real danger to her, but because of a deep scar that she carried in her heart.

"That's enough for now.", she said at last. "Let's go for that after dinner walk you wanted. The stars should be beautiful tonight."

#

It was a clear, cool night with a waning moon that had not yet risen. The sky was dazzling and the Milky way looked like a mist draped high across the sky. My namesake constellation shone high above.

We held hands at first, then I turned to kiss her for a long while. She broke it off, and we resumed walking, this time arm in arm. Starting on the east side, we turned south to go around clockwise. The tower she held Diana in loomed over us. I could see no light coming from it.

"Why are there no lights in the tower windows? Are you keeping her in darkness?"

"I will not speak of her now, and neither will you. Diana is well treated, but I cannot allow her to see out or fly out or communicate with her mind."

"But what can she do? Why do you hurt her?"

"She is not in pain, nor is she being mistreated. She is asleep. Diana will remain in a deep sleep until you return for her. Now those are enough questions about her!"

I wanted to know more, but I knew she wouldn't budge now. Better to change the subject. I was going to have to find a way to get to Diana and wake her before I could escape with her. All the more reason to study the "History of the Psychics" and learn all I could.

"How is it that together with your Ravens and your Snakes you cannot defeat the Morifati and yet they remain outside the castle and do not enter?"

"They are afraid of you my love."

"Afraid of me? How can they be afraid of one man? I watched your Snakes kill some of them on the river, and the Ravens attacked some and gouged their eyes out."

"They know you have the amulet, and they know you can see around the corner. They fear what else you may know now that you are here."

"Why don't they retreat? Why linger and lay siege?"

"Their orders are to capture you and retrieve the amulet at all costs. They do not fear death, only defeat."

"They are indeed a strange bunch of people. They are more like animals than men. For them, all that exists is pleasure in the here and now. They feel justified no matter what they do. There is no remorse for them, no pity, no love, and no meaning to their lives."

"You speak the truth. You know them well. You learned much while you were with them. Don't you see now why we have to kill them?"

"Is there no alternative? Can I not reach them some other way? Maybe I can help them to feel the Spirit of God."

"They deny that there is any spirit of any kind. They believe that your mind and your self are physical. Just electrical waves. Than is just the universe of electricity to them."

"Electricity? What is electricity and what are electrical waves?"

"You've seen lightning? That energy, that light and heat is all electricity and magnetism. The History of the Psychics has a section that will explain it to you."

"How can I hope to understand something like that?"

"The ancients did. Before the great third war they understood all those things. That's how the Nukes worked. There is a fantastic amount of energy stored up in matter, in metals. The ancients knew how to release it. The Nukes were so hot they blew all the air away from the cities and knocked everything over and burned everything up."

"How can they deny the evidence of their senses? If I enter their minds and show them the Spirit, won't they understand?"

"You do not have that kind of power. There is no guarantee they would accept the truth even if you did. You risk being corrupted yourself by joining with them that way. And they would see inside your mind and know what you know. That knowledge is too dangerous to share."

"I still think I ought to try."

"You are trying to be too good, Rion. There is a time for compassion and a time for ruthlessness. Now is the time for ruthlessness with them. You must learn to balance these desires within yourself. It's possible to be too good, and it's possible to be too bad. The Morifati have never shown compassion to anyone and they will show none to you."

I thought she was right. Everything I had known them to do had an evil motive, even when they were kind to me. I knew enough to know that someone had to show remorse on their own. I could not make them feel remorse, or make them feel anything else, for that matter.

"So when do I start my studies?"

"Tonight. I am going back to my boudoir and you are going to go to the salon and start your reading. Start with the history sections. When you get tired, come to me, but spend some time with it first. You must be serious about this Rion. You must be a man, more than that you must behave as a King."

"What's the goal of studying this book? What am I supposed to learn?"

"You will learn how to kill with your mind."

"That seems wrong."

"I do not mean you to bring peace, Rion, but a sword! Free your people from this evil! Free me from this evil!"

She leaned into me and put her arms around my neck. I knew she wanted to be kissed. As soon as I started, she kissed back without restraint.

"Do this thing for me, darling. Let neither me nor Diana down. Everyone is counting on you."

And with that, she turned and left me looking at the stars.

#

I found the book exactly as we left it. How was I ever going to prepare in the short time I had? Dorothea believed in me, but she would not do, could not do for me what I had to do for myself and for everyone. If I didn't get this right, I was going to wind up roasted human flesh for sacrifice to Than and Blackheart John was going to slice and eat my liver. Diana would remain a captive, Dorothea didn't say what would happen to Diana if I died. Would she let her go?

On top of that, the Morifati were going to launch their attack on the Free State unless I succeeded. The pressure was on. Still, I couldn't help but just page through the book looking at the maps and the artwork before I got started. Then I broke down and started reading the history.

I got bored with reading all the history after a while, so I flipped over at random to the section of the book that listed and taught all the Psychic powers. Whether by accident or whether someone or something guided me, I cannot say, but I landed directly in the middle of the section that explains how to assume animal forms. More than that, it explains how to find what forms are compatible with your own spirit and how to develop the ability to transform yourself.

Like I said, I landed in the middle of the discussion on how to transform. The section I found described how to transform into your Spirit Animal. I thought I better find the beginning, so I flipped back to the start of the section on Spirit Animal transformations.

The first thing anyone has to do is determine what their spirit animal might be. I began reading. Determining your animal form is not a choice you can make for yourself ordinarily. You have to discover what your animal form is. Some rare individuals can assume more than one form.

Finding your Spirit Animal requires guided meditation and active imagination. It cannot be forced. You must perform these techniques in a totally relaxed state. When you have achieved the proper state of mind, an image of your animal will appear to you.

It has to be something you can live with for an extended period. Some choose to remain in their Spirit Animal form for the rest of their lives. The Wolves and the Ravens are some of these. You are not, of course, truly the animal. You will become a being that is manifesting itself in the animal form. Higher powers of the mind are retained and abilities like telepathy and telempathy remain.

I got up and walked over to Dorothea's chaise lounge and got comfortable and relaxed. I closed my eyes and allowed my mind to wander. I opened them and looked for something to concentrate on. There was a candelabra in a corner of the room I could gaze at without turning my head. I watched the candles flicker. I allowed myself to drift toward sleep. I thought about things that were happy. When something reminded me of something that made me anxious, I practiced breathing techniques to dispel the anxiety and relax.

The image of a Grizzly Bear appeared to me. That caught me by surprise, but I knew it made sense for me. This had to be my Spirit Animal. If not my Spirit Animal, then it was at least a form I wanted to master if I was going back to the Morifati village.

If the goal was merely to escape, that was one thing. I could use 'seeing around the corner' for that anytime. Dorothea wanted me to fight them. It would take something more than a wolf or a raven or a snake to do that. As a Grizzly I should be able to hold my own, even against a crowd of them, especially if I combined it with seeing around the corner.

Something told me not to tell her, though. This should be my secret, a secret I could use against her. Could snakes and ravens fight against a Grizzly Bear? I doubt it! I knew if I could escape from the Morifati this way I could escape from her as well. I would study this in secret.

Dorothea wanted me to learn how to kill with my mind. Her idea was that I should use that technique and 'seeing around the corner' to surprise them and defeat them and open up the gates of their village when everyone assembled outside.

She wanted me to read all that damn history first. I would have to, I suppose, but I wanted to explore the book a little farther first. So I started paging and flipping around. It was then I found the key technique I had been looking for. Why had no one taught me this before? Knowing what the Morifati wanted to do to me, this would have been the best thing for me to know. I now had two things to learn that I would keep to myself until the appropriate time. When I had these powers, I would hold the key to defeat the Morifati, rescue Diana, and restore peace to the world.

The book explained how to survive being burned in a fire. There was a whole section on how to walk through fire and live. How to touch fire and not be burned. Even how to survive being burned at the stake.

It would require great courage from me to accomplish these things. There was no other way left for me now. If I still wanted to defeat them my way, or if I was to defeat them the way she said it had to be, I was going to have to pass through the fire.

THIRTY-FIVE

MY DESTINY

When I returned to Dorothea, she was asleep. That was a good thing. I didn't want to talk to her just then. I didn't want to lie about what I had learned. Besides, there is little point in talking about what you are going to do or plan to do or want to do. It is always better to just do it.

Before that, no one really cares.

I undressed and slipped under the covers next to her. She was surprisingly warm blooded for a snake. Dorothea lay completely nude under the covers with her back to me. It was almost as if she lay coiled. She was fast asleep, though, so I didn't wake her.

I couldn't understand myself. I was in love with Dorothea now, but I didn't trust her. I was in love with Diana, but I couldn't remain faithful to her. Was there no way to master myself? Maybe there was something in the book on Limerence Spells or on love and lust in general. I had self-control everywhere else. Why not with women?

I snuggled up to her, close enough to feel the curve of her back and the touch of her soft bottom. I felt tired, and I didn't want to talk just yet, so I fell asleep.

I woke the next morning before Dorothea woke up. I slipped out of bed without waking her. I wanted to get back to the "History of the Psychics" and find everything it had on love and limerence, so I snuck out of the room.

#

When I got back to the salon, I grabbed the book off the shelf and began paging through it to find anything on Limerence Spells. There had to be something on it, since Dorothea claimed the book was a compendium on all Psychic powers. It was there, and maybe some other things as well.

Unfortunately, the chapters were numbered but without descriptions. I gathered they had compiled the techniques by orders of difficulty. It was possible that each numbered chapter represented all the knowledge taken from single individuals, omitting any duplications of techniques. No need to repeat something described earlier in the text, especially if it was simple to master.

I became frustrated though, because I just couldn't seem to find it. Then I hit upon an idea. I would leaf through the book page by page until I found it, making note of each page number as I went along. Then, once that process was begun I would see around the corner into my own future to the time when I found it and looked at the page number.

That worked. I saw the page and the page number and I flipped straight to it. There it was, the section on how to produce limerence in another person. There was more than one technique, of course, and a discussion on the various reasons for needing a spell of this type. Warnings about side effects which were numerous. A Limerence Spell was considered an advanced technique which could easily create complications. Novices were warned not to try it.

I saw nothing on how to remove one. Was it in this section at all? It turned out it was not. And what about blocking or resisting a Limerence Spell when it was cast on you? I paged through the chapter, and there was nothing. I would have to use my technique again.

I soon found the section on how to remove a Limerence Spell. There was more than one technique, in fact. One of the techniques, well really two of the techniques, were being used on me now. Sneaky, very sneaky. They were conspiring against me. For my own good, but I could see now how I was being manipulated.

#

I did not hear Dorothea enter the room. Lost in thought, bent over studying the "History of the Psychics", I had entered into a kind of trance. I felt her presence gradually, the way you feel when you slowly become aware of something behind you. She was not behind me, though. She stood off to my left and a little behind, watching me and smiling.

"So what have you learned, darling?"

"Much. Something I should have known all along."

I stood up and walked over toward a candelabra that was placed on a nearby table to give light to the room. I stared into the flames and concentrated. I looked into the flames and looked into myself. I wanted to find any fear that was hidden away inside me and silence it.

"Watch!"

I held my hand over one of the candles. I lowered my hand into the flame, palm first. I felt no pain, not even any heat! I turned my hand over to examine my palm while keeping the back of my hand in the flame. My palm had not burned. I withdrew my hand completely. Nowhere on my hand were there any burns. I had not felt pain nor heat.

I turned and walked back over to Dorothea. I held my hand out to her.

"Look!"

She took my hand in her hands and brought it up to her mouth and kissed it. She looked deeply into my eyes.

"You have done very well, Rion!"

"I wish I had known that before!"

"It is a wonderful thing to know. Especially when dealing with the Morifati and their barbaric custom of burning people alive."

"Why haven't you used this on them before?"

"Because I don't know it daring. I do not have this gift. You do! This is why I need you, Rion. Through you, together we can defeat them!"

"Whether I want to or not?"

She looked deeply into my eyes then. I could feel her entering my mind. It was going to be next to impossible to conceal anything from her.

"You are not being manipulated, darling. I can assure you that we both love you and want the best for you and that little Morifati witch Anna wants nothing good for you at all. She would enjoy watching you die and she is looking forward to it. She hopes she can play a major role in your sacrifice. Everything she has done, she has done for her true lover, Blackheart John!"

"She's Blackheart John's lover?"

"She is his mistress, his consort. She is hoping that one day soon she will become his Queen. Anyone who stands in the way of that will feel her wrath. Anyone who can help her gain that power will be used for her purposes."

"Aren't you doing something similar to me? Don't I hold the key to your power?"

"There is much more at stake here than you and me, Rion. What is it that you want to do after all? What do you want me to do? You cannot postpone your fate. You cannot, you must not avoid your destiny!"

"And what is my destiny?"

"You are the one who will defeat the Morifati! You were foreseen long ago. I have waited for you for three centuries."

"I am that important?"

"Your life, your decisions, will determine the fate of your people, and the fate of the Wolves, and me, and my Ravens, and Snakes, and even the Northmen. The Morifati have to be stopped now before they grow stronger in military power and Psychic power. They are preparing to expand out into the world as far as they can go and steal and kill and burn everything in their path. They will not stop until you stop them, or until they have lost themselves in some faraway land, a land they have conquered but cannot hold."

"I see. I can see now that you are right. This is not something that I should walk away from. You are right. I agree to go."

"Good! Excellent! That's excellent news!"

She rushed over to me and kissed me. I could tell she wanted to be held tightly, so I did. We sat down, reclined really, on the chaise lounge, and began making love.

Her long blonde hair was pulled into one braid. She wore a little tunic which barely concealed her breasts and exposed the entire length of her exquisite legs. She wasn't wearing the medallion. I wondered why, but I would not stop and ask. The only jewelry she wore was a pair of dangle earrings with gemstones that had to be diamonds.

I felt madly in love with her then. I had not had the time to remove any Limerence Spell she had put on me. At that point I didn't care any more. I wanted her then, more than I ever had. I was ready to pick her up and carry her back to her boudoir.

"We mustn't do this now, Rion. There are so many techniques you need to master, and you must leave soon."

"There are some techniques I already know that I want to use on you right now."

We looked deeply and meaningfully into each other's eyes. It didn't seem like I needed to carry her anywhere. Dorothea sat back and pulled her arms from under her tunic, releasing pendulous breasts. She stood up and let the tunic fall to the floor. There she stood, in all her feminine glory, smiling at me proudly. After all, she literally knew everything I was thinking.

She pulled off my shoes and unbuttoned my shirt and pants. I stood up and stepped out of my clothes. Lying back on the chaise lounge, she held her arms out to me.

"Come join me now. Let's take our fill of each other."

I didn't care anymore. I was prepared to give in to her desires. Her desires had become my desires. Her seduction of me was complete.

#

Afterward I held her in my arms on the chaise lounge. I felt comfortable and relaxed, holding her in my arms. She lay reclined on me peacefully, like she never intended on getting up.

"That walking through fire without being burned trick is good to know, and it will keep you alive when they try to sacrifice you to Than, but it is not enough by itself to defeat them. Have you learned to kill with your mind as I have asked?"

"I found something better that I want to learn. I will metamorphose into a bear! Between that and seeing around the corner they cannot defeat me!"

"That's not what I asked you to do, darling."

"I know, but this is how I have decided to defeat them."

She sighed deeply. I could tell it frustrated her, but I could not help her. This was my decision, it was my life being risked.

"Will you not listen to me?"

"It's my life being risked, my divine Majesty. I know these methods will work. I don't have the Sight, but I have good instincts, intuition, if you will. Use the Sight, see if I am right or not."

"There's something else."

"What? What are you so afraid of?"

I turned to her and kissed her then. To reassure her of my love and sincerity of purpose. I pulled back and looked into her eyes. I reentered her mind.

"I had hoped that you could become a snake like me. So you could become my consort."

"That's not what I saw. I saw the Bear. I saw a Grizzly Bear!"

"That's not the future I hoped for, Rion. That's not the future I want for us."

"What about what I want? Does that mean nothing to you?"

"Well, of course it does! But I was hoping you would want the same things I want for us both! Can't you see?"

"All I can see is you say you rely on me, but you do not trust me to make my own decisions. You don't seem to want me to be my own man."

"I only want what's best for you! What's best for us both!"

"I will decide what's best for me! Didn't you see in the future that I would be King? Does a King let his Queen make every decision for him?"

At that point, she burst into tears. I never thought I would see that. It seemed out of character for her to cry. She never asked or begged me for anything. Dorothea had ever and only made demands to me and to Diana. She acted like someone who was accustomed to being in control of everyone and everything all the time.

That she wanted me to increase in power, I had no doubt. Did she have the courage to trust me to live as a free man and as a King? Independently from her? I think she was afraid of what might happen. Considering her powers, there must be some basis for her fears that she would not share with me.

Now I had to think of how I could get out of this without making her angry, but still get my own way. Whether her tears were sincere or whether it was an act to get her way, I could not tell. Grandfather had warned me that women would pull this kind of stunt.

"Wait now. Can I defeat them as a snake? You know I can't. So for now I will master the art of becoming a Grizzly Bear. I can slaughter them with that and even break through their village wall. Later, when I have returned, I can become a snake and we can continue as we are now only closer."

"What about your little virgin?"

"Well, you promised to wake her up, didn't you?"

"She can remain asleep until you agree to all my demands as far as I am concerned."

"That wasn't our deal."

"We didn't have a deal. I had to do what I did to get you to go back to the Morifati. To behave as though you have a backbone."

That hurt, and it pissed me off, so I pushed her off of me and stood up.

"Don't you ever insult my courage or doubt my bravery! I won't listen to that! I went to the Morifati willingly! I let them capture me! I risked my life on your word alone!"

"Calm down, darling. You are still my hero, and I'm counting on you to defeat them. I know you can do it!"

She lay there demurely, completely relaxed and composed, self assured in fact. She wasn't smiling, though.

"Rion. I want you to promise me that you will do what I have asked you to do."

She said that in a voice that was completely calm. I couldn't help but feel a slight menace to her words, though. I was convinced now that she had to stay in control, no matter who she was with or what was going on around her. I was gaining an understanding of what she was really like. Being in control was more important to her than anything else, more important even than defeating the Morifati.

She had made me angry now. I felt rage building within me. I thought about the transformation technique. I started concentrating on the image of a bear. Then I felt it happening. Right there, in her salon, I became an enormous Grizzly Bear. I glowered at her.

"I told you to calm down, Rion."

"I don't feel like taking orders from you right now.", I said with my mind.

I tried to stand on my hind legs and tower over her, but the room was too small and I bumped my head. I got back down on all fours and turned and started for the stairwell that lead to the roof of the keep.

"Rion come back! Please come back!"

"I need room! I'm going to the roof where I can stand up."

As a Grizzly I could move fast, much faster than she could. I was on top of the roof and outside before she could catch up to me. I stood up, stretched, and roared. Just then she came out to join me.

"Rion! Don't let them see you or hear you! The Morifati must not know you can do this. They will have a trap prepared for you if they know."

"They won't know."

I searched the Morifati out in my mind. None of them had seen me. Some had heard, but they thought it was the cry of a bear hunting in the wood.

"Please transform back Rion! Please!"

I had not gotten it completely out of my system, but I didn't want the Morifati to know anything, so I transformed back. Her Ravens were watching us, as always. They had not flown away when I let out that roar. They saw it coming. They saw everything. It was impossible to startle them.

"Happy Dorothea?"

"I didn't intend for you to get angry with me."

"What did you intend then?"

"I just want us ......"

"To what?"

"To rule together!"

This discussion was going to go nowhere. I was going to fight the Morifati my own way and rule my own way, no matter what her heart's desire was. I would not leave Diana asleep in that tower either. Even if I had to marry Dorothea to establish peace between the Free State and the Snakes, I would not let Diana remain there a captive.

"It's time for me to go back to the Morifati."

That remark caught her off guard.

"But Rion you ...."

"I know enough now to defeat them. There's no point in postponing it any longer. I will leave in the morning. I'll walk out of here and go to them. They are waiting for me out there like vultures."

"What about tonight?"

"What about it?"

"I'd like to say goodbye to you before you go, darling, to wish you well. We won't see each other for a long time, and despite the powers you now have, success isn't guaranteed."

She walked over to me then and put her arms around me and lowered her gaze. Then she looked back up into my eyes. I knew what she wanted me to do.

THIRTY-SIX

I SURRENDER TO THE MORIFATI

"Rion, there is something I need to warn you about."

It was the next morning, the day I decided I was going to walk out of the castle and hand myself back over to the Morifati, to be taken captive and taken back to their village to be sacrificed to their god Than.

We were having breakfast in her dining hall. Too big of a breakfast, really, considering the ordeal I would undergo. I thought I better eat up, though. I did not know whether the Morifati would starve me or fatten me up like before. They would probably fatten me up, but you couldn't count on them. How could I trust a Morifati?

The champagne and the egg casserole tasted wonderful though, so I stuffed myself. The alcohol might help numb the pain a little.

"So what is it? What's the great danger now, Majesty?"

"There is a way they can defeat you."

"Really? How? With the powers I've got?"

"You can't use those powers if you are unconscious."

That made sense, but I still felt like arguing.

"How am I going to wind up unconscious?"

"Any number of ways. You could pass out from pain and fatigue. They could drug you. If they get any hint that you can do what you have learned, they will surely drug you. It will disappoint them not to see you writhe or scream in agony but if they know you won't burn, they will certainly drug you so you will."

I had to admit she was right. The potion the High Priest gave me before put me right out of my mind. Could I transform into a Grizzly in that state of mind? And the beatings they gave me before, they had whipped me and carried me around on poles and dragged me in the dirt and starved me and gave me no water until I passed out from the pain and fatigue. And when I was asleep or under the influence of a potion, they had entered my mind. The Old Hag, the High Priest, Blackheart John. They had all entered my mind at one time or another.

"I need a way to keep them from entering my mind. I need to hide my thoughts."

"Yes, you do. Now are you beginning to see my point? Will you listen to me at last?"

"So what's the answer?"

"Go get the book, bring it back here to the table."

"I haven't finished eating."

"Then finish and go do as you are told!"

"Watch your tone now, Majesty. If I turn into a bear, I will be even hungrier. I might eat you."

"Just go!"

Dorothea sat back and sighed. She acted completely put out with me. I couldn't decide whether she loved me or hated me. She seemed at times to both love me and hate me, or to swing between the two emotions like a pendulum.

I pushed back from the table and went and got the book from the salon, which was of course the next room over. I wondered why she hadn't just ordered her Snakes to fetch it. It was a short walk and a simple task, so I was back with it quickly.

I pushed my plate out of the way and plopped it down, and grabbed my champagne glass.

"Careful Rion! That's enough champagne for now, you've got some work to do."

She motioned to her Snakes, and they came over and cleared away my plate and glass. I closed my eyes and saw myself paging through the book to the correct page. I found it and opened up the book to that page.

"How did you know where to turn?"

"That's a little trick I learned using seeing around the corner."

"I see."

"Will this keep anyone from seeing into my mind under any circumstances?"

"Not if they have this amulet."

She gestured to the amulet, which she was wearing around her neck again.

"Also, Rion, you have to know that when someone is probing you, trying to enter your mind. You must keep your wits and stay on guard. They have potions that make it hard to know what's going on."

"Yes, I found that out the hard way."

"Now let's try it. Read the instructions."

I read over the technique. It basically goes something like this. You imagine yourself deep down in a room, surrounded by thick walls, or you can imagine yourself underground, in a mine or a cave or a dungeon. The idea is to go someplace where nothing can get to you. No one can hear you or see you, they don't even know where you are. You don't even have to go underground if you don't want, you just have to go someplace in your mind where you can't be found, can't be seen.

"I'm there now Dorothea. Try it. Try to find me. First without the amulet."

I imagined that I found a cave that went deep inside the Forbidden Land mountains. The last mountain that we had to cross before we got to the great river. I kept going. I didn't have a torch, but I could illuminate the cave the way Diana does.

When I got to the center of the mountain, I found a big void with a lake in it. I sat down next to the lake. I was alone. No one knew where I was and I couldn't see out past the chamber myself. I had separated, isolated myself completely.

"That's good darling. Very good. Now let me show you what I can do."

While I sat there by the lake, I noticed a motion in the water across from me. A snake was swimming toward me. It swam up onto the shore and then transformed into Dorothea. She smiled at me triumphantly.

"Behold the power of the amulet."

"Did I not create a deep enough hiding place?"

"No, Rion, you did well, very well. They will never be able to see into your mind here. The amulet reveals all. It has that power, grants that power to its wearer. Nothing can be hidden from it."

"Why couldn't the high Priest see everything I knew?"

"That fool doesn't know how to use it properly. He has never seen or read the History of the Psychics. I don't think he even knows of its existence and we must keep it that way until we have destroyed them completely."

"I'll do my best. Any time I can feel them trying to enter my mind I will come here."

"That's really all you can do until it's time to attack. They will know you are hiding something but they will not know what it is."

"So it's as simple as that."

"No, not quite. Whenever they torture you, come here. Here you can block the pain out of your mind. Everyone has a breaking point. Here you will feel nothing, so you can endure indefinitely. They will not kill you until it is time to sacrifice you to Than."

"Why is it necessary for me to let myself be sacrificed to Than?"

"Because when they see you defeat Than, that you have defeated death, they will lose their faith in Than and Blackheart John. They will have no reason to believe anymore."

"But why me? And why in this manner?"

"It is an initiation that you must go through to become the being that you will become. There is no other way than this. Do not be afraid, Rion. You will be reborn as a new man. As the greatest Psychic that ever has been. You are fated to be the King of this world."

And then I was back in her dining room. I brought myself back. Dorothea was staring off into space, holding the amulet in both hands, and then she snapped out of it and looked at me.

"A little warning would be nice, please."

"So, do you think I'm ready now?"

"You will still need some luck. But yes, you are as ready as you are going to become."

"I'm ready to go. I don't see any reason to wait any longer. What can you see with the Sight?"

"I see success. The future can change at any time when human will is involved, however. When it's something that appears random, or something from the physical world, there is no doubt, but human will and human fate are in constant conflict. Nothing will be decided for you until you bring it into being. Nothing is ever automatic."

I got up and walked over to her, and placed my hand on her shoulder.

"Shall we?"

"I will not watch you go, Rion. I can't bear it."

"Then let's have a toast."

I motioned to the Snakes to bring champagne. Dorothea stood up to face me. We were handed our glasses. I held mine aloft toward her.

"To victory Majesty!"

"May you return to me soon, Rion!"

We clinked and drank our toasts down. I looked at her and she looked at me. We embraced and kissed deeply.

I broke it off and gestured once more for her to join me. She turned away and shook her head, saying nothing. I felt a little stupid standing there, a little awkward. I wanted to speak, but I had no words. I walked out of the dining room.

So it was time now. Dorothea would not see me out. The Morifati were waiting out there, where they had camped the entire time, while Diana and I were inside. The Morifati did not lay siege. They simply waited for me to come out.

It was as if they knew I was going to come to them. I think they did know. In fact, I am certain of it. Had the Ravens told them on Snake's behalf, or did they have their own way of knowing? I never found out. It didn't matter. Things were going to turn out the same way, no matter what.

They thought they were receiving a sacrificial victim. They did not know that I was really a Trojan Horse, the means of their downfall, their nemesis, their fate. How amusing.

I had a big surprise in store for them. I was looking forward to it. It would not be easy, though. They would whip me, torture me, bind me and bring me before their King. It would be another ordeal for me.

In the end I would be victorious over them, but I had to let them have as much line as I could before I set the hook. I was going to let them do their worst. I was going to let them believe they had succeeded, that they were about to embark on a campaign of conquest that would cover the known world.

Then I was going to yank it all away from them.

I left her behind. But instead of going down the stairwell right away, I went up to the roof of the keep and looked out over the ramparts. I looked ahead in my mind to see as far ahead as I could. I couldn't quite see them yet. They were camped over in the forest to the northeast of the castle. I guess they expected nothing at this point, they were just waiting.

I tried to see ahead on my journey. I wanted to know what I would face when I got to their village. I couldn't see anything. I could imagine, I could plan and strategize, but I could not see. I just didn't have the Sight. I didn't have that gift. I could 'see around the corner', but I could not know the future far in advance.

I better make my way out now. Waiting would not make it easier.

#

I unlocked the gates and walked through them. There was no way for me to lock them behind me, so I just pushed them shut. I guess the Snakes would come in human form and lock the place back up behind me.

I looked ahead again. This time I could see the Morifati. they had become so relaxed that I could just walk into their camp and appear without them seeing me until I was among them. They immediately rushed me and knocked me down and bound me and began whipping me. I tried approaching them in different ways to see if I could get a different outcome. There was no way around it. Each and every way I approached them, they did the same thing. This was going to be a long day.

#

In the end, I just walked quietly into their midst. They did not even notice me at first. One of them was staring into the fire. He looked up blankly. Then an expression of horror and surprise covered his face. He let out a war cry. He practically screamed like a girl.

They rushed me then. I didn't resist. It would be easier that way, for me and for them, not that I cared about them. They brought out a pole, and they bound me to it. Some of them started off with me, then stopped when they realized they needed to strike camp.

I thought things were going to be easy until the leader of this little group came over. It was the Captain from before. The Ravens had not killed him, but they had pecked out one of his eyes. He wore an eye patch now, and he carried a grudge.

He ordered his men to set the pole in the ground on one end. Then he laid into me with a bullwhip. I took that for as long as I could, then I went deep inside the mountain to the underground lake. It was quiet and peaceful in there, and I felt no pain.

Snake did not appear to me, but I heard her voice.

"I'm sorry Rion. I wish it did not have to be this way."

"Don't worry. I'm having fun right now. They won't know what hit them when I reveal my surprise."

"Be careful. Don't get overconfident!"

"I'll be careful alright. Careful to rip their guts out and let them have a look at them before they die."

"Be careful, darling! Keep your mind on your goal. Your life depends on it, and all my hopes."

THIRTY-SEVEN

A CAPTIVE AGAIN

When at last I emerged from inside the cave inside my mind I was lying inside one of the Morifati boats. They were taking me back upriver.

To say I was sore was an understatement. The blood had dried on my wounds. I lay where I had been dumped in the bottom of the boat. The state my body was left in while I was in these trances must be something akin to sleep. I was sore and my muscles cramped the way they would, as if I had slept a long while in an uncomfortable position on an uncomfortable surface, which was, I guess, the circumstance I found myself in. Then on top of that they had lashed me until I was bleeding freely, but now the blood had dried. My muscles were cramping from dehydration.

Nothing is worse than a cramp in your hip except a cramp in your hip and a cramp in your calf at the same time. Then again, a cramp in both legs and both calves is excruciating, especially when trying to move and relax your muscles just increases the pain even more.

All I could do was yell in agony. I didn't care whether they liked it or not.

"Water! Give me water!"

"Quiet! Shut up you Freeman dog!"

Then I felt a kick on my backside. That didn't stop me from yelling and demanding water. Never at any time did I beg. I knew water was the only thing that would relieve the pain, or a little vinegar, but I would never let the Morifati hear me beg for it.

Finally, a voice barked out a command. They lowered a bucket over the side. They splashed a bucket of water on me and laughed. Then they yanked me upright and held a cup to my lips. I drank deeply. Fresh water straight out of the Great River. Water never tasted so good.

"I want this one kept alive for sacrifice to Than! King John has commanded it!"

I drank as much as they would let me have, then I demanded more. They kept giving it to me; I guess to follow their Captain's orders. It didn't really help. I felt gripped by intense pain in both hips as cramps set in again. I yelled. I couldn't help it.

"Give him salt! I want him alive to be brought to King John!"

I waited just long enough for them to press some salt into my mouth and wash it down with some more river water. Then I gave in to the pain and rolled over on my side. I went deep into the mountain again. They might do things to me while I was out, but I didn't care. I was beyond caring.

I found the peace and the relief from the pain I was seeking deep inside the mountain next to the lake. I thought maybe I should just wade out into the lake and swim in it. Was it shallow enough that I could lie down in it?

I walked out into the lake and found it to be too deep to lie in, so I swam out. Then I just let myself sink. To my surprise, I did not need to breathe. It was, after all, a lake, deep inside a mountain that existed only inside my own mind. I wasn't anywhere at all, except down deep within my unconscious.

Curiously, it felt cool. It was relaxing and comfortable to just float, like I was lying in a big, comfortable bed. I didn't want to go anywhere. I felt like a baby again swaddled in a crib. I fell into a deep sleep.

\#

When I woke up this time, it was night. I was no longer in the boat. I was lying on the sand. Somehow I had healed myself or the water had helped because I was no longer cramping. I twisted myself a little and sat up. I looked around.

We were back to the island where Diana and I had camped. That was not a promising turn of events. I had made no effort to cover our tracks there. I left the campsite and the firepit as it was. There was discarded Morifati equipment lying around when we left, taken from the boat the snakes attacked.

Had they found it yet? If they did, they would know where it was from and have some idea of how it got there. Still, their orders were to bring me back alive so I could be tortured and sacrificed. If they took revenge on me now, Blackheart John would be more than just a little angry. He would be furious. They would surely all take my place over the coals.

No one was watching me. That was curious. Then when I tried to stand I discovered they had tied a tether to me. I was not going anywhere.

I was starving. The stars were out in the night sky, shining brightly. My namesake constellation was up again, and clearly visible. Orion, the hunter. Yet here I was, trussed up like some captured game.

It turned out I should have been called Ursa Major; I mused. The temptation to transform into a Grizzly was strong, but it was too soon, way too soon. I needed to wait until I had them all together, Blackheart John, the High Priest, the Old Hag, and Anna. I needed them close enough to tear their throats out as they stared in shocked horror.

While I sat there thinking it over, a figure approached me. It was the Captain. He had a cold and angry expression on his face. He was gritting his teeth.

"You camped on this island before, didn't you? You and that little dove-witch."

There was no point in lying now, since I couldn't conceal information that they already knew, and knowing wouldn't do them any good. Any advantage they thought they had was an illusion now. I could tear their hearts out if I wanted.

"Yes. We camped here and fished. While you looked for us downstream."

"Clever. You think you are brilliant, don't you, Freeman? What happened to my men?"

"The Snakes attacked them."

"Then why are their weapons and fishing gear here? You killed them! That dove-witch used her magic!"

"Snake killed them. She sent her Snakes to kill them. All I did was salvage the boat."

"You stole! You're a liar! Where are their bodies?"

"I found their boat and towed it here. I took only what I needed and left the rest. I put heir bodies in the river and I scuttled the boat. I used their bait to fish for catfish. You should try fishing here, it's a delightful spot."

With that, the Captain grabbed me and stood me up.

"If not for my orders, I would barbeque you right here on this beach!"

Then he stood back and landed a roundhouse, open palm technique punch on my jaw. I was out cold then. I didn't go to my mountain cave. I slept a deep sleep, punctuated by nightmares.

#

The sunrise woke me up. I lay still, waiting for them to return. Now my jaw was sore along with everything else. My head ached as well. I wondered if the bastards would feed me or give me water before we got underway.

While I lay there, I noticed something flying overhead, a dark shape. A large raven landed in the trees above me. It was Raven.

She looked down at me, blinking. She appeared to be happy and amused, as she always did.

"So how are you this morning, Rion?"

"Not that great. Having thoughts of revenge."

"You look terrible. Have they mistreated you?"

"Thanks. They are behaving just as you'd expect for Morifati. If they weren't under orders to bring me back to their King, I would be breakfast now."

"This is the place where we camped, isn't it? Where you caught those delicious fish? And made love to your little dove?"

"That's right. And I dumped the dead Morifati in the river here and scuttled their boat. These Morifati know that now, and they are pissed."

"That's too bad, but don't worry. We Ravens will feed on their flesh before they feed on yours."

"Thanks for the vote of confidence. Snake is afraid I won't succeed. I've learned new powers, and we must not allow them to know that, or they will try to find a way to defeat me."

"Can you do nothing now?"

"No. I've got to let them feel confident now. I've got to appear helpless."

"That will be difficult, Rion. They suspect you. I have seen it. They are asking themselves why you would just give yourself up to be sacrificed. It seems crazy to them. No Morifati ever gives his life for another. All act out of greed or out of the belief that death overtakes us all. You are someone they cannot understand, cannot explain. You have been with Snake a long while now, long enough to learn from her. They know you are her ally. They are convinced the two of you have a strategy, a strategy they must find out from you."

"I'll never tell them that. When they find out, it will be too late. In the meantime I will have to endure much, but when the new moon comes, they will have to sacrifice me and launch their attack on my people. Be ready then with your Ravens. I can promise you a great battle with many Morifati dead."

"Think of something to tell them, something misleading. It won't be enough to just withdraw from them."

"But I can't allow them to see inside my mind. If they know what I can do now, if they see the powers that I now have, they will defeat me."

"You must find an explanation they will believe. If you don't. If you just curl up and go away and block them from entering your mind, they will know that something is wrong. They will know you are hiding the truth. They don't know about the History of the Psychics, but they know that Snake and the other Psychics have many powers and that powers can be taught and learned. You could have learned anything while you were with her, and you are her ally. They have no doubt of that."

What had I told them before? They had broken me down with all the potions and the Limerence Spell. I must have told them that Snake had sent me to them, but did I tell them exactly why? I don't think I knew exactly why myself. No one had told me anything other than that I would learn to see around the corner, and that I could stall them and keep them from crossing the Forbidden Land and entering the Free State.

Up until now, I would expect the Morifati to be as confused as I am about all this.

"All they really have now are their suspicions, Raven."

"But they know Snake is their mortal enemy, and now so are you!"

Then I heard voices from down the beach.

"Can you hear that, Raven?"

"They are coming, be quiet and still, lie back down."

I thought she might fly away, but she stayed where she was and watched. I guess she knew they couldn't see her from anywhere but directly below, and if she flew now, they would see her flying away.

There were three of them this time, the Captain and two men. They cut me free of the stake they had tethered me to and yanked me to my feet.

"Who were you talking to?"

"No one. There is no one here with me."

Then Raven did something I did not expect. She released a dropping right on top of the Captain's head. The Captain of the Morifati looked up then, but it was too late, Raven was flying away.

"What did you say to her? What message did she bring you from the Snake-witch?"

"I don't know what you are talking about. Birds can't speak."

I got one right in the gut then. It blew out all my air. All I could do was gasp for breath.

"Get a blindfold for this smartass. Better yet, let's black bag him."

They produced a bag and put it over my head. Everything went dark. They tied it too tight at first.

"Don't kill him, you fool. I want to see him roasted alive. I am going to ask King John for a piece of your liver as reward for bringing you back."

They started dragging me off down the beach. Then they made me walk on my own with the bag over my head, goading me along with their hands and pulling me with the tether.

"Don't think that you can outsmart us, Freeman."

"Captain, what if he can speak to that vulture with his mind?"

"You're right! We should have thought of that before!"

They yanked the bag off my head. One of them fetched a jug and held it to my lips.

"Drink! Drink or it will go worse for you!"

I tasted the drink from the jug. It was liquor! Smooth but very strong, some kind of whiskey. Morifati moonshine! I hoped that was all that was in it, alcohol. They had given me mind altering potions before.

I could tell this was potent stuff. Their intent was to confuse and disorient me. They knew they couldn't stop me from speaking with my mind, but they could make sure I had nothing sensible to say.

After just a couple of shots, they put the bag back over me. I could feel the liquor taking effect. They sat me down in the boat and left me to wait. I called out to Raven.

"Can you hear me?"

"Yes Rion, I can hear you."

"Will you follow me to their village?"

"That was my intention."

"Gather your Ravens together, and the Wolves, and my people. We will all attack on the day of the New Moon."

"Dorothea has already commanded it, Rion. Have no fear, take concern only for yourself. We are all counting on you to fulfill your fate."

THIRTY-EIGHT

RETURNED TO THE COURT OF BLACKHEART JOHN

I did not go back into my mountain cave on the way back. They ceased beating me or even talking to me, except to give me orders to move here or there, or to lie down or stand up.

On the day we left the island, I passed out from the liquor soon enough. I slept as soundly as I could in the bottom of their boat. When I woke up they poured more liquor into me, so for a day and a night and a day afterward they kept me drunk and disoriented.

When we got close to their village, they relented and began feeding me again. Feeding me quite a lot, mostly fish, but still everything they had. They liked to fatten up a sacrifice. That was their custom.

I wasn't allowed to see what we were doing or where we were going. They literally kept me in the dark with that bag over my head. I guess it terrified them that I might contact Raven or Snake or Diana or even someone else. The Morifati were a distrustful, paranoid bunch, suspicious of everything and everybody, including each other, which told me you couldn't trust them at all.

I could see now why the Psychics couldn't bear their presence. Especially the highly empathic Psychics like Dorothea, the inside of a Morifati's mind was a nightmare of greed, lust, treachery, and deceit. I was sick of them myself.

The worst thing was there was no way to reach them. They were too far gone. At first I hoped I could reach them. I hoped I could reach them through kindness and compassion. I could see now that nothing could change their hearts, they were wholly given over to evil.

When we arrived at their dock, they snatched the black bag off my head. It was broad daylight then, and the sun hurt my eyes. I had a little trouble adjusting to the sunlight after not being exposed to it for that long.

"Are you there Raven?"

"Look up."

I shaded my eyes with my hands which were tied, and looked. There she was, soaring high up. I got a slap on the back of the head for that.

"He is trying to contact that vulture Captain."

"Keep your eyes downcast, Freeman. Those birds can't help you now. They dare not attack here. No one will come to help you."

"I don't need help."

That was greeted with guffaws of laugher. They thought it was the funniest thing they ever heard.

"Don't need help? You'll be screaming for all those witches by the time we are through with you. But no one will come. They can't come, their magic is not strong enough."

I wanted to answer that, but I knew I would show my hand. Wait, just wait. Let them feel confident. Let them get the bonfire ready and spread the coals. I was going to enjoy this after everything I had been through.

#

They took me to the gate where a throng of Morifati had poured outside to jeer at me. They made a path for us, our triumphal victory parade. The escaped captive returned to be sacrificed.

They all had their war paint on, just as I described it earlier. It made me feel deja vu a little, but things were different now. Before I was helpless and did not know how to escape. Now I knew exactly what to do. It was just a matter of timing.

A boy threw a mud clod at me. That angered the Captain when some of it splattered on him. He started yelling at the crowd not to throw things and to stay in their places. The crowd grabbed the culprit and sent him to the back.

It seemed they still wanted me alive and intact for the sacrifice at the New Moon. No lynchings here, just deliberate ritual torture. That was the Morifati way.

The crowd hemmed us in all the way to Blackheart John's longhouse where he held his court. It appeared as sinister as it had before, with its black paint and its red trim. A large guard of warriors flanked its entrance. They had determined not to let me get away this time.

We entered the longhouse where a guard and spectators assembled on both sides, almost like a wedding ceremony. At the far end sat King Blackheart John on his throne with Anna sitting on his right and the Old Hag sitting on his left. The two maidens stood in attendance next to Anna, and the High Priest stood next to the Old Hag.

They brought me to them with my hands bound in front of me and a tether tied to my neck. The Captain held my lead. The company dragged me toward the throne and then threw me down on my face before the raised platform where they all sat.

"Here he is, my King! The coward turned himself over to us!"

"It's a trick, Majesty! This fool has something planned! Or the Snake-witch does, and she has sent him here!" said the High Priest.

"Is that true? Have you and the Snake-witch been plotting against us? You ran away from us last time and ran straight to her. Who are you and what are you after here? I can tell you right now you will fail.", said Blackheart John.

The Captain yanked on my tether to make me sit up. I tried to stand, and he shoved me back down to my knees. I would have to kneel in front of Blackheart John.

So I knelt there and said not a word in reply. I just stared at him.

"He is insolent, Majesty! He dares to remain defiant! He must be executed at once!"

They all shouted accusations at me then. Just a bunch of nonsense and hysteria. I wondered if they were sane at all.

"Silence! All of you! I will question the prisoner! You will only speak when spoken to!"

Blackheart John was getting angry with everyone, not just with me. Something was going on, and he did not understand what it was. That was not a situation he liked to be in, he liked to be in control all the time; he preferred to fight from a position of strength. He hated and feared uncertainty.

Anna leaned over and whispered in his ear. He acted angry at what she said, but then became thoughtful. He looked at me again.

"Will you not answer me? Will you not speak for yourself?"

"I have nothing to explain."

He snorted at that.

"You truly are an arrogant son of a bitch. You have no notion who you are speaking to. I could have granted you a rich life with a share in our conquests. Money, women, anything you could desire. You could have become one of us."

"I'd sooner die first."

"You will! We can easily grant that request. In fact, I am counting on it now. You have earned the slowest death that we normally provide, according to our customs. I will sacrifice you to Than. Tomorrow night at the New Moon festival, you will slowly roast over the coals. You will not receive the mercy granted to the Northman, a slit throat to hasten your death. No, we will roast you properly, slowly, to keep in all the juices and flavors. I will personally carve up your liver and present slices of it to our greatest warriors."

"I have no fear of what you can do!"

"Really? You want it the hard way, don't you? Well, that is how you are going to get it."

"Is this supposed to make me afraid? Am I supposed to make some sort of confession now? Beg for mercy?"

The temptation to transform into a Grizzly was almost too great to resist. I knew it was not the time, though. I wanted them to see me survive the fire. If they could see me hanging over the coals without burning, without cooking, with no pain or fear. That I knew would inspire more fear and confusion in them than anything else I could do. They were always claiming that they did not fear death, but I had seen inside their minds. Deep inside, they had more fear of death because they had no hope. They had convinced themselves that this life was all there was, and for them, that was true.

"Get this Freeman dog out of my sight. Interrogate him, whip him until he pisses himself."

"Majesty, shall I interrogate him?", said the High Preist.

"No. I have something else in mind for him. You had your chance. Soon it will not matter what he knows or what he says."

"Please Majesty, I would like to revenge myself upon him for the theft of the amulet."

"Without the amulet, I'm afraid your powers will not be enough. I want to give Anna some time alone with him."

"As you wish, Majesty. You will permit me to perform the sacrifice to Than as usual?"

"Of course! That is your duty. I just think some feminine power is in order for this one, he seems susceptible."

#

They left me alone in a large empty room, hanging from a chain attached to a rafter. I wondered what would happen next, so I looked ahead. Anna and the two maidens were walking toward me, along with the Old Hag. They were carrying jars of something and other tools, including bull whips.

I waited for them. Presently they entered and, without saying a word to me, they walked past me and set everything on a table behind me. The Old Hag came around in front of me and stared at me intently. Anna joined her. They had expressions of curiosity on their faces, but there was no love or friendship there.

"The Limerence Spell has been lifted.", said the Old Hag.

"Yes. It's the work of that Snake-witch, no doubt."

"Is she your lover now? Have you been unfaithful to me?"

I had to think that one over. The logic was so convoluted. It was clearly an attempt to regain control of my mind. Should I say anything? It might be better not to speak to them at all. There was nothing to be gained by arguing, and volunteering information, no matter how innocent it might seem, would be foolish. Why tell them anything? The less they knew, the better it was for me.

I looked ahead. The best course of action was indifference. Complete indifference to anything they said to me or did to me. And I dared not drink anything they offered me.

"I have nothing to say."

"What! You will tell us all! We know you went with the Dove-witch to the Snake-witch! What are you planning? Do you dare to defy me?"

"A King does not have to explain himself."

They screamed with laughter at that. I remained completely calm and indifferent, like I couldn't care at all what they did. When they stopped laughing, their faces turned hard.

"There is no King but John! You Freemen have no King! Just a bunch of old men who sit around and do nothing. Elders, I think you call them. Isn't that right Cluthera?"

That was the first time anyone spoke the Old Hag's name. It was either a slip up, or Anna just didn't think I could gain anything by knowing. Cluthera grinned at me with sheer malice.

"No, they have women on their council too, but they all behave like Grandmothers if you understand my meaning. They hide from us. They avoid us. They know what we can do and they fear us. This one was sent here to spy on us. He is no King, just an errand boy."

"But how does he know the Snake-witch? Why did she send him back to us? What does she know about him? What can she have planned?"

"She can appear to men in their dreams. The Snake-witch has that power. She has many powers but she cannot defeat us and she knows this. This one is dangerous. He can 'see around the corner'. That's how he escaped before. And he stole the Amulet. The Snake-witch has it now. She can use it to see into minds. She may even be able to control others with it. We have been trying to master it but the High Priest can only see into minds. He does not know the other powers of the Amulet."

Cluthera turned to me then.

"You have heard everything, Rion of the Free State. What has that witch done with the Amulet? What does she expect from you? Why are you here?"

She stared at me intently then. She had not entered my mind before, not without a potion first. What was she trying to do now? I entered her mind.

They were planning to get the information out of me any way they could. First with physical force, then with a potion. They would create another Limerence Spell if they could, but they were running out of time. The New Moon feast was the next day. If they could not get me to talk, it was time to get it over with and sacrifice me to Than whether or not they learned anything. They would take their chances.

They felt confident they could defeat the Wolves and the Free State. They believed that Snake and the Snakes and her Ravens could not attack them directly and succeed, but they weren't sure they could attack her. It had never worked in the past. She had always outsmarted them.

Each time they attacked her castle, they found it empty. They could not find her, they could not kill her, and they could not burn it down. Nothing in the castle would burn. The Ravens harassed them constantly, and the Snakes attacked at night and struck stealthily at all hours of the day. They always lost men without gaining anything until they had to withdraw.

What they really wanted was a way to get to Dorothea. A way to find her, or a way to draw her out and kill her. They were really hoping that she would come and try to rescue me. Or that they could learn something from me they could use, or perhaps even turn me against her.

I could feel Cluthera's despair at the loss of the Limerence Spell. She had really hoped I would love Anna enough to kill Dorothea.

"You did not do as we asked.", said the Old Hag

"It's obvious to me now, Rion, that you no longer love me. You have betrayed me with the Snake-witch and the Dove-witch, too. You are a traitor and a deceiver.", said Anna.

She nodded her head to the two maidens standing behind me. I felt the bullwhip before I heard it crack. The two maidens were taking turns whipping me. It was painful, but not un-bearable. Anna and the Old Hag watched me with unconcealed amusement. They thought they had me in an inescapable situation.

They could keep this up as long as they liked, and I would not talk to them, so I checked out and went deep inside the mountain again.

THIRTY-NINE

PREPARED FOR SACRIFICE

The problem with withdrawing into my mountain cave was always how to pass the time. It was sometimes boring poking around in there. I learned nothing about the inner workings of my mind. I could only escape suffering in the real world, and only for a short time, really. The drawback was that they could do anything to me while I was there and I would neither know it nor feel it. I needed a way to look out.

I had been wandering around in the cave when I decided to take a swim in the lake. It was a funny sort of lake, one I couldn't drown in. I could fall asleep in it as I had done before. I found I could create features in the lake and the cave just by imagining them or wishing for them. The whole thing was, of course, a creation inside my mind. Where was I, after all?

As I contemplated all these things I came to a small island in the lake, just a flat rock sticking up, but big enough to pace back and forth on or lie down and rest. I sat and wondered how I should go about finding out what they were doing to me and whether to revive myself, when I noticed Snake swimming toward me.

"So how are things going now, Rion?"

She had swum up and slithered upon the rock and lay curled in front of me.

"They were whipping me when I checked out."

"I guess they are still mad at you?"

"I'll say! They think that you and I are plotting against them but they don't know what exactly. All they have are vague suspicions right now. They don't know about my powers."

"You can't pull this trick for too long at a time. You will have to come to, eventually."

"I need to look out. Is there a way to watch them without feeling anything?"

"There is. Look in the water."

I walked over to the edge of the rock and looked into the pool. There, like a reflection on the water's surface but more like a vision, I could see myself being whipped by the two maidens while Anna and Cluthera watched.

It didn't seem to bother them that I wasn't conscious. Cluthera gestured to the girls to stop, and she and Anna went over to examine me. They could see that I wasn't responsive. Anna tried to give me something to drink. I guess the Limerence Potion. But it just dribbled out of my mouth.

To my surprise, they all just turned and left me hanging there.

"Looks like they have gone now. That's a neat trick. I wish I had known that one before. Why didn't you teach it to me?"

"It's really better if you learn things on your own. I can't teach you everything."

"How am I going to do that without the book?"

"Use your imagination. Experiment!"

"I'm going to have to tell them something. I need to tell them something to throw them off."

"Then think of something."

277

"Like what?"

"Anything but the truth. I must go."

And with that, she slid back into the water and swam away. I looked at myself hanging from my bonds in the room where they left me bleeding from my wounds. This was going to hurt. I would be sore. I knew what to tell them now, though.

I was right; it hurt. I felt sore and my muscles ached and my open wounds stung. Just what you might expect from being bullwhiped. It was easier to tolerate this way though, psychologically. There wasn't any of that wondering when it would all be over, and fearing that maybe it would never end.

Still, I was tiring of this. Tired of the Morifati, tired of enduring their tortures and threats and insults. Looking inside their minds was disgusting. It was hard not to hate them. I wondered if there was ever any point in feeling any kind of compassion for them. Grandfather had taught me to 'Love my enemies' though, so I had been trying to see some humanity in them.

I could not find any. There was none left. After three hundred years of living this way and believing what they believed, I don't think they had any humanity left. I never saw a spark of compassion in them. In fact, they enjoyed themselves. They enjoyed having power over another human being, enjoyed the thought of taking whatever they wanted wherever they found it.

The Morifati had so long been victorious in the past they could no longer conceive of losing. That's why they had hatched this plan of going on a raid around the world. Everyone had withdrawn from them. The Northmen had gone as far North as possible. We had hidden ourselves on the other side of the Forbidden Land. The Wolves and Snakes and Ravens all withdrew from them.

The Morifati were predators, merciless human predators. It was their way of life and their religion. All they knew, all they could conceive of, was preying upon other human beings. They did not create; they stole.

They left me hanging there for a good long while. The bonds on my wrists cut into me. It was going to be tough to endure. I wished for the sacrifice to begin. I was ready to get things over with.

I was actually glad to see them when they came back in carrying jars of ointment. The two maidens started rubbing the ointment into my skin and my wounds. It didn't help that much. I kind of got the idea they were basting me.

Anna and Cluthera stood in front of me, staring intently. They were so intent I knew they were trying to read me. I didn't let them in my head. I had learned how to keep them out.

"What did you do during the punishment Rion?", said Anna.

"I passed out from the pain."

"Liar! You used some kind of Psychic magic!"

"The Snake-witch has taught him to resist interrogation!" said Cluthera.

"Are you a Psychic? What else do you know?", said Anna.

"I am just an ordinary Freeman."

"Why did you come here?"

"Snake contacted my people. She warned us that the Morifati were about to attack. They sent here me as a scout. Only as a scout."

"Why did you give yourself up to us so easily?"

"I had to. I had no choice. Your High Priest saw me spying on your men. They surrounded me. I had to take the chance that I might escape later."

"Then why did you come back?"

"He lies. He can see around the corner and he can block our mind probes and he can resist torture by going somewhere else in his mind. Those are all ancient techniques of the Psychics!" said Cluthera.

"What can we do then?", said Anna.

"We must inform King John and Murdock the High Priest. They will know what to do. We are wasting our time on this one. His fate is sealed now."

So they left me hanging again.

#

A guard came and surrounded me. They put a tether around my neck and cut my wrist free from the supporting beam. I collapsed from my own weight.

"Get up!" the Captain barked.

"Pick him up! Drag him if you must!"

"On your feet!" said some Warrior next to me.

Two Warriors grabbed me under the arms on both sides and stood me up. When they felt my legs steady, they rushed forward with me, which of course made me stumble. They held me up, though. They didn't let me fall, and they would not let me get away.

They walked and dragged me back to Blackheart John's throne room. Everyone was assembled as before. The guards brought me before Blackheart John, but instead of making me kneel, they stood me up and held me upright.

"So you admit to being a spy for the Snake-witch, huh?"

I remained silent. I knew they would twist my words no matter what I said at this point. I was ready for them to throw me into the fire, ready to reveal myself. Why not get it over with? They clearly loved these little theatrics. I could transform into a Grizzly right now, I thought. I wanted to see the look of surprise on their faces.

"Answer!", screamed Cluthera.

"Confess! Tell his Majesty what you told us!", said Anna.

I just stared at them defiantly and said nothing more.

"We need do nothing more, your Majesty. Let us prepare him for sacrifice.", said the High Priest.

"Agreed. You will make the preparations we agreed upon, since the Snake-witch has taught this one powers?"

"Yes, we must take precautions. We cannot perform the usual ceremony. The risk is too great."

"Freeman! Look at me! Stand him up straight so he can face me!" said Blackheart John.

The guards obeyed and stood me up, almost on tiptoe. I stared into his eyes, but remained silent. Something told me I should 'see around the corner'. I knew they had something extra planned, but I didn't know what.

Then I saw it! The Captain was walking up behind me with a sap in his hands! I could see him approach and knock me out cold while Blackheart John distracted me. I could not let this happen! If I was unconscious, I would burn! I had to be conscious to resist the flames and transform into a Grizzly!

I had to stop them somehow. I had to get free. I struggled, but it was no use. In desperation I went inside my mind to transform into a Grizzly. Then the Captain knocked me out cold.

FORTY

SACRIFICED TO THAN

I was unconscious. The worst possible condition for me to be in. Psychic powers require conscious effort and concentration. At least the powers that I had learned did. This was what Dorothea warned me about. The possibility the Morifati would learn or would suspect what I could do and find a way to prevent me from doing anything.

This was the Achilles heel for any Psychic. To be unconscious, or to be in any way rendered insensible. The Morifati must have learned this trick long ago, which was one more reason why the Psychics were afraid to approach them. It was not just the terrible pain of being an Empath around their disgusting minds; it was the fact that they could trap and kill a Psychic.

Dorothea had been less than totally honest with me. I could see it now. Well, not now, but after I woke up and had a chance to sort things out. She was using me as a Cat's Paw. I was here to do something she could not do herself. She had told me that much, but she had not told me why. I would learn the hard way.

She wanted me to succeed, though. I knew she was counting on me. If she could help me she would, but I had to find my way through this on my own, or so I thought.

That's why I was surprised by what happened next. I dreamed. I dreamed about Diana. I could see her waiting for me in her tower room. She could not see out. The windows had been barred and covered, so she could neither see out nor fly away.

I could see her clearly, vividly. The room was filled with the light that she radiated. It was a comfortable room, well furnished, but still a golden cage for my little dove. Then she spoke.

"Rion, can you hear me?"

"Where are you Diana? Where am I?"

"We are in a dream. We are sharing a dream together."

"How? How is this happening?"

"You have done this many times before with Dorothea. Do you not remember?"

"I know I have, but I remember nothing about it. What has happened to me?"

"The Morifati knocked you out so they can sacrifice you to Than. Don't you remember that?"

"I don't remember anything. As far as I know I have always been here."

"Can you feel anything?"

"I'm...., happy. I'm happy to see you!"

"Do you remember anything about me?"

"We love each other. We grew up together. You are a prisoner somewhere."

"Rion. You have got to wake up!"

"How can I do that?"

"Will it! Say, I am going to wake up now!"

"I am going to wake up now!"

I could feel myself struggling against sleep then. Against the paralysis, my arms and legs were heavy. I wanted to roll over but couldn't.

"I feel like I am lying under something heavy."

"Keep trying! Wake up! You have to be awake to fight them! And one more thing! I cannot come to you physically, only like this. If you fall asleep again, I will come to you and wake you, if I can. It is better that you try to reach me in your dreams, if you can remember. That is all the help I can offer."

As I struggled, I felt pain and soreness in my muscles. Then the back of my head felt sore. I woke with a groan to find myself bound in a sheet from shoulders to ankles. They were determined that I would not move.

Diana had disappeared. All my aches and pains had come back. They had taken me back to my former prison, the little shack where they kept me before. I lay on the bed where I slept previously, but that was the only comfort I had.

Well, I was awake now. What would I do when they came for me? Could I play possum? Should I escape deep within my mind, back to the mountain cave? They seemed to understand what that was. I didn't think that was going to be safe.

The problem with going to Diana in a dream is I could not will myself to dream. My dreams occurred in the regular cycles as everyone else's dreams did. I did not know how to force it, especially not when I was unconscious.

I heard them opening the door, so I closed my eyes. Soft footsteps approached me. I looked into their minds. It was Anna and Cluthera. They were here to see if I was still unconscious and to make sure I remained unconscious. They had brought a vial of poison with them.

"Shake him.", Cluthera said.

Anna shook me roughly. I didn't respond.

"He can't still be out.", Anna said.

"Let me try.", said Cluthera.

A moment passed, then I felt a flame touch my toes. I yelled and jumped reflexively. I opened my eyes.

"Stop that! I am awake!"

"See! He is awake! Soon you will feel more pain than that King of the Freemen!" said Cluthera.

"We've got something for you. Something to make sure that you cannot escape or fight back.", said Anna.

They rolled me over on my left side.

"Do not struggle. If you make it difficult for us, we can just bring guards back to hold you or knock you out.", said Anna.

"It is better to let the potion work its spell. This way you might not feel any pain at all. If the guards knock you out, you might regain consciousness over the coals. Then you will know what it feels like to be roasted alive!" said Cluthera.

"What a pity. That's what he deserves!" said Anna.

"We don't dare trust this one. I know he has learned something else. He has powers he is hiding. Quickly! He may have some way to fight back."

Anna started pouring the potion into my right ear. She did it carefully to make sure none leaked out. It took effect right away. I felt that side of my head going numb.

"Careful, not too much. We want him to regain consciousness after it is too late, but we want him to be confused, powerless."

"There. Is that enough?"

"It should be."

I was going under. There was nothing left to do. I had to take the chance. I went deep inside the mountain cave, dove into the lake, and swam out to the rock.

#

Time passed. I watched myself through an image in the water as I had done before. They left me alone for a long time. What would happen if I reentered my body? Would I remain unconscious from the poison? Was there anything I could do now?

285

Could I protect myself from the fire remotely? Where was I, anyway? I had to still be in my body, even if my mind was here. Here was inside my mind, anyway. It had to be. My mind was not inside a mountain sitting on a rock in an underground lake. Whatever I am, whatever makes me Rion had to still be inside my body but living inside this perceived world created by my mind. It was the only chance I had.

I would have to use the fire resistance technique from here wherever here was and then transform myself into a Grizzly. Would I still be unconscious? They had given me enough poison for a man, but not enough for a Grizzly. It might work, it had to work, or I was cooked. I couldn't risk reentering my body now if it would render me unconscious.

How could I test it? If I could do anything, then I should be able to 'see around the corner' remotely. I tried that. I concentrated to see if I could see anyone come into the room. It worked! I could see two guards outside! They remained motionless though, it was not yet time. It had to be soon however because as I scanned around through their eyes I could see that the sun was setting.

I thought I ought to start. No sense wasting time, so I concentrated on the technique. It should work and it should last as long as I maintained my concentration. But how to know?

Soon after the sunset I could see Cluthera and Anna returning through the guards' eyes. They entered, and the guards entered with them. I returned to watching them through the pool. I had hoped that they would touch me with the candle flame again, but then I realized that was the last thing I wanted since they might notice that I was not burned.

They didn't bother with me though except to dump me unceremoniously on a stretcher and carry me out in a procession, with Anna in the lead, Cluthera following, and then me on the stretcher carried by the two guards.

Six Warriors joined the little procession in front and behind, each carrying torches. There was no light anywhere in the village except from those torches and the light from an enormous bonfire up ahead of us.

The glow from the bonfire and the torches of the entire village lay ahead of us. I looked ahead to see a large ceremonial space I had not been taken to before. So this was where they performed their ghastly sacrifices. It was a much more elaborate arrangement than I had seen with the Northman.

Here there was a large circle of totems arranged in a ring around a massive central totem made of stone. Stones lay linking each totem to the central one like the spokes of a wheel. It looked very much like the sky wheels we built in the Free State to observe the night sky, but oddly different. We did not carve grotesque figures and paint them in red and black and white.

No one stood inside the ring except the High Priest. They had built an enormous bonfire in front of the central totem, which I could see now was a graven image of their god Than. The god of death. They had painted his image black with red eyes and mouth. The totems were more elaborately painted. I guess they were meant to represent kings and priests and priestesses from the past.

The Morifati chanted and danced around the circle in a procession, just as I had seen them do before. They all had their war paint on. They screamed out war cries. Their women wailed and screamed.

"Than! Than! Than! Than! Than! Than!"

I could feel the tension building in the crowd as we approached. When we got near, they stopped circling and made a path for us. We entered the circle, and they brought me before the High Priest.

They brought a long pole out to barbeque me on. They had built the bonfire in a stone pit with rotisserie posts on each side. They placed the pole in a slot in front of the statue of Than, as it had been for the Northman.

They stood me up and tied me to the pole. There was a raised dais directly in front of the statue of Than, and the High Priest went and stood on top of that so he could address the crowd.

The High Priest held up his hands for the crowd to be silent. The Morifati stopped chanting.

"Than! Grant us victory!" the High Priest said.

"GRANT US VICTORY!" they answered in unison.

The High Priest turned and knelt on one knee in front of the statue of Than. He muttered some sort of incantation or prayer to himself. Then he stood, turned, and addressed the crowd again.

"You are all fated to die!" he said.

A great cheer and war cries rose from the crowd. They didn't stop until he raised his hands.

"That is why we are strong! We do not fear death! Death is our god! We know that Than rules over all men and decides the fate of all men! He owns your soul, you cannot escape from him! He made the strong to rule over the weak. We, the Morifati! We are the strong!"

Another great cheer rose from the crowd.

"Than is your god because death is your fate!"

"Than! Than! Than! Than! Than! Than!"

The High Priest of the Morifati held up his hands for silence.

"We are here to prepare to attack the Free State. They think they are free. They are not free! No one is free from Than! Death is the fate of all men. All men are fated to serve Than. No one can escape from Than! We have one of their own to sacrifice before we attack. He thought he could escape from us! Escape from Than! Escape from his fate!"

He paused to let that sink in.

"Has he escaped? Can anyone escape? Will the Free State escape from Than?"

He gestured for the crowd to respond.

"Than! Than! Than! Than! Than! Than! Than! Than! Than!"

Their chant ended in a war cry.

"Than is pleased when men do their own will. It is the will of Than that we live as we please, that we do what we please, that we take what we please. It is his will that the strong survive! It is his will that the weak perish! We, the Morifati, may do whatever is necessary to survive! No one will stand in our way and live!"

A team of Warriors rushed up then and took hold of the pole they had me spitted on, turned it over, placed me in the center, then hung me over the coals produced by the bonfire which had already been spread beforehand to roast me over. They danced wildly around the circle, chanting and screaming out war cries.

Not long after they lowered me over the coals, the sheet they had wrapped me in caught fire. It blazed, I blazed like a torch for a while, but my body did not burn. The technique was working. The Morifati got agitated. They could see I was not cooking. That was something they did not expect and could not understand.

I was going to have to transform into a Grizzly now. I concentrated. It worked. I burst through my bonds and broke the pole they were trying to barbeque me on. I just lay there on the coals, though, not burning, but not moving, either.

Could I make myself stand up? I tried hard; it took great effort but the big bear my body had become stood on its hind legs. Was the poison nullified now? It had to be if my Grizzly body could move around. I could not be one hundred percent certain, but I had to take the chance.

I reentered my body. There I stood in the middle of the coals. The Morifati were in a frenzy now. I 'saw around the corner' quickly. Some of them threw spears at me, but I dodged out of the way, knowing where they were coming from and where they would go.

Raven called out to me. "Rion! Is it time to attack?"

"Prepare to attack, but wait for my signal. I want to speak to them one last time."

I knew it was a big chance to take, but I wanted to return to human form and appeal to them one last time. There was about to be a great battle. In any battle, even in a just cause, good men die and women and children are often killed, and I wanted to avoid that if I could. We men of the Free State do not believe in killing and bloodshed for its own sake or in a war for conquest. We do not steal or pillage.

I looked deep within myself to see if I could still feel the effects of the poison. I could not, so I transformed back into a man. I stood in the middle of the coals. I turned and walked over to address Blackheart John.

"King John! Hear me! Tell your Warriors to hold their fire!"

"Who are you? How dare you order me around! That snake -witch has taught you some black magic, I see. It will not save you. It will not save you from us!"

"Listen to me! We have assembled a great army! The Freemen, the Wolves, the Snakes, the Ravens, and the Northmen are all waiting for my signal to attack. If you do not surrender now, all will perish inside this village. Every Morifati man, woman, and child will die. Your race will cease to exist! Turn away from death! Turn away from Than and live! You can live in peace with all the surrounding tribes if you will it! Choose life not Death!"

"You fool! I do not fear you! We do not fear you! We do not fear Death! Death is Than and Than is the god of death. We do not fear him or his will, we obey it! We obey the will of Than! You will know the horror of being defeated in battle by us today! I will eat your liver yet!"

The High Priest spoke up then.

"That is why we are strong! We do not fear death! Death is our god! We know that Than rules over all men and decides the fate of all men! He owns your soul, you cannot escape from him! He made the strong to rule over the weak. We, the Morifati! We are the strong!"

The Morifati went wild then, running around preparing for an attack. A guard remained behind, ready to attack me. It was time now. There was nothing left to say. There was no appeal I could make.

"Start the attack now Raven!"

"We will! We will defeat them at last!"

I transformed myself into a Grizzly and stood in the fire towering over them. Blackheart John's court had remained behind. Every one in it, Anna, the High Priest, and Cluthera. I looked ahead to see how to make my attack.

When I could see how they would attack me, I rushed forward to deal Blackheart John a death blow. That would have worked, but I forgot about his ability to jump. Just as I swiped at him with my paw, a blow that would tear anyone apart, he jumped away, out of sight.

I turned aside to the High Priest. He just stood there, frozen. One stroke with my paw left him wide open and bleeding to death. I picked him up and threw him on the coals. Let him die the way so many others had died.

Cluthera and Anna turned to run, but I was quicker. I was on them in an instant. I threw Cluthera into the fire as she screamed curses. I turned to Anna next. She had frozen to the spot, trying desperately to work some kind of spell. I leaned in and tore out her throat with my jaws. Her head nearly came off.

I threw her remains onto the coals as well and spat her throat out.

Blackheart John's guard tried to circle in on me, so I dove into them, slashing with one paw and then the next. A Grizzly is faster than any man and I could 'see around the corner' so I cut my way through them before they had time to react properly.

I had to get to the gate to open it so the allies could get inside before the Morifati could organize a counterattack. The Ravens began swirling around overhead. They dove in to pick up branches from the bonfire and carry them over the Morifati village and drop them on the rooftops. Some of them brought branches of their own and lit them in the coals. They were going to set the entire village on fire!

"Raven! What are you doing?"

"We are going to burn the whole village down! Get out! Get out now and join your people! They are waiting for you to lead them!"

I looked ahead to find my way out. Before I had found a way that avoided the Morifati, this time I planned to fight my way through them and break the gate open from the inside.

I found the gate and troop of Warriors guarding it. I dove into them, avoiding their spears and arrows and slashing left and right with my paws. I was large enough in this form simply to walk over many of them. Despite their bold claims about death and fear, many of them danced back out of the way and others fled. They were used to fighting weaker opponents and believed themselves to always be the strongest, always the victors. They did not know how to attack a stronger opponent.

Soon I found myself at the gate where I lifted the bar, swung it around and threw it at them, knocking many down in the process. I burst through the gate, then shoving with all my strength against the left door. I tore it right off its hinges. I turned back and did the same to the right.

I attacked some Morifati who had been foolish enough to follow me out. I made quick work of them and then looked around. Morifati bodies were strewn everywhere. I guess I killed as many as a hundred Warriors in that melee. The combination of a Grizzly's quickness and strength, my enormous size even for a Grizzly, and my ability to 'see around the corner' had transformed me into a deadly monster. The Morifati had not expected this and neither had I.

It was time to find my people! I ran across the field to where I thought they might be.

FORTY-ONE

ALLIES UNITED

When I drew close to their camp, they all drew back in fear. There were Wolves there, and Freemen, and Snakes, who Dorothea transformed into human form to swell our ranks. They saw me come running toward them in the form of an enormous Grizzly and were terrified.

I saw them draw back to encircle me and draw out their weapons, so I called out to them in my mind.

"Do not be afraid! It is I! Rion of the Free State! I have come here to lead you!"

Then Wolf called to me.

"Rion! What has become of you? Have you transformed into a bear?", and then to the army he said.

"Stand down! Put away your weapons! This is our leader! He will be our General and our King! This is Rion of the Free State!"

"Do not be afraid. I will reveal myself to you." I said.

So there, in front of the crowd that had assembled around me, I transformed back into human form. Now, I stood before them as a man. I stood before them as their King. Everyone spontaneously took a knee.

"Rise! Build a bonfire at once! Where are the Ravens?"

"They've gone to attack the Morifati village.", said Wolf.

"We need to gather up as many branches as we can so the Ravens can light them and drop them on the rooftops of the village."

The men dispersed at once to gather up wood and tinder and branches for the ravens to carry.

"Raven! Bring your Ravens back here! We are building a fire for you to light your torches in."

The men improvised and built several small fires quickly. The place lit up by the glow from the fires. I could see that there were many more men than I could see at first. The Ravens circled overhead, silhouetted against the night sky. I could see no Northmen.

"Where are the Northmen? Aren't they coming?"

"They have sent word that they are on their way to us, but I don't know how far away they are."

I looked ahead, and I couldn't see anything, so they were not close in time. I needed every man I could get. The Morifati were going to come pouring out of their village in a rage after we set it on fire. We needed to surround the village so none could escape.

"Raven? Can you spare a few scouts to go look for the Northmen and hurry them up?"

"I have already done so."

"Really? I need some scouts to be my eyes in the sky and make sure the Morifati don't escape from some other gate or a hole in the wall."

"I have done that as well."

"Don't you wait for orders?"

"I can see what you are going to do before you do it. I can hear what you are going to say before you say it."

I had forgotten again about their ability to "see around the corner". It was even better than mine. It was impossible to sur-

295

prise her, that's why she hopped around smiling like she knew a secret all the time.

"And now you, Wolf! How are you, my old friend?"

He stopped holding back then and rushed forward to rub himself against me, and his pack joined in. He stood up, put his paws on my shoulders, and licked my face. That was their custom, so I put up with it. It felt good to see him again after everything I had been through.

"To answer your question, I have learned to transform into a Grizzly. Snake has a book she let me study that reveals many secrets. I can also withstand fire and endure torture without breaking. And I learned to 'see around the corner', Diana taught me that."

"We heard you escaped to Snake's domain from the Ravens. They bring messages to us from Snake. They gathered everyone together here. We knew you would appear to us, but we didn't know how."

"Hail King Rion!", said Lara.

"So you've come too?"

"We have all come. All the Wolves of the Forbidden Land. We even brought our pups! But where is your mate? Where is Diana?"

"She is being held captive by Snake."

"Snake is your enemy? How can that be?"

"No, Snake is my ally, but there is a rivalry between them. Snake wants me for herself and she didn't trust me to come back here on my own."

"I see. A competition over you. I had to fight off many contenders to claim my mate."

"Enough of that Lara, we have a battle to fight.", said Wolf.

It was then that Raven spoke up.

"Rion, I must go. We need to keep dropping fire on their rooftops until everything in the Morifati village is on fire. They will try to stop us, but when they see that they can't, that is too late to save their village, they will come pouring out of that gate. Be ready! Get your men ready!"

"Go then! Keep watching them from the skies! Call out to me before they attack!"

She flew off toward the village, which was burning by then. I turned to Wolf.

"How many men do I have here now? And Wolves?"

"There are at least three thousand Snakes, a great force. They fight well, but they cannot think for themselves. Snake is directing them from her castle. Every available man from the Free State is here."

"And Grandfather? The elders?"

"They are in the rear. They told the men to follow your orders."

"How large a force are they?"

"Several hundred men, from your village and the others."

"Who is in charge of them?"

"You are!"

"No! Who brought them here? Their Captain?"

"Your Grandfather of course."

"Summon him for me. Have him brought here. We need a plan of attack. Have you been in contact with Snake?"

Wolf turned and sent three of his Wolves to find Grandfather. Then he turned to me.

"She has not spoken to me. She is directing those Snakes remotely. Using the Ravens as her eyes."

"I need to contact her. Let her know what the battle plan will be. Is there a place nearby where I can sit quietly?"

We were near the edge of the field the Morifati had planted. A forest began there which stretched toward the Great River, with only a few gaps where meadows could be found. I saw a big oak I could lie back against.

"I need to lie here undisturbed for a little while, Wolf. I and going to contact Snake. I will appear to be unconscious."

"I will stand watch and be ready. I would contact her for you, but I don't know how. She only contacts me when she wills to do so."

So I leaned back and got comfortable. I went back inside the mountain cave. I dove into the lake and swam out to the rock.

#

I watched myself through the pool again, then I pulled back until I was high overhead. Until I could see everything in relation to everything else. I could see where all the men where, I could see the Morifati village burning. It was not completely out of control yet, but it was getting there. I could see the Ravens flying around, busying themselves with feeding the fire.

Dorothea appeared behind me, startling me.

"We need to talk. I want to plan this battle."

"You don't have too much time for a plan. You must take action now!"

"I didn't want a massacre Dorothea."

"You've got one whether or not you wanted one."

"But to kill women and children, to kill everyone in the village. Is there no other way? Can they not be made to see?"

"They have darkened their minds with their obsession with death, with greed and stupidity. They corrupt their children from birth onward. They do unspeakable things to them. They have bred evil into them. It is part of their nature now."

"I wish there was another way. Is there no Psychic Power that could enlighten them?"

"No. None. Nothing they would respond to, and besides, do you not know what they have done to the Northmen? To the women and children of the Northmen?"

"I had not thought of it. I can imagine now that I have seen their ways firsthand."

"Imagine what they plan to do to the women and children of the Free State."

She had me there. There was no sense in pursuing it any longer.

"Ok. I see. We still need a battle plan. I need some way to control your Snakes."

"That's not possible. I alone can control them. Just tell me what you want them to do."

"I want them to attack first. When the Morifati come pouring out of the gate, they will try to overwhelm us. I want to send in the Snakes first to block their exit. I will hold the Freemen and the Wolves in reserve and they will attack if the Snakes' line breaks."

"What about the Northmen?"

"They are not here yet. I want them to attack the flanks of the Morifati as they advance on the Snakes. Send word to them through the Ravens. Tell them to hurry."

"That's a good plan, but you have forgotten something. Blackheart John is still alive, and he is looking for you. What you did has filled him with murderous rage. You must duel with him personally. You are the only one who can anticipate his moves. He will take many by surprise and kill them before you can find him."

"You are right. He doesn't stand much chance against a Grizzly with the Sight."

"You must fight him as a man. Hand to hand. He will not approach you in your Grizzly form. He is too clever for that."

#

When I came out of it, Wolf was lying there watching me. A man stood a few feet away, quietly waiting. It was Grandfather!

"Grandfather! Come here!"

"What did Snake say?", said Wolf.

"We will talk about that, the three of us."

I got up and breathed deeply to shake the spell off of me and stretched. Grandfather came over and embraced me.

"My heart soars to see you again, Rion."

In spite of myself, I cried tears of joy. But how did he get here? I assumed that Grandfather and the Elders would all remain behind, that in fact all the elderly, and the young, and those who cared for them would remain behind in the village.

"I can't believe how good it is to see you, Grandfather. I have been on a great journey. I was held captive here, but I escaped to Snake's castle, I was held captive there, Diana is still her captive there, I returned here, Snake demanded it, I was held captive again and now we are preparing to raze the Morifati village."

"You cannot destroy evil Rion."

"What do you mean? Do you not approve?"

"You can destroy the Morifati, but you cannot remove evil from the world. There will still be evil men. There will still be evil Psychics. There will still be cruelty and indifference to suffering."

"What must we then do?"

"Whatever we can. Follow through on what you are doing here, but know that it is not the ultimate battle against evil, only the final battle against the Morifati."

"I feel great sorrow now, Grandfather. Even though I know we are on the threshold of a great victory, I feel sorrow for all the loss of life, for all the Morifati women and children who will die, and for all our people, the Wolves, the Snakes, and the Northmen who will die to achieve our victory."

"You are a good man, Rion. You have empathy, not just telepathy. You will become a great King. My heart's desire is to see you rule over all this world. Your Kingdom will not be gained through conquest, but by uniting the Psychics with all the Tribes and Nations."

"So there is nothing else to be done?"

"You did not create this situation, the Morifati did."

We both fell silent then. There was really nothing more to be said for now.

"Come on now Rion. We need to arm ourselves for the battle. We do not have much time. Soon the fire will be too great for them to fight and they will have to fight their way out."

He turned then, put his arm around me, and we walked to the place where the warriors of the Free State were waiting for us. Wolf followed us.

The first light of dawn was on the horizon before us. So was the glow of the fires from the Morifati village. The fire had grown to where the Morifati could not wait much longer. Soon the battle would begin.

FORTY-TWO

THE FINAL BATTLE

The army assembled on the plain next to the forest. The Snakes were all out in front of us in advance lines, facing toward the Morifati village. Without a word they advanced toward the gate of the village, which luckily for us was the only entrance or exit. The Snakes stopped when they were close enough to rush the gate.

The Ravens were keeping up their attack. Circling high over the Morifati village with branches in their talons, then diving down to feed the fire. The flames over the village had grown tall in places. The glow of the fire was bright enough to illuminate a small cloud which grew from the smoke that rose up. A light breeze blew as the heat from the fire sucked in air.

The men of the Free State had assembled in a ceremonial circle, with the Wolves joining them. Grandfather and I passed through the men until at last we stood at the edge of the circle. The men wore the war paint of the Freemen. Three colors, red, white and blue. Red and white stripes on their cheeks, blue on their foreheads with white stars. Arms and legs and every bare spot painted in unique ways to identify each man.

Grandfather already had his war paint on. Warriors came up quickly to paint my body and present me with weapons, a machete, and a bow and arrows. When I was ready, Grandfather turned to me.

"Rion. The time has come for us to sing our death song."

"Our death song? You are not preparing to die, are you? I will not allow it!"

"Do not interfere with a man when he sings his song. He alone knows what he faces. He must face the Great Spirit alone. If he has done well he will be received as a son."

"But I don't want you to die. I am not ready for you to die. I have seen a future for you in my dreams."

"Indeed, I will not die. You have seen correctly. As the eldest, it is my duty to lead the men in our death song, then they can sing a song of their own. Many will not survive this battle."

"Will I die in this battle?"

"You will die, but not today. Today you will lead our people, and the Northmen, and the Wolves, and Snakes, and Ravens to a glorious victory. Many years from now, after you have ruled over all the known peoples as a King, you will die. It is the fate of all men."

I started to speak again, but he motioned for me to remain silent and to remain where I was. We were gathered in a circle, and Grandfather walked out to the center. He lifted up his hands and turned around slowly to look over the men.

"Hear me! Warriors of the Free State! Are you with me?"

The men let out their war cries in unison.

"The Morifati believe in Death! Death is their God! They call their god Than and claim that none can escape him! Do we believe that?"

"No!"

"Our God is life! Our God is the Creator of all living things! The Creator of the universe and the stars! The Great Spirit!"

Grandfather paused, and the men were silent.

"The Great Spirit does not bring death. You are not fated to die! Your fate is to live forever with the Great Spirit. We are his sons! Our women are his daughters! The Great Spirit gives all beings life!"

The men called out their assent.

"We are going into battle soon. Some of you will die and go to live forever with the Great Spirit. The time has come to sing our death song."

Everyone sang.

"I am a child of the Great Spirit, I am a child of the Great Spirit, I am a child of the Great Spirit."

The men sang that way for some while, and then let out a war cry in unison.

After the song ended, Grandfather held up his hands for the men to become silent. Then Grandfather sang his own song.

"I am a son of the Great Spirit, I am a son of the Great Spirit, I am a son of the Great Spirit. Great Spirit, have mercy on your son. Great Spirit, have mercy on your son. Great Spirit, have mercy on your son. Show me your way, Show me your way, Show me your way."

When Grandfather had finished singing, he raised his hands again. Everyone fell completely silent. A glowing aura shone around him. He transformed into a red-tailed hawk. He flew above us all.

Grandfather circled and soared above us. The Ravens circled below him. To me he said, "Lead your people wisely, Rion. Bring them victory!"

"Grandfather, why did you not tell me that you were a Psychic?"

"The time had not yet come. There is too much for one man to know about this life, about this world we live in now, and about how to live in it for one man to take it in all at once. Be patient, do not resist the Great Spirit. Go wherever he sends you. Do not resist him but swim along with him as you would a swift stream."

#

A tall column of flame grew near the center of the Morifati village. The wind rose, the fire drew it in to feed its flames, which circled up to form a cloud of smoke in the shape of a mushroom.

Just when I thought no one could remain inside any longer, they burst forth from the gate. They poured out, screaming and raging. To my amazement, they sent out women and children first. I guess they thought it would give them a better chance to escape. The women were armed with machetes and bows, and some had infants strapped on their backs. Children of all ages, boys and girls, held machetes and bows.

The Snakes rushed forward then and quickly blocked off any path of escape. The Morifati would have to go through the Snakes to get out. The two armies rushed together, and a melee ensued.

The fighting was brutal, and many died on both sides. The Snakes had the advantage in size and strength. The Morifati could not break through their lines. Soon I could see what the purpose of the attack was to weaken the Snakes. Many of the Snakes lay dead by the time the Morifati warriors poured out. The others were growing tired from the intensity of the fight.

The Morifati fought in earnest now. The Snakes slowly fell back. Would their lines hold? Where were the Northmen?

"Raven! Can you hear me? Where are the Northmen? We need them now!"

"They are almost with us. The Snakes will have to hold out on their own until then, unless you and your men want to join the fray."

I was tempted to do just that, to send my Freemen in now, but something held me back. I looked ahead, and it did not end well. It did no real good. It was better for us to hang back and launch volleys of arrows at the Morifati if they got too close, pushed the Snakes back too far. We were in total only nine hundred men. The Snakes had numbered three thousand to start with. I don't know exactly how many Morifati there were, but my guess is there were at least six thousand warriors at the beginning, not counting the women who fought. Their total strength could easily be twelve thousand men and women.

I had forgotten to ask about the Northmen's strength, but I reckoned it to be at least six thousand, maybe more. The Allies would need all the support we could find. I knew I had to keep the Morifati contained on this field. They were extremely dangerous on open ground and also in forests where they could attack from cover. The Morifati had generations of experience in fighting tactics.

My captains had assembled around me by then. I turned to them.

"Have your men ready their bows and form into ranks. We will advance close behind the Snakes, and launch volleys of arrows into the Morifati. We are waiting for the Northmen to reinforce us. The Northmen will attack their flanks. Together with the Wolves and Snakes, we will hold the middle ground. When the time is right, we will join the fray. If the Snakes' lines fail, we will join the fray. Under no circumstances will we allow the Morifati to break through the Snakes and gain the field."

The captains cheered and rushed off to join their men. Everyone assembled quickly, and when they did, I motioned for them to advance. I wanted to lead, but one of the captains, an elder named Jim, stood before me and said, "A general leads from the rear. We need you to use the Sight to lead us. Stay back where we can protect you until the time has come for all of us to fight."

So we marched up double-time then, and when we were in place behind the Snakes, we launched volleys of arrows into the middle and the rear of the Morifati ranks. The thing that made the Morifati dangerous in an open field was their ability to form into phalanx formations. They had formed into multiple phalanx formations, standing close together. No gaps between their formations. This slowed them down, but it made it almost impossible to penetrate their lines.

The Morifati were pushing the Snakes back. They almost had them on their heals. Our volleys were helping, but not enough. Morifati continued to exit the gate of the village in formation instead of rushing out like berserkers, as they had done at first. As they came forward, they pressed the ones ahead of them further out. At this rate, they would gain the field soon.

Finally, the last of them were out, but the Snakes had fallen back and so had we. We were killing them, but not enough of them, and we could not stop them from advancing. If the Northmen did not arrive soon, we would lose containment and they would be free to move around and capture the center ground.

Their grain lay trampled, watered with the blood of the dead. Many men, women and children lay dead or dieing. Stepping over the dead held the Morifati up but little. The sun began to rise.

I looked ahead to see if the Northmen would get here in time. They had come! They were just then dividing up! One division to go around the burning village and attack from the right, and one division to attack from the left.

"Raven, what can you tell me about the Morifati village now?"

"Everything is on fire inside. The wall of the village still holds. All the Morifati are outside now. No one else remains.

These are the ones we must kill. The Northmen are here and they are preparing their attack!"

The Northmen on the left flank waited for the Northmen on the right flank to get into position. The Morifati had pushed us all back into the field and there was an open space behind them between them and their burning village. Their rear was exposed, but there was no one attacking it. The Snakes lines were breaking. They retreated as the Morifati advanced.

All at once the Northmen were in place, and they attacked immediately. The Northmen plunged headlong into the Morifati. They attacked from the left and right and from the rear. The Morifati stopped to regroup. The Snakes held up their retreat and rested for a moment.

Looking at this scene, I knew the time had come. I looked around at my men. They were ready. The Wolves could barely contain themselves any longer.

"Charge! Charge! Charge! Kill them all!"

I had forgotten about Wolf.

"Wolf? Are you with me?"

"I am at your side!"

I looked and Wolf and Lara had been waiting next to me the whole time. I was so focused on the battle; I had not seen them. We rushed forward behind the Freemen and the Wolves then as they charged into the fray to fight with bows and machetes and teeth.

The Snakes jumped back in the fight. In their human form, they were quick and struck their blows with great force. They had already killed more Morifati than they had lost as casualties, but the Morifati were so disciplined as fighters that the Snakes could never defeat them alone.

#

We pressed them until at last we had killed them all except for the elite Warriors of the Morifati, and Blackheart John.

They were surrounded, about three hundred men in all. The Northmen were on their flanks and behind them. The Snakes and the Freemen stood in front of them, blocking their way as they fought to break through our lines and make for the Great River.

The Morifati stood together in one phalanx. No one of the allies could break through their lines. We could only kill the ones along the outside, or shoot arrows into their midst, which sometimes found a target, and sometimes bounced harmlessly off their shields.

Blackheart John kept jumping around in and out of their phalanx. Striking our warriors unawares, killing as many as he could, and then jumping away when he sensed we were about to close in on him. He was killing many men.

The Ravens circled overhead, screaming out cries of frustration that they could not join in. They could of course see what was going to happen before it happened and they tried and tried to warn the men where the Morifati would strike.

The Wolves had made their way to the front lines where they lunged at the Morifati, pulling them down off their feet whenever they could and attacking the Morifati from behind whenever they broke free of their phalanx and tried to fight in single combat.

My men would not let me advance to the front lines. I needed to get up there so I could fight Blackheart John in single combat. No one would allow it. They kept holding me back, protecting me.

I looked ahead. What should I do? I saw the best thing. I transformed into a Grizzly Bear. I stood towering over my men and over the Morifati. I pushed my way forward. My men tried to hold me back, but they gave up as I pushed them aside.

"Stand back, men! Make way for me! I want to fight Blackheart John alone!"

All my warriors and the Wolves pulled back and stopped pressing the fight. The Morifati stood their ground. I suppose Blackheart John ordered them to stop advancing. They maintained their phalanx inside of a ring that the Allies formed when they pulled back and ceased firing.

I stood in the ring my men had cleared, before all my Allies and before the Morifati. The Morifati barely contained themselves. They wanted to continue the fight. The spirits of the Allies were high, too. Everyone was in a rage. I called out to Blackheart John.

"Blackheart John! Will you come out to fight me?"

He appeared in front of his Morifati Warriors, facing me with pure, murderous hatred in their eyes.

"Will you fight as a man? And not use your cowardly magic?" said Blackheart John.

"I will fight as a man! Hand to hand, or with any weapon you choose!"

"Let's fight with machetes!", he was grinning at me so I thought he must be lying. He might use anything. There were no rules to observe here.

Some men rushed forward to form a guard around me. I transformed back into a man. I motioned to my men to bring me a machete and a bow. I slung the bow and quiver across my back and stood ready with my machete.

To my men I said, "Leave me now. I have the Sight. I know where he will strike."

I looked ahead to see what he was planning to do. I responded in my mind. Then he did something I did not expect. Maybe it would be best if I did not try to see too many moves ahead.

My men drew back slowly, reluctantly. Then I stood alone, facing him. With my men behind me, and with the Morifati behind him, we stared each other down. I 'saw around the corner' again. He kept changing where he would pop up. Was he trying to confuse me, or was he just uncertain? What would he do if I rushed forward? I saw it, so I acted on impulse.

He appeared just behind me and lunged to stab me in the back. I whirled around and parried. We fought a while with no one able to land a blow. Then he jumped again, back into his ranks.

This was going to be trickier. There was no way I could rush his decision this time. He appeared here and there. This time, he was going to use his bow. So my hunch was right. He was not interested in a fair duel. Revenge was what he was after, no matter what.

Just before his next move, I saw it. I dropped to my knees and ducked an instant after he appeared. His arrow flew right over me, right where my heart would have been. He got behind me again, so his arrow sailed over me and went into the throat of one of his Morifati Warriors.

Blackheart John screamed in rage and started to reload. But I jumped to my feet, slotted an arrow, drew back, and he disappeared.

I kept my bow at the ready. Where would he appear this time? He never gave up, you had to give him that. First here, then there, trying to gain some advantage. I knew I could do it, but I also knew I had to do it. I followed his thoughts.

Finally he appeared, not behind me, but off to my right, in front of my men. This was going to be a tougher shot for me. I had to make it just before he jumped but after he had committed. If I missed or miscalculated, one of my men would be injured or die.

I turned and released the arrow toward my men. Everyone gasped when I did. No one knew what was going on except for me. I timed it well. My arrow buried itself deep in Blackheart John's chest.

He slumped, a look of abject horror and surprise on his face. With fear in his voice, he cried out.

"Than! Avenge me!"

It seemed he was afraid, after all. Everyone was stunned silent and motionless, then a Hawk cried out overhead!

"Grandfather!"

All the Ravens screamed. The Wolves howled. The men of the Free State, and the Northmen and the Snakes all let out their war cries. They rushed forward and past me without having to be ordered. Their momentum carried them into the Morifati and broke their ranks. In minutes, all the Morifati lay dead.

I turned around, and the Northmen had cut off Blackheart John's head and stuck it on a pole and were dancing around it. Good for them. After what the Morifati had done to them, their women and children and their ancestors, they had a right to celebrate.

I let them go on celebrating. I walked out of their midst toward the Morifati village. The heat of the fire could be felt even from where I was standing. A breeze rushed past me to feed the flame. Flames so hot that they drew in air and produced a kind of upside down tornado.

"Grandfather, show me what you see."

I looked through his hawks' eyes at the scene of the battle and saw that we had trampled the field into a mass of mud and blood and dead bodies. There were many to be buried now, and heroes to be remembered. The Morifati would have to be piled up and burned.

I should have been happy, but I wasn't. I only felt sorrow for the ones who had died. What could I say to the families of our men?

It was time for me to go back to Snake's castle and rescue the woman I loved.

FORTY-THREE

I RESCUE DIANA

I stood at the edge of the wood outside Dorothea's castle, wondering what to do next. It was a beautiful day. The sun shone out of a deep blue sky through only a few wisps of white. The castle, though still overgrown with vines, did not look so gloomy as it had before. The Morifati were not waiting for me to cross the field, watching and waiting to strike.

The Morifati would never threaten anyone again. When I left their village, it was a burned out ruin. It looked as bad as the ruins of the cities from the Great Third War, or at least that's what Grandfather told me. Nothing remained standing except for portions of the village wall. The houses and buildings were all reduced to blackened charcoal and ash. There were no remains of anyone or anything behind.

Soon after the battle, the Ravens began eating the remains of the Morifati dead. That shocked me. I wasn't expecting it, but it made sense when they explained that it was their custom. Ravens were, after all, carrion eaters.

I persuaded them to let us pile the bodies up and burn them in funeral pyres. They relented and allowed it. What would we do with our dead now?

Grandfather said, "Build a cemetery here just inside the forest."

So we did just that and placed memorials over each grave and one memorial in the center of the graveyard. We sang our death songs while we worked. Grandfather consecrated the memorial when we had finished it.

I asked the Wolves, "What do you do with your dead?"

"When a wolf is ready to die, there is a place we all go, if we still can, and dig a hole and lie down in it and wait. If death comes suddenly, then a wolf lies where he died.", Wolf said.

"Dig holes for your Wolves and we will carry them over there."

So next to our own cemetery we placed the bodies of the wolves that had died in battle, but we covered them over with stones so their remains would not be exposed. The Wolves howled over them and the Ravens flew round and round overhead, and we sang songs to salute their courage and loyalty.

The Snakes, both the living and the dead, transformed back into snakes and then either slithered away or lay there and decomposed. We did not touch them. They stank horribly right away.

The Northmen carried their dead back up north with them. It took more than one trip. They lost half their force.

Our casualties numbered three hundred. The Snakes lost about two thousand. The Northmen lost three thousand. The Wolves lost two dozen. The Ravens lost no one. The Ravens with their ability to see what would happen next were untouchable.

The Morifati of course lost everyone, man, woman, and child.

The area was ruined. The crops were all trampled, blood and mud and grain mixed together. The stream was polluted now with blood and bodies. The village was one blackened mass of burned wood which still smoked.

Grandfather said to the Northmen, "You can have this land now, since it was yours to begin with. We will return to our Free State, the Wolves will return to the Forbidden Land, Snake has her domain, and the Ravens will live in the eternal sky."

"We thank you for what you have done. May all our tribes, man and Psychic, remain allies and live in peace and freedom from evil from this day forward until the end of the ages.", said the Chief of the Northmen.

And to me he said, "Rion of the Free State. You are the greatest war chief we have ever heard of or seen. Your courage, your strength, your Psychic powers, have surpassed all, including Snake herself. If you need us. If you need anything. If we can be of service to you in any way, you have only to ask. We will follow if you will lead."

So after everything was in order and the Northmen left, and the Ravens left, I turned and found one of the Morifati boats that had not been destroyed in the battle and left in it. No one called out to me, neither Grandfather nor Wolf. They all must have known what I had to do now.

But how to rescue Diana? I wanted to enter, go and find her in her tower room where she slept, and wake her if I could. If the spell could be broken. If the spell could not be broken, I would have to go and find the "History of the Psychics" and learn how to remove the spell.

There was no way I knew of to get past the Ravens without being seen. They probably knew where I was right now and were watching me.

Dorothea was another matter. Should I confront her? She still held the amulet. She could take control over me if she used it. I could get stuck inside there. Living like one of her servants. What did she have in mind now that the Morifati were gone?

Would she be happy to see me? I guessed so, but everything we had done before was done on her terms. It was time for me to be my own man. To rule as King with Diana as my Queen, not Dorothea.

I would have to confront Dorothea. There was no other way around it. If she would not release Diana, then I would have to stay there until I could get to Diana, wake her, and escape.

A pretty tall order when there were eyes everywhere. I would have to get in and get to that book, "The History of the Psychics". If there were methods I could use, they would be in there.

Dorothea would be happy to see me after this glorious victory, but she liked having things her own way. I doubted she would let me just walk in and walk out with Diana. She would want me to stay. I knew she would. She would want to crown me as her King.

While I stood thinking this over, planning my strategy, I heard a voice overhead.

"Rion, what are you waiting for?"

It was Raven. She had been perched overhead the whole time, watching me. So that answered one question. No, I could not get past the Ravens.

"I want to see Diana again."

"She is inside, waiting for your return."

"She sleeps. Locked away in the tower by Dorothea."

"Dorothea waits for you too. And why are you not happy to see me? You have been quiet for three days now. No contact with anyone!"

"I am happy to see you, little one. I never properly thanked you for all your help."

She fluttered down then and landed on my shoulder. I held out my arm so she could walk out to my hand. I gave her a little kiss on the side of the head and beak. How do you kiss a raven?

"Who are you most loyal to, Raven?"

"What do you mean?"

"Who is your leader now? Who are you loyal to the most? Me or Dorothea?"

"You! You are the leader of all now, but I will not betray Dorothea. We have been allies for too long."

"Can I trust you, Raven? Will you keep a confidence?"

"Yes, of course!"

"I want to free Diana. I want to go in and wake Diana and leave here with her."

#

So I entered Dorothea's castle with Raven perched on my shoulder. This time there were Snakes there to open every door and gate. They still spoke not a word and had blank expressions on their faces.

Dorothea had not come down to greet us. A little power play on her part. There was more light in the grand entryway this time. Curtains had been pulled back and torches lit. It still looked ancient, but it no longer looked gloomy. The whole place still looked like it was hiding snakes underneath it, but it no longer looked abandoned. There was no longer anyone to hide from and nothing to hide from them.

"Where is she Raven?"

"She waits for us in her throne room."

"Her majesty does not deign to come down to greet us, but waits for us to come and pay tribute."

"If you say so, but she will be happy to see you. She worried about you. Dorothea hides her feelings."

That was the problem with Dorothea all right, always hiding something. I could guess what she was expecting now. No, I knew what she expected now. I had to tell her that it would not happen without making an enemy out of her. It was bad enough to scorn a woman, but what if the woman was a Psychic who could transform into a snake?

When we entered the throne room, Raven took flight and alighted on the back of Dorothea's throne. Dorothea sat on her throne, wearing the amulet.

"Behold your Majesty! Rion of the Free State! Hero of the Massacre of the Morifati! He returns to you now to show his affection!" said Raven.

"Come forward Rion! It's so good to see you again! I thought you might not make it when they knocked you out. They have killed Psychics that way in the past. I worried. I didn't let you know, but I worried."

I went forward, but she did not stand to receive me. Instead, she sat and extended her hand to be kissed. I knelt and kissed it.

"Leave us now Raven, I want to speak to Rion alone."

"As you wish, Majesty." Raven said. She fluttered off and the Snakes let her out.

"The conquering hero returns. Why have you not contacted me since our victory over the Morifati?"

"I wanted to talk to you in person."

"Here we are, together again."

"I want you to let Diana go now."

"And if I don't?"

"You agreed to let her go if I went back to the Morifati!"

"And then you agreed that it was necessary to go back."

"I have fulfilled my end of the bargain."

"Have you? Have you forgotten about the two of us ruling this world together as King and Queen?"

"I never agreed to that!"

"You are unfaithful Rion! You love another! After everything I've done for you! You are still in love with Diana."

"I have been unfaithful, but to Diana, not to you."

Dorothea grasped the amulet in her hands. I thought she was just about to put a spell on me with it, but instead she took it off. She stood up and slipped out of her gown, raised her arms over her head and transformed into a snake. She grew into enormous size, an impossibly large anaconda.

Dorothea advanced on me until she towered over me. She gazed into my eyes. It was the dream! The dream that started all this! Our eyes were locked, and she was big enough to swallow me in one gulp.

"Don't move Rion!"

I looked ahead to see what would happen and to my astonishment; she meant it! If I turned or moved one way or another, she would swallow me!

"Would you really kill the man you love, Dorothea? Would you really swallow me whole?"

"I can. I will if you force me to."

"What do you want from me? I know you don't want a man who would surrender to you or anyone."

"I want you to admit that you can't live without me, that without me you would not be complete. That without me you would never have gained any power, or won any victory, or stood up to torture."

I had to admit all those things were true. Though I didn't know about not living without her. I reckoned I could live without her, all right.

"I do love you, and I know I couldn't have succeeded without you. I would not even have tried, but Diana and I are destined for each other, and you know that. You have the Sight!"

"This conversation is over, Rion. Leave now!"

I turned and went. I didn't like being dismissed like that, but after a few quick looks 'around the corner' and I could see it was my only choice. Dorothea was angry with me, no doubt about it. I never imagined how powerful her anger was. It made me feel angry too. I resented her for all this. I walked off into the hallway as far away from the throne room as I could go.

I was left alone after that. I suddenly realized I had been given what I wanted, time to find Diana. Surprised by good fortune, I decided to explore the castle to find the way into the tower. I had wondered how I would ever find Diana and free her. When I was here before, Dorothea had always been my constant companion, or I had always been hers. The only time she left me alone was when I studied "The History of the Psychics."

This was the first time she gave me free rein. I thought I better take the chance and try to find Diana. The tower was in the northeast corner of the castle. I knew that, but I had never gone through there. Dorothea had been careful to avoid that part of the building.

I cut through the library. That might distract anyone who was watching. They would just assume I had gone there to resume my studies. Nothing unusual about that.

I stopped to look at the shelves. "The History of the Psychics" was right where I left it. I ran my hand over it. It could be worthwhile to continue where I left off. There just wasn't any time.

There was an exit from the library on the east side that I had never used. I never saw anyone else use it either. I tried it. It opened into a dimly lit hallway that ran north and south, or at least that was my best guess.

I followed it as far as I could until it ended and I had to try going to my right. At the end of that hall, was a curved wall with a door. I stopped, looked around, and listened intently. I looked around in my mind. I had not been followed, and no one was coming.

The door opened into a stairwell with a spiral staircase. I followed it up and passed some windows that gave a view outside. This was the tower, no doubt about it. At last, at the top, was a landing and a door.

The door to the tower room was locked. Why wouldn't it be? The door was locked, the windows were covered with drapes and barred to keep Diana from flying out, or seeing out. She could project herself if she could see out. As an added measure, Dorothea had placed Diana under a deep sleep.

All that kept her prisoner. She could not get out or to communicate with anyone outside at all except for the time when she came to me in my dream. Or had I gone to her? It was hard for me to know. I had no control over my dreams. I simply went wherever my mind took me. I guessed the same was true for Diana. That would explain why she had not come to me after we shared a dream.

Dorothea, I suspected, could control her dreams to some extent. How else could she have come to me in the depths of my mind, to the underground mountain lake? There was much that she knew and kept secret.

So how do I get in? Steal the keys? Pick the lock? Go back to "The History of the Psychics" and look for a lock picking technique?

I heard a fluttering of wings behind me and a tinkle of something metallic hitting the floor. I turned and there was a small golden key lying on the floor. How did that get there? It wasn't there when I entered.

"Is that what you need?" said Raven.

She perched on the rail of the stairs. I had not seen her in the dim light up there. It was black behind her.

"How did you know.....? Nevermind. Thanks little one."

"Move quickly Rion! Dorothea won't leave you alone for long!"

Then she flew off again. I tried the key, and the door opened into a darkened foyer leading to a suite of rooms. Diana lay on a bed, radiant. There was no light from the windows or candles. There was no light to illuminate the room at all. It would in fact have been pitch black in there except that Diana herself glowed with the radiance that Diana herself shown with when she was about to appear, or transform into a dove. Not too bright, just enough to see by.

This soft glow suffused the room. She lay fully dressed on top of the covers, as if she had been laid out that way purposefully, lying in state maybe, but she was clearly alive. She breathed softly and her chest heaved, arms folded with her hands crossed over her heart. Diana's hair had been washed, combed out and braided.

I went over to the side of the bed. I was going to lean over and kiss her before I tried to lift the sleep spell, but just as I did, she opened her eyes and grinned at me.

"I thought you were never going to make it back, Rion!"

FORTY-FOUR

CONSPIRACY

"Diana, I thought you had been asleep this whole time!"

"I have been. I had to sleep so I could watch over you."

"I'm confused. I thought Dorothea put a spell on you."

"She did, but we agreed on what to do beforehand. You needed a little push. A reason to fight. Someone or something to live for."

"I'm really confused now. What's been going on while the two of us were here? While I was away?"

"We need to have that conversation with Dorothea. In her presence. Aren't you going to kiss me?"

I forgot to do what I had intended to do before she woke up. I thought I was going to have to break the spell Dorothea had her under. It turned out she was waiting for me all along. The two of them owed me an explanation for this.

I leaned over and grabbed her. It had been such a long time since we were together. I had been through so much. I kissed her with all the passion that comes from being held captive by the Morifati. I had been Dorothea's captive as well. I suddenly realized how much I had missed Diana, how much I had longed for her.

"Dorothea is going to have to wait on us this time, darling. We have something to catch up on."

#

When we got back to the throne room, things had changed. Three thrones had been set on the dais. Dorothea sat in the center. Raven perched on the back of Dorothea's throne.

We walked down and Dorothea gestured to Diana to join her. Diana sat on her right side. They both regarded me with amusement. I could tell I was the butt of a private joke.

"The conquering hero returns with his lady love.", said Dorothea.

"So what's going on here?" I said.

"It was necessary to deceive you, Rion." said Dorothea.

"Just a little white lie, for your own good.", said Diana.

"I don't get it. Why lie to me at all?"

"You were under a Limerence Spell, remember?" said Diana.

"To remove a Limerence Spell is very difficult, Rion. There are many techniques, but few guarantees of success. You had to be given someone else to live for, another future, with another woman.", said Dorothea.

"The Morifati didn't know everything about you, but they knew enough to realize that they had to defeat you any way they could. To completely control your mind. To corrupt you by all means if at all possible.", said Diana.

"So you thought that when I went back to them, I would fall back in love with Anna?"

"We couldn't take that chance. Remember when you got here you were still pining away over her.", said Dorothea.

"And you made a complete fool out of yourself while you were with them the first time.", said Diana.

"You humiliated yourself, Rion." said Raven.

"Thanks. Thanks a lot. You couldn't let stupid old me handle the Morifati all by myself."

324

They all laughed at my discomfort then. Sitting there smiling at me in a knowing way. A female conspiracy, no doubt about it. It even seemed like Raven was smiling.

"Now don't get your ego bruised. None of us could do what you did. We needed you, and we love you very much. In the real way, not limerence, love.", said Dorothea.

Dorothea gestured to the throne next to her, on her left.

"Come and join us, Rion, take your rightful place."

I sat in the throne on Dorothea's left and I thought, here I am sitting on the opposite side of my bride to be, and everyone has told me that I am King of Kings, and Chief of Chiefs now, so why am I not sitting in the middle? I thought I would dig them back a little, since they were in a mood to tease.

"Shouldn't I be the one sitting in the middle, Dorothea?"

"Indeed, you should, but not until your coronation, and not until after your wedding."

"So what comes next, then? Where will these things take place?"

"Be patient Rion. Remember, we have been alone together for over three days so in the eyes of the Free State we are already married.", said Diana.

"Just shut up and do as I'm told. Wait until I get my instructions?"

"That's right!" they both chimed.

"In that case I am going to go study 'The History of the Psychics'. Let me know when it's time for dinner." And then I walked out and left them sitting there grinning at me.

FORTY-FIVE

A WEDDING

Two weeks later I found myself back in the Forbidden Land, this time in the Wolves' domain. I made the journey alone, retracing the steps I had made and that Wolf and I had made together, until I found the path next to the stream that led down to their territory. Diana had not gone with me.

"You are not to see me until you see me waiting for you at the altar.", she said.

When I arrived at the place where they dwelt, Wolf was there to greet me.

"Are you prepared to meet your fate?" he said solemnly.

I couldn't tell if he was kidding. He had rarely kidded before.

Wolf led me to the place I had seen in my dream. The Cathedral of the Wolves. It was a natural formation in the side of a cliff that formed an oval shape that was open on one end, surrounded by tall cliff faces all around, except for the entrance.

Rocks had fallen down at the far end to make a raised platform above the floor of the little gorge, and a monolith had fallen to make an altar. The place was a naturally formed chapel, and the rays of the sun illuminated the whole place as it set. By chance, the opening faced west.

Everyone was there waiting for me. Grandfather stood in front of the altar. The crowd had divided between women and she-wolves standing behind Diana on the right side and men and wolves standing on the left, waiting for me to take my place. Such was the custom of the Wolves to marry in this way.

Dorothea stood with Diana as her maid of honor, and so did Lara. Wolf would be my best "man". Only Grandfather stood in the center. The Ravens watched us from all around, perched high on the cliffs.

Diana wore the same gown I had seen in my dream that night we camped at the start of the mountain trail. It was exactly like the dream image in every detail.

Everyone turned to watch us approach. Wolf walked in front with me directly behind. Everyone sang. Wolf and I took our places at the altar on the men's side. I met Diana's eyes. Grandfather gestured for us to stand together. I took her arm.

"What the Great Spirit has brought together, let no man put asunder.", said Grandfather.

We then said our vows. The same vows that people have said since before the Great Third War, and for thousands of years before that.

Grandfather then anointed our heads and placed crowns on us and declared, "You will rule together as King and Queen, over all the people, and over all the Psychics."

Turning then, we walked down the aisle, making a procession on our own. When we got to the end we turned, handed our crowns over to attendants for safekeeping. Then I transformed into a Grizzly, and Diana transformed into a dove. She alighted on my shoulder and we went off into the wilderness to be alone.

Born in Mobile Alabama, V. H. Mizzell spent most of his childhood there, except for a year in Summit New Jersey. He holds a BS in Physics from Auburn University and almost but not quite an MS in Mathematics from UAH. He has spent thirty years in the Defense/Aerospace industry, most notably working as a Fortran programmer on the Burst and Transient Source Experiment (BATSE) and as a Systems Engineer for the Boeing Company, Lockheed Martin, and Northrup Grumman.

He developed a love of Science Fiction when he found Heinlein's juvenile series in the Mobile Public Library Bookmobile. That was also the year that Star Trek premiered on TV and his big sister bought a telescope.

The Sight is his first published novel.

Lightning Source UK Ltd.
Milton Keynes UK
UKHW010411190821
389088UK00006B/353